Generational Payment

Generational Payment

COUPLES & CRIME BOOK ONE

LYV LAMERE

Tuxtails Publishing, LLC

Tuxtails Publishing, LLC

www.tuxtailspublishing.com

First Tuxtails Publishing Print Edition August 2023

ISBN: 978-1-957211-16-9

eBook ISBN: 978-1-957211-17-6

This book is a work of fiction. Unless otherwise indicated, all the names, characters, businesses, places, events and incidents in this book are either the product of the author's imagination or used in a fictitious manner. Any resemblance to actual persons, living or dead, or actual events is purely coincidental.

Cover design by Lyv Lamere and Tuxtails Publishing, LLC

Learn more about the author at www.lyvlamere.com.

To the one who feeds me.

1928

He looked down at her body and knew that, yes, he had understood her.

For a long time, they had built a life together. Famous actors, shining careers, and the parties they had given. Prohibition hadn't dimmed the light of Hollywood, and with their private haven outside of town, the press had been a nuisance at best until now.

So much had felt like a dream, but seeing her dead in front of him now reminded him of the darker side of their fame, of things secretly going on.

He slid a paper into his suit's inside pocket, while he frowned at another note demanding money in his other hand. And he knew he would do whatever he could to protect the family name.

Therefore, he would pay. Not to support the crime, the greed, but to be the one to explain to the public how a childless marriage had finally taken its toll. It was all that was left for him to do now.

Chapter One

S ome days Scarlette questioned her own sanity.

Today was definitely one of those days. There had been no seat on a direct flight available, that's why she had chosen multiple connections to get from the East Coast to the West Coast. Now, after more than ten hours at airports and on planes in the middle of a heat wave, she considered committing herself to the nearest psych ward. No sane person would jump on a plane to search for background information on some pathetic blackmail attempt just because she had a few days off and nothing else planned.

Sure, the letter was intriguing, but for Scarlette, the real interest was to find out if the family it mentioned really had been her ancestors. Her parents had always been honest with her, and she knew she had been adopted as an infant nearly thirty years ago — and she couldn't be happier. She would never want to replace them, and from what she could tell from the letter, she now seemed to be the last one of that unknown bloodline anyway.

But who could resist finding out if your great-great-grandfather had indeed belonged to the old-time Hollywood league of silent film stars?

So, here she was: sweaty, annoyed from the travel, waiting in line for a cab at the airport in LA. The rental and the trip outside of town to the old villa where she hoped to find out more would have to wait until tomorrow. The day had been too long to take that on today. For now, she wanted to get to her hotel, get some food, take a shower, and fall flat on her face.

Of course, that didn't happen. Her body's clock was screwed up. As a result, she devoured a burger on her way to her room and now stood in the bathroom drying her long, thick hair after her shower. It was a decent room for LA: nothing overly fancy, but clean, and the water didn't get cold after five minutes. Celebrating that fact, she had taken her time and thought after getting dressed she might feel human again.

She picked up a fresh pair of jeans — the practicality of pockets won over the still lingering heat — and a black tank top and decided to go to the hotel bar for a drink and some more research.

Tyler studied the picture he had taken of the note on his phone again while sipping his beer. It had been hard enough to bury his parents after the accident, but hardly a month later he had gotten the letter threatening to ruin his family's name. As a biographer, he of course knew most of his family history back to the early 1900s. It wasn't hard; his family had kept as good as all the documents, pictures, and many keepsakes over the years. Tyler himself had written several articles and more than one book on different family members. He knew they had gotten lucky and could live comfortably even today. But they all had worked for it, and they gave back to the community. That was why he took this threat seriously enough to look into it personally. It might have happened about a hundred years in the past, but in this case, it would only worsen the situation. They had built an empire on their name; to think all of it could be based on a lie could destroy everything.

"Hi. Are you waiting for someone?"

With his concentration interrupted, Tyler glanced over with annoyance shimmering in his eyes.

"What?"

"Sorry, I didn't mean to disturb you. Are you waiting for someone, or can I sit here? The place is packed, but if you're saving the seat, I can try my luck somewhere else," the woman next to him elaborated.

His brain needed a moment to catch up with her question. "Ah, no, please sit."

For a second there, he had only been thinking about getting his hands into her mass of dark auburn hair, dragging her head slowly back, and tasting that full, inviting mouth. When she thanked him and the friendly smile brightened her green eyes, he was mentally tumbling to the floor with her.

His mouth went dry, and he lifted his beer. What the hell? He had never before had such a reaction to a woman. A general attraction, sure, growing into a wave of lust when he went to bed with someone. But this was a punch straight in the gut.

And he realized she really just sat beside him, ordering her drink and taking her phone out. No attempt to keep talking, getting his attention so he might buy her beer. He should have seen it coming, he thought. She was a looker, and the tank top and tight jeans didn't try to hide the curves. But it was all straightforward with no fuss, and if the light didn't play a trick, she didn't even wear make-up, or if so only the slightest touch of it.

What he didn't realize though, was that he had the same effect on Scarlette. Seeing his profile at first, she had made out part of a well-defined face and wavy, close-to-curly dark blond hair falling over his shoulders, a nicely toned body in a basic black t-shirt and high-quality jeans. Then he had looked at her with those sky-blue eyes and her heart had skipped a beat before starting to race. She felt her abs contract, her breasts tingle as she imagined him sucking on them. She needed that drink.

Taking a deep breath, she unlocked her phone and blankly stared at it. She was the first person to admit that she might be less shy about sex and lust than other women. She knew attraction, either the instant, easy kind ending in the occasional and simple one-night stand, or the kind blossoming with a series of dates, a relationship. She was okay with both. But this felt like a hand around her throat, a slap in the face.

Tyler wanted to focus on his own phone again, but he saw her staring at her home screen for several seconds, and when he studied her more closely, he could see her pulse beating rapidly in her throat. A smile slowly spread on his face.

He gave her a few minutes to scroll through some texts and open a web page before he shifted a little and bumped her thigh with his. Her sharp intake of breath made him grin.

"Sorry."

"No problem," she said with a quick side glance and caught the last of his grin. Thinking two could play, she ran her hand through her hair to hide her own smile.

In the crowded bar, the noise level grew steadily, much like the blood alcohol of the guy on Scarlette's other side. When that guy tried to convince her to let him buy her a drink, she could almost physically feel Tyler shift his complete attention to her. *Time to see where this is going before anybody gets more insistent and ends up bleeding,* she thought, and politely but firmly declined the offer before turning towards Tyler.

He was already looking at her, and she beamed another smile at him. "Feed me, will you? I can't get to the pretzels over there."

Whatever it was between them, he decided it felt like too much fun not to go with it. Reaching into the bowl behind him, he got a few pretzels and held one to her lips, then followed his instinct and leaned in, brushing his lips over hers.

"So, I had the best-looking girl in here sitting beside me, kind of had a drink with her, fed her, kissed her. Do I get her name?"

Laughing, she reached for his hand to steal another pretzel from his fingers. "It's Scarlette," she said and placed the pretzel between her lips, leaning over to offer him half. "I shared my party snack and two kisses with this seriously good-looking guy. Do I get his name?"

He laughed just easily as she had. "It's Tyler. Nice to meet you, Scarlette."

"Nice to meet you, too, Tyler."

Getting comfortable on the bar stool, she rested her arm on the bar and kept smiling at him. "And what brings you to LA?"

"Family business," he answered and did his best to keep his voice from hardening. "What about you?"

"Oddly, something similar. A little genealogy, I'd call it. Got some info that sounded interesting on some long-dead relatives and wanted to check it out. But it's hardly exciting until I know more. What are you doing for a living?"

"I'm a writer. Biographies mostly."

Studying him a moment, something clicked. "Wait, are you Tyler O'Brien? The guy who interviewed the Queen before she passed away and got the contract to write her biography?"

"Yeah, that would be me." He shifted uncomfortably, and it was obvious to her he'd been through this far too often over the past weeks.

"Don't worry, I won't ask about it. But I read about it and remembered I actually read one or two of your books. I'm usually more of the horror novel kind, some classics, too. But your biographies are well written, and you manage to portray interesting people, actual people, not the usual 'high-class businessman needing an ego boost' sort of book."

"Oh, I write those, too. They pay well and offer the chance to finance the more interesting ones."

Grinning, Scarlette toasted him with her beer. "You're honest, I like that. I loved the one about the sherpa guiding people up on Mt. Everest. The things he does, what he has seen... puts all our check-out-where-I've-been-social-media-bullshit into perspective."

He nodded slowly, took a long sip of his beer. This woman could kill him.

"You okay, Tyler?"

"Yeah. I'm good. I just wondered what I did right in my life to run into you here and now. I haven't met anyone before who understood exactly that and managed to put it so simply and so on point."

"No reason to circle around any point there might be, right? I wouldn't say I'm a simple, well let's say 'uncomplicated,' person, but I'm straightforward and honest myself, so I appreciate it in others."

"I can see that. What are you doing for a living?"

"Pet consulting." When he stared, nonplussed, at her, she chuckled. "Don't worry, I'm not playing *Dr. Doolittle* and have a therapy couch for the spoiled poodle with anxiety attacks whenever she sees a patch of actual grass. I studied zoology and realized that as much as I love fieldwork and even the lab, we have great scientists working on conservation, habitat rehabilitation, and so on. But people are still fucked up and keep animals as pets that shouldn't be kept as such. But what can you do with a koala who's lived in captivity for years, whose digestive tract couldn't even deal with being pushed into the wild again because of mismanagement?" Letting it sink in for a second but not expecting an answer, she took a sip from her bottle.

"So I opened a consultation business. I usually try to advise people before they even get a pet — all kinds that is, also cats, dogs, fish — about costs, best living conditions, and so on. Or, after they get one, on how to do better. Which is, in the end, less expensive because they will pay less for me than for their vet who has to cut open the dog the fourth time to get something out of its intestines instead of them securing the apartment so the dog can't get to the rubber duck in the first place." When he grinned, she gestured with her drink. "Trust me, I've been there. And for those with exotic pets, some get fined by the authorities, but zoos and sanctuaries can't take in all those animals. So to reduce fines, or because some truly want to do better, the authorities have agreed to work with me, consult on improving conditions, so some animals will stay with their owners, but differently than before."

Tyler studied her over his own bottle for a moment. "I get the feeling I could already write a whole book about you even now. That's an impressive and interesting business. And I see why you're so direct."

"Yeah. Some people need a little pampering, but for most, a clear, concise approach works best."

They both had shifted so their thighs were touching, and studying his eyes, she was pretty sure she saw the same itchy desire in them that boiled in her. "So, let's see how you deal with me being direct. Wanna get out of here? I couldn't really concentrate on my research in the first place, and when I saw you even the last bit of focus went down the drain."

"I feel like you read my mind. Yes, let's go."

They both tossed some money on the bar and slid down from their stools. Their hands brushed against each other and something close to an electric shock ran up Scarlette's arm. Feeling the same energy, Tyler grabbed her hand harder than he had planned. She was small, about 5'4", and her hand seemed delicate in his. But the way she tightened her fingers around his told him not to underestimate her strength.

When she led him through the crowd towards the exit, he

could smell her hair and the lingering scent from her shower on her skin. And when she had to stop to let a waitress pass by, Tyler bumped into her. His hands gripped her hips, and he could feel the blood rush down when he heard her hum in response to the contact. "Get out of here."

"Working on it. Where's your room?"

"Fifth floor."

"Okay, we might make it that far."

They dragged each other to the nearest elevator, but inside the cabin, Scarlette held up her hand, slightly pushed Tyler to the other wall. His heart hammered against her palm. "If you kiss me now, we'll rip into each other right here, right now. And I'm not in the mood to search for a new hotel tonight because we got kicked out of here."

"Fair point. You smell incredible, I can't wait to taste you, every inch of you," he told her, and saw her shiver in reaction.

"Good thing my body lotion is flavored. I hope you like pomegranate." She could see him tense, drew in a sharp breath when he pushed himself from the wall and caged her in with his hands beside her head. His eyes burned into hers.

"I will make you scream."

"I believe you could."

For a few seconds, they didn't move, didn't even breathe. Lust thickened the air. When the doors opened, they stumbled out together, and Scarlette let him maneuver her a couple of doors down the hall.

Tyler fought with his key card and finally managed to open the door to his room, pushed her against it from the inside, and crushed his lips to hers. Sighing, she got a hand in his hair and dragged him closer. Her other hand fought its way under his shirt, and her lips curved in approval when she felt his muscles tense under her touch.

They both tasted greedily, and when his lips roamed down her throat and his teeth nipped at her neck, she moaned. Pushing her hips forward, she felt the bulge in his jeans pressing against her. A fresh wave of lust rolled through her body. Riding it, she dragged the shirt over his head and sank her teeth in his shoulder, starting on his belt.

"You're fast."

"Then you better keep up."

He raised an eyebrow, a cocky grin spreading on his face. "Okay."

He ripped her top down the front. She gasped, then laughed.

"Good job. Left back pocket," she said before she pushed his jeans and shorts to the floor, closing her hand around him. He fumbled in her pocket and found a condom. "You come prepared."

"Fieldwork. Same as Girl Scouts: always be prepared. Gimme." She took it from his hand, ripped it open, and rolled it over him. He groaned, fought for some control. "I support the enthusiasm, but I want more from you."

"You can have it, don't worry, but the way this goes, we could both forget. And I don't see any problem with you staying up until you're inside me."

"No argument there. Come."

He took her hand and drew her in for a deep kiss on their way to the bed. His busy fingers unhooked her bra and let it drop to the floor, and when his mouth found her breast, sucked on it, scraped teeth over it, she cried out. "Damn, you're good."

He only smiled and shifted to her other breast, his hands working on her pants. He needed to have her. He wanted to savor her. He only had her for this one night, so he wanted to take everything from her. Fighting himself and her seeking fingers, he cuffed her wrists with his hands. "I need to taste you, remember? Let me."

His lips roamed over her, from her neck to the valley between her full breasts, down her ribs. His tongue ran over her skin, tasted the lotion, and he approved it with a murmur. He lingered on her hip, his tongue playing around the tattoo of a dragon riding there.

Under him, she shivered, she felt her heart pump blood to every part of her body that he touched. He wasn't just good, he was amazing. She couldn't think. And when he slowly slid a finger inside her, she moaned once more. His tongue followed, playing her from the outside.

She simply exploded. Crying out, she arched, pumped her hips against hand and mouth in demand. "More, Ty. More."

"All you want. Hell, you're something else."

She tasted dark and sweet when his tongue slid inside her. Hot and soft and wet, all of her waiting for him. She rushed over the next peak and went limp, before gathering her strength and rolling him over. "My turn." She explored, she teased, and she tasted just like he had. "You've got a damn fine body."

Not ripped, but defined. Scarlette ran her hands over it in appreciation, let her gaze wander over the whole six feet of him, skin gleaming with sweat and muscles all tense. "And you taste delicious, too."

Her mouth ran from his chest down to his belly, making him quiver before she closed her lips around the solid length of him.

She put every bit of his control to the test, and when she shifted and finally took him inside, he ran his hands to her hips, held her in place. Sheathed tightly in the heat of her, he felt her shudder. And she rolled her hips. No lover before could have prepared him for what it was with her. With all the want between them, he understood she was holding herself back as much as he was.

The dim light of the lamp on the bedside table let her eyes flash green at him when she gazed down, made her skin shimmer golden. *Like a lioness ready to pounce*, he thought. And just like that she quickened her pace, purred a deep, feral groan from her throat.

She was still contracting inside when he dragged her down and rolled on top of her. "My turn again." He heard her breath catch when he slipped even deeper inside her. And with her cry, he thrust hard and fast until she fisted around him again and shattered with a scream, dragging him over with her.

Tyler collapsed on her, but couldn't find the strength to shift his weight from her. But since she was panting under him, it seemed like she could breathe. He was panting about as much as she was, but finally managed to form a few words. "What was that? Are you okay?"

"No idea what it was, but it was freaking great. So yeah, I'm good. You?"

"Very good. Guess the neighbor next door will hate us, because I'm not done with you. And somehow I don't think we'll be much quieter next round."

Scarlette giggled. "You just screwed the next-door neighbor into pure bliss. As long as you keep the next round as entertaining as the last, she won't complain."

Tyler raised an eyebrow in consideration, then took her mouth with a grin. "Yes, she looks quite blissful from my perspective. Let's see what we can do to keep you like that."

Two extremely satisfying rounds later, Scarlette picked up her pants and wiggled into them, then inspected the remnants of her top. She slid it over her shoulders, knotted the front, adjusted a bit, nodded. "This should be okay, I only have to go one room down the hall. Thanks for the evening, Ty. This was... fun doesn't really cover it. Sure, it was fun, too, but I'd say this was exceptional."

"Exceptional sounds appropriate. Thanks, Sparks, it was an adventure."

"Sparks? Really?"

"You haven't seen yourself from my perspective. It's your eyes, there's a fire in them. And then there's all that amazing hair of yours. It fits, believe me."

Finger combing her hair, Scarlette laughed. "Okay. Well, who knows, maybe we will see each other again someplace. For now, good luck with your family business."

"I wouldn't mind running into you again. Good luck with your genealogy project."

"Goodbye, Link," she said, and tapped the Triforce tattoo she had found on his shoulder earlier when she took a step over to give him a quick kiss, then vanished out of his room with a smile.

In the morning, Tyler cursed himself. How could he have let her go just like that? As soon as she had been out the door he had realized he still wanted her, still needed her. No other woman had ever caught his mind so completely. And that was ridiculous. They'd had great sex. Amazing, mind-blowing sex. But it was sex, nothing more. It hadn't seemed like it had been anything else for her, had it? An interesting conversation before and an engaging personality didn't mean they had a special connection.

And now she was gone, and he didn't have her number, not even her last name, and no idea where exactly she came from except the general direction of East Coast. That much he had found out between roughing up the sheets. She was careful, didn't give too much information to a stranger. And that's what he was to her, wasn't it?

So why was he standing in front of her door and felt desperate when she didn't open? "Shit, she must have checked out already. You're such an idiot," he mumbled to himself and shuffled back to his room to get his things and check out himself.

Scarlette was out on a run to clear her mind. She couldn't get Tyler out of her head. She couldn't say what it was, but it had been different from everything she had experienced before. She had been sure the lust would fade overnight. She knew how that went. But he had reached her like no one else before. She had always enjoyed sex, had never heard any complaints about her ability there. But the way she had given him total control of her, that was new.

And damn it, woman, you're not here for this but to find out about your family. Enjoy the fact that you had some incredible sex. You both knew it was only one night, and you were both totally fine with that, she told herself and turned back to the hotel.

The open door of his room and the maid's cart in front with all the sheets and towels from inside it popped the last bubble of hope that she might see him again this morning and at least give him her number. Frustrated, she went into her own room, put out the "Do not disturb" sign, and stripped to take a shower before packing her things.

She was annoyed with herself when her thoughts kept circling straight back to last night. Giving up, she closed her eyes and with the hot water running over her she glided a hand over her breasts, let the other wander between her thighs, and sighed while sliding a finger into where she felt her pulse beating frantically already. Shuddering, she climaxed. *Damn it, Ty, how's that supposed to hold me over?*

Chapter Two

S carlette used the drive from the hotel in LA to the Airbnb close to the old house outside of town to make some calls to her friends and let her family know where she would go next – you could never be sure what might happen, and having some trusted people know the steps of her trip was always a reasonable precaution.

She brought her things into her bedroom and, relieved to have the small house to herself, she made some coffee to take outside.

The back porch gave her a view of the villa overlooking the houses down there. Hadn't she told Tyler she liked horror novels? That didn't mean she planned to star in one, and the villa reminded her eerily of one of the ghost stories she had read in the past. *Definitely going up there before it's dark,* she decided, then studied the note again:

It's time somebody told you about your real family.
We can't say much about your father, but your mother
recently died of cancer.
Our sincere condolences.
But it doesn't change the fact that it is now your turn to pay.
Your dear great-great-grandfather killed his wife and covered it
as suicide.
It wouldn't do the career any good to be a known murderer.
Especially when he was on the brink of losing everything
because he couldn't make the jump.
Silent film to talkies, it was a big change.
Eton Barret wasn't cut out for change.
And his dear Cecille paid the price.
We have proof of him killing his wife.
If you want to save the family name from a scandal, you will
do as we say.
You have ten days to get $10,000 together.
We will contact you with instructions for the payment.

The note had made her curious. But she had no intention to pay anybody even one cent. Even if it was all true, it didn't truly concern her. Should they decide to publish it, even her connection to it, she wouldn't be harmed. Her real family, the one giving her a home, supporting her, being honest with her, weren't involved in any of it, so nobody would be hurt. And, if worse came to worst, she knew a consultant to spin it to her advantage so her business wouldn't suffer.

But it was still interesting, and she figured if she wanted to find out anything more about her ancestor, the former silent film star, than she had already googled and dug out from the library, she would find it in or around that house.

Packing a few things she considered essential, she shot a text to her mother and walked through the backyard toward the foot of the hill.

Turning a corner, she ran straight into Tyler. She wished she could enjoy the pleasure shortly rising inside her, but it was overshadowed by suspicion. "Now that's interesting. Tyler, hello."

"It is. Scarlette, what are you doing here?" Confusion and hurt made him answer colder than he wished. He had sensed her even before she had bumped into him, and all he could think was, *Why else would you be here, if it wasn't you?*

"You really have the nerve to ask what *I'm* doing here, Tyler? Was fucking me a bonus on top of the blackmail attempt? Look, we had fun, really, but just because you're a great lay it won't magically make me pay. You should realize I don't know those people, I don't even know if they really are my ancestors, or if he is, so make public whatever you want. Guess I should change my mind and hope not to see you again. Bye."

She had spoken too fast, turned around too briskly to get away from him, but damn it if she wasn't hurt. Well, she would get over it.

She hadn't even taken two steps when he grabbed her arm.

"Scarlette, wait one damn minute! What do you mean? I wanted to ask you basically the same thing. So let's start over. You got blackmailed? You aren't here to collect?"

"Of course not. I don't have to lower myself to something so pathetic. I didn't even know about the Barrets before this."

"Barrets? I'm confused. What are you talking about? I thought this was about Charles and Mary-Beth O'Brien."

"You aren't making any sense here, Tyler. I didn't get anything about the O'Briens. Here, that's what I have. Either you're involved, then you know it anyway, or this is even crazier than I thought," she said, and handed him her phone with a picture of her note.

After reading it, Tyler shook his head and wordlessly handed her his phone.

It's time somebody told you about your family's secret.
Your parents will have kept this from you up to now.
But their accident has sped up your involvement.
Our sincere condolences.
But it doesn't change the fact that it is now your turn to pay.
Your dear great-great-grandfather killed his wife and covered it
as suicide.
It wouldn't do the career any good to be a known murderer.
Especially when he was on the brink of losing everything
because he couldn't make the jump.
Silent film to talkies, it was a big change.
Charles O'Brien wasn't cut out for change.
And his dear Mary-Beth paid the price.
We have proof of him killing his wife.
If you want to protect the family name from a scandal, you
will do as we say.
You have ten days to get $250,000 together.
We will contact you with instructions for the payment.

"Seems like they know you're loaded. And like they are pretty lazy, since they used essentially the same note twice."

"Not exactly funny, Scarlette."

"Sorry. But what do you want me to say? If this isn't some sick joke, then it follows that our families paid some other people a lot of money before this, for god knows how long. And at least I didn't even know about this family. I was adopted as a baby. Whatever would come to light wouldn't mean anything to me, wouldn't hurt my family's or my reputation. I came here because I was curious, not because I intended to pay. And if you consider doing that, you are a lot less smart than I thought."

Tyler sighed. "No, I don't intend to pay, but I need to figure all this out. *My* family's reputation might be severely damaged. And aside from the stress for all family members, it might cost us money. Money we use for charity, and that's what would hurt all of us the most."

She studied him for a moment and gave him back his phone. After sliding her own into her pocket, she decided to trust her instincts and took his face in her hands, kissed him sweetly. "Then let's figure this out together and make those idiots pay instead of us."

Baffled, he stared at her. "Just like that?"

"Ty, I was angry because I thought you were behind this. And I was even angrier because thinking that hurt me. I still don't know what happened last night. I really thought it would be sex, straight and simple. But I can't get you out of my head. I cursed myself half the morning for not giving you my number or anything, because when I came back from my run the maid was cleaning your room already. I know this probably sounds as crazy as these notes, and I don't want to make more of it than it is. But I also don't want to make less of it. I'm not saying let's jump into a relationship or anything, I'm merely saying perhaps we should see if there's any potential for more than we had last night."

She still held his face, and now he wrapped his hands gently around her wrists, laid his forehead against hers. "I'm pretty lucky you said that, because I was cursing myself this morning, too, for letting you walk out of my room like I did. But I thought if I told you that right now, you would either think I want you in bed again — which, yes, I definitely want — or you would start to evaluate my stalker potential. But damn it, you know a Triforce when you see it, and you know who's who."

Tilting her head, Scarlette grinned. "Good points. Since I want you in bed again, too, we can scratch that off the cons list. As for the rest, should you turn out to be a creepy stalker, I promise you I wouldn't have a problem contacting the cops about you, so I suppose we would deal with that, too. But you don't strike me as the type. And I even have a neat 'Zelda is the girl' shirt. So, life is complicated enough, why complicate things unnecessarily between us, when we can take it day by day, see how it works out?"

"Be careful. If you keep talking so rational and make it so easy, I could seriously fall in love with you."

"Could be nice. We'll see. For now, where are you staying?"

"I rented a trailer, easier to extend if this takes longer than anticipated. What about you?"

"Small house via Airbnb, about five minutes from here if you cut through the backyard. I think I might have the better kitchen. Should we go over there? You can park the trailer up front, and we can throw something together for dinner later while we do a deep dive into what we have both found out so far?"

He ran his hand over her hair, smiled. "Sure."

Interlacing his fingers with hers, he walked down the street and around another corner to guide her to the trailer. She wasn't the least bit surprised when the first thing he did inside was pick her up and tumble onto the bed with her.

Later, Tyler was sitting at the kitchen table in Scarlette's place and nodded in approval. "Nice work, Scarlette."

"To be honest, most is public knowledge and articles from the early 1920s. There isn't an offspring mentioned for Eton and Cecille. All I could find was that she committed suicide because of that; there were rumors of fertility problems and associated depression."

"That sounds oddly familiar to Charles and Mary-Beth."

"Mhm, strange. For Eton, it reads like he remarried about five years after her death. He had a child with his second wife, and if those idiots are right, that's where my biological family stems from. But they weren't public figures anymore, so I couldn't find out about them so easily. I didn't exactly have a lot of time, and that's not the kind of research I'm trained to do."

When she leaned against the table with two glasses of wine in hand and passed him one, he took it and faced her. "Thanks. And that might be the case, but it's mine, more or less. I have everything on my family I need to know or can find within our documents. If you let me, I can dig into yours."

She took a sip from her glass, shrugged. "Yeah, why not. Maybe there is something more behind this. It's too convenient that those women both killed themselves for the same reason at the same time. From all I could find out, it reads to me like all four were close friends. It took a bit to click, to really connect them, but there were those huge parties in the 1920s right at the house up there. I think Cecille and Mary-Beth often arrived a day or two before, setting everything up together. That sounds like connection, like support, not like double suicide however dark things seemed."

"You are right, and now that it clicked for me as well, I only agree even more. I have seen pictures from some of the parties. Not many exist today, but a few, and in them the women strike me as close friends. I think we have a long night ahead of us going over all this."

"Yeah. And tomorrow we should try to find a way into that house."

Playing with the hem of her shirt, Tyler grinned at her. "You looked like you already wanted that today."

"Right. And then someone distracted me with multiple orgasms."

"Despicable."

"Absolutely."

She giggled when he drew her into his lap. "Uh-uh, not now, the lasagna will be ready in a few minutes. And after dinner you can start researching my family, while I go over that archive you've brought along on yours."

"Okay." But he indulged them both in a long kiss before letting her get up again.

When she was getting plates out, he topped off their wine, watched her for a moment. She moved easily but efficiently, and when she checked the oven and the smell of food put a bright smile on her face and made her wiggle her hips, something warm ran through him. He couldn't say what it was, but she fascinated him.

With a short spike of panic that settled equally fast into contentment, he realized he had told her the truth – he could very well fall in love with her. And that was crazy, he barely knew her. For now, he would just enjoy her. She was smart, well-organized (if her files were any indicator), could appreciate simple things in life like good food, and they were amazing in bed together. Everything else, they'd evaluate later.

He lost his train of thought the second he tasted the lasagna. "Oh my god, where did you learn to cook like that?"

"My dad. He owns a small restaurant, together with my grandmother. And once you've spent a month eating trail rations and powdered soup, you put some effort into learning how to do better at home. Can't you cook?"

"I can, but not like this. Tell me about your family, your real one."

Everything inside her warmed. He knew, he understood that for her it wasn't blood making a family.

"Okay. My grandparents immigrated to the US in the early sixties from Italy and had my dad here, he was their first child. My grandpa died two years ago, but grandma is still going strong and even though dad has taken over most of the management aspects of the restaurant, grandma still cooks, talks to the patrons, sometimes even waits tables."

"And your mother?"

"She is an obstetrician. She always wanted to get into medicine, but when she couldn't have kids of her own, after she had two miscarriages, she wanted to understand why, help others. She has a small private clinic, but most of her time she helps around several hospitals in New York."

"So smarts and ambition were ingrained from early on."

"Yeah, you could say so. But they always said I should do what makes me happy."

"And now you do?"

"Yeah."

Watching her smile, Tyler reached out to play with her hair. Then something fell into place.

"Wait, is your mother Dr. Cynthia Langella?"

"Yes, that's her. How do you know?"

"One of our charities has worked with her several times. Due to our family history with Mary-Beth committing suicide because of fertility problems, that's one of the areas my family has always tried to help."

"The world is a strangely small place."

"Agreed. Your mother does great work."

"Yeah, she does. I'm enormously proud of her. She's somewhat disappointed that she won't ever help me with a pregnancy, but she's learned to live with it."

"Is it okay if I ask why?"

Scarlette shrugged easily. "Sure. Kids just aren't my world. I like them fine when I babysit for friends or my cousins, but then I can hand them back to their parents. I'm not a mother type, never have been. In the beginning, my mom especially had problems accepting it because she couldn't understand. But now she spoils the rest of the kids in the family all the more."

Tyler sat back in his chair, studied her for a long moment. "You really mean that."

"What? That I'm not a mother type? Yes. For all the good my mother does, I have also seen children being conceived in an attempt to save a marriage, or because there was an inconvenient accident, or sometimes because the woman thought it was expected of her simply because she had a uterus. None of these are reasons to have a child. If you decide to have one, you need to be okay with giving a lot of yourself up for a long time. And as egoistic as it might sound, I'm not ready to do that. So any child I would have of my own, it would never be fair to the kid. I like myself and what I have done with my life. I'm happy. I don't need a kid to define myself. Lots of people tell me that's heartless or selfish — and with the selfish I agree to a point — but I think it is a lot more heartless to have a child and then not being able to care for it or give it all it should have."

Tyler thought about it over more lasagna before he answered her.

"I think most people have an instinctive need to say you'll change your mind at some point, that yes, especially as a woman you would feel the need to have a child of your own."

"Heard it often enough, yes. You know, whenever I answer them and ask if they think guys make the biggest decisions of their lives with their penis, and if not, why I should make them with my uterus, they always goggle at me and don't know what to say."

Instead of staring, Tyler started to laugh. "Oh, I can see that clearly. And I see your point. It's still unusual for a woman to say she doesn't want children, so people are confused, and a basic human reaction is denial. Guys have been, let's say, socially allowed to say that for a lot longer. And because men are in a way less involved in having children, at least in the pregnancy aspects of it, we don't get depicted as heartless because we already are more distant in people's minds. I can say, I like it better to know you know yourself well enough to be able to say you couldn't give a child completely everything it deserves, so you would rather not have one than involuntarily deprive it of anything in the end only to accommodate society. And it takes guts to voice it so clearly."

"Perhaps I like being contrary." She winked at him. "No. I don't mind that, but the rest is true. And while the uterus example is highly simplified, it sometimes gets people thinking. There are other reasons for not wanting kids — overpopulation, fucked up state of the world in general, to name a few — but those are easy reasons. Not less true, but too easy, and usually something to work on. But your heart has to be in it, and mine wouldn't be. A person deserves better, especially an innocent child. So, no kids for me. I had a sterilization years ago, best decision of my life."

Reaching over the table, Tyler brushed his thumb over her knuckles. "I think the heartless argument is absolutely ridiculous. You have the biggest heart I know. You think of a child not even in existence, while I also know a lot of people who had children for very selfish reasons, and I've seen how those children suffer."

"You're the first one to get that, and just accept it."

"You understood an incredibly important point of some of my books. I would say we work well together."

"It seems so. I never had this conversation after knowing somebody for only a few hours. But you're right, we work well, so you need to know things like this before this goes somewhere other than the bedroom."

"I was thinking about the kitchen counter next, actually."

She chuckled, nudged his hand. "Tyler, I mean it."

"So do I. Here's the deal. Yes, I also think things with you could go in a different direction than anything I had before. And absolute honesty here, with most women I had fun, I had maybe a casual relationship. There was one I thought things could become more serious with: Veronica. Then we were talking about kids. She would have been a great mother, is one now as far as I know. But I couldn't see me as the father of these children. You love your work, I understand that. Because I love mine. I travel for it. A lot. When I write, it's sometimes at highly inconvenient times for a family. I have interviews in the middle of the night because people live across the globe. All those are things you'd have to deal with, by the way. So..."

He ran his hand through his hair in a restless gesture, because it still made him feel guilty that he hadn't talked with Veronica a lot earlier in their relationship and by that had hurt her so much in the end. "I broke her heart when I told her I don't want children of my own.

"Scarlette, I understand and accept your point so easily because I share it. What I want to give up of myself, I give up to a consenting adult or to my work. I couldn't give up my work to bring a kid to a soccer game. If I get an inter-view with the freaking Queen, I need to take it. She wouldn't reschedule because my kid has a birthday party. And you are right, no kid deserves to be put in second place."

She stared at him for a very long moment. "Fuck, Ty."

"What?"

"I could seriously fall in love with you, too," she mumbled

and ran her hands over her face, back through her hair. He grinned at her, gave her a quick kiss. "I'll take it."

"We'll see. But at the moment we have other things to think about."

He helped her clear the table after dinner, and because lust hadn't burned itself out just yet, cleared the counter, too, before having her on it.

They worked until late at night. In the end, Scarlette felt like she already knew most of Tyler's family personally. When it came to her own, she found herself surprised when he showed her one of her biological grandparents had worked as a veterinarian. "You start to wonder what's nature and what's nurture, don't you?"

"You know who you are, Sparks," he said and kissed her hair when he set a new mug of coffee in front of her.

"Yeah, you're right. It's just a little weird. And from how you followed and found things, also pretty convincing that this was really my biological family. Thanks for the coffee. Ty, can I ask you something?"

"Sure."

"If this whole thing turns out to be true, which I sincerely doubt, but *if*, what would you do? About your great-great-grandfather and what he might have done?"

He leaned back in his chair, crossed his legs at the ankles, and looked at his coffee. "I've asked myself the same thing. I still wouldn't pay."

"But you also didn't involve the police, yet."

"You're right. And I think it's because, should it really be true, I want to be the one to reveal it. It would still dent my family's reputation, but as long as I control the story, it won't control us, and *they* won't control us. Contacting the police, there's always some way something could leak."

"And you'd lose control."

"Exactly. What about you?"

"Good question. I never intended to pay, but I also didn't have anything to protect. So I figured, in the end, I would hand everything to the cops, make those idiots pay. Now I'm afraid once I do that, you and your family would unavoidably be dragged into it, without us being the ones steering things in the right direction, and I can't do that."

Sincerely touched, he held out his hand. "Come here."

When she stepped over to him, he drew her into his lap and gathered her close. Framing her face with his hands, he kissed her softly. "Thank you."

Sighing, she kissed him back. "You're welcome. Let's go to bed, I can't focus anymore tonight."

"All right."

Comfortably snuggled against Tyler, Scarlette woke to the insistent ringing of her phone.

"It's five-thirty in the morning, who the hell calls at this hour?" She reached for the phone, saw that the caller was her friend Julia and, ignoring the fact that she was naked, she answered the video call. A mass of long, blond curls appeared on screen, almost covering a face with still-swollen eyes and cheeks red from dried tears.

"July, sweetie, what's wrong?" Seeing the worst crying jag must be over, Scarlette relaxed a little.

On the other end of the call, Julia studied her screen. "Oh, are you still in bed?"

"I am, but it's no problem. Just give me a second to get a shirt."

Beside her, Tyler stirred and blinked at her. Scarlette shortly glanced at him, ran a hand through his hair. "Sorry, I'm getting up, you keep sleeping."

"No, don't worry, I'm mostly awake anyway. My body's clock is screwed up from my last weeks of travel. I'm gonna make us coffee. Stay where you are," he told her and pushed himself up to give her a kiss before rolling out of his side of the bed, hunting up his shorts.

July heard the conversation, saw some dark blond hair and a shoulder with part of a tattoo lean across the camera before Scarlette came back into view.

"Shit, I'm sorry. I can call later, I..."

"July, it's okay."

Scarlette saw her friend sigh with relief. "Who was that?" July asked.

"Tyler. Tyler O'Brien, who might just turn out to be the love of my life, as he's making me coffee," Scarlette explained with a grin towards the door where Ty had just left. He heard her and, with a huge smile spreading across his face, called back to the bedroom on his way downstairs. "I'll hold you to that, Sparks!"

Laughing, Scarlette shifted her attention back to July. "So July, what's wrong?"

"You've never said that about a guy before."

"I never thought a guy could be before. But something clicked between us. But we're not talking about me here.

Sweetie, you sound half drunk, and I see ice cream next to you, and the tissues. Just because you're working in Australia right now doesn't mean I'm not here for you when you need me."

"I know. Thanks. I was down, and I thought I'd catch you before you headed out for work for a little whining and to complain about that guy. I completely forgot that you're on the West Coast, I'm sorry."

"No need, really. What about 'that guy?' Do I know that guy? Do I need to know him? Do I need to fly over there and kick his ass?"

Sniffling, Julia managed a laugh. "No, you don't have to. He's... well, he's good-looking, works at the law firm next to my office building, seems very friendly and sweet, and we've been running into each other at the coffee shop for a bit now, smiling at each other mostly, you know how it is."

"Sure." Scarlette scowled at the screen. "Don't tell me he stole your coffee today. I'll personally drag him to court for it." It had the desired effect, and Scarlette heard her friend laugh again.

"No, that's not it. He actually asked me out last week."

"Okay, that sounds... reasonable when you've been some-what flirting before. Wait, did he hurt you? Have you called the cops? Are you okay?" Concern all over her face, Scarlette studied the image of her friend for any signs of injuries.

"No, no, nothing like that! He didn't even go out with me."

"Now you've got me confused."

July huffed out a breath. "Guess I had him confused, too. I told him no, when he asked."

"Come again?"

"I said no, because, well, I didn't want to seem too easy to get. It's not like he asked me to spend the night in a sleazy hotel, just a movie and dinner, but... anyway. He was kind about it, said 'okay' and wished me good luck. And I think he really meant it. And today I heard from a colleague that he had a date for tonight with our boss's secretary."

Careful, be careful what and how you say it, Scarlette told herself. Sometimes there was such a thing as being too direct, and a crying girlfriend with wine and ice cream needed gentle handling. "Sweetheart, in solidarity with you, I will say once: 'He has a dick, so he is one.' But as much as I love you, I can't really mean it. Okay, a few days between asking you and someone else seems short, but I can't blame him for moving on when you told him no."

"I know. I only figured he'd put a little effort in there and pursue me if he was really interested."

Scarlette nodded at the screen in understanding. "Yes, I can totally see that, and how you were hoping for that. And I understand it. But you know how it is right now for guys, too. Put too much pressure on a woman, go after her when she has said no once, a lot of them end up being slandered online, getting branded as a stalker and whatnot."

Seeing Julia already drawing in air for a passionate reply, Scarlette held up her finger. "I know you wouldn't do that. And I'm not saying many guys don't deserve an eye-opener when they keep pushing and not accepting a no. I'm just saying it's unlikely absolutely every guy vilified online has been exactly as terrible as he's made out to be. And I understand a man when he retreats and protects himself instead, when he does exactly what you asked of him and respected your no. It's not easy, neither for the guys nor for us. We want to be treated like equals and still feel like a princess. That's a difficult road to navigate, especially if you don't really know a person first. How was he supposed to know you wanted him to go after you, hm?" All sweet and gentle, but still not pampering July too much. For Scarlette, friendship came with absolute honesty, even if it meant nagging about her own gender.

Heroically swallowing her automatic defense, July instead spooned some ice cream into her mouth, then stared at her friend. "Okay, and what am I supposed to do now?"

"What about this? You try to find out how his date went. If it went very well, I personally wouldn't interfere. But if there was nothing between them and he's still on the market, why don't you talk to him next time you see him at the coffee shop? Tell him the truth. Not that you changed your mind about the date, but that you would like to explain to him why you said no initially. Tell him women are complicated, we're a piece of work, we annoy ourselves half the time, but if he's still interested you'd like to go out with him."

"Seriously?"

"Well, yeah. What's the worst that can happen? He says no, too. And most guys at least mean it, so you'll know. Maybe he'll complain to a few of his friends about how screwed up women are."

"I guess you're right. Thanks, Scarlette. I mean it."

"No problem. I'll come over soon, or you come back to visit me once I'm done with this whole thing here. Then we'll talk and properly get drunk together."

"Sounds perfect to me."

"You better?"

"Yeah. Yeah, I am. You'll have to tell me more about Tyler."

"I will."

"Now, girl. Important things first. How's the sex?"

"Seriously incredible."

"How and when did you meet?"

"At the hotel bar, when I landed here the day before yesterday. We clicked, had an epic night together, and later he actually offered me his help with finding things out about my supposed ancestor." Yes, it wasn't all in there and in the perfect order, but for now, she didn't want to include his connection too much.

"And you're sure he isn't behind the blackmail attempt? Scarlette, this is all so strange."

"It is, but yes, I'm sure. He isn't Patrick, he seriously wants to help. He's a biographer, he knows how best to find things like that. And he's coming back with coffee right now."

Taking the mug from him, Scarlette thanked him, turned the phone around for some introductions. "July, Tyler O'Brien. Ty, Julia, or July, Stone. We've been friends for about twenty years now."

"Hi, Julia."

"Hello. Sorry I woke you both up."

"No problem, we have a full day ahead of us, an early start only helps."

"Okay. Uh, nice to meet you."

"Nice to meet you, too."

Scarlette turned the phone back, grinned at her friend. "See, he's cool and doesn't look like a serial killer. Call me or text me about your guy."

"I will. Thanks, honey. Love you! Bye."

"Love you, too. Bye."

After hanging up, Scarlette gulped down some coffee, sighed. "Oh, thank you, coffee gods."

"Junkie."

"Yes, and not ashamed to admit it."

"Well then. Julia seems charming."

"She is. Best person I've ever known aside from my parents."

"So if I ever need to know any deep, dark secret about you, she's the one to go to."

"Maybe I should keep you two far apart from each other."

"I doubt there's any danger of her telling me anything. Polite as she was, she watched me like she'd contact the FBI and would nag them until they tell her all there is about me."

Scarlette lifted an eyebrow. "You have an FBI file?"

"Not that I know of, but she might get them to open one."

She shook her head, played with his fingers. "She just might. She tends to worry."

"Because of... who was it? Patrick?"

"You have bat ears. Yeah. You know how I joked about handing you over to the cops if you turned out to be a stalker? I did with Patrick. We went on one date, it didn't work for me, but he got obsessed. It ended with him breaking into my old apartment and trying to slip some tranq into my food and drinks, probably to abduct me when I was out cold. I walked in on him in the kitchen in the middle of the night, grabbed a knife and pinned his hand to the counter, then called the cops on him."

Tyler's fingers gripped hers, squeezed, his other hand came to her cheek, rested there. "Holy shit, Scarlette. Did he hurt you?"

"No, I was faster, and he would most likely have run."

"When was that?"

"About two years ago." She waved it away with an easy gesture of her hand. "I moved, he doesn't know where. I have a restraining order against him. I know how to defend myself. I'm good."

He kept his hand on her face, brushed her cheekbone gently with his thumb. "And it explains why you're so careful about giving details about yourself."

"I've always been. But yes, the incident made me even more aware of how and what I say and to whom, and confirmed why I don't really use social media to share anything about me."

"So I'm the exception?" His sweet smile shot straight to her heart.

"It seems that you are."

"I am happy to hear that." He leaned over to kiss her. But instead of the heat he had expected, her story now pushed a need to protect, to cherish, to the surface. He deepened the kiss without any haste, tasted lavishly, played with her tongue, and ended it with his lips curving against hers. "Very happy."

The gentleness had surprised her, the kiss had dazzled her, so Scarlette shook her head. "Man, you can fuzz my brain even with a kiss."

"Happy to hear that, too. Should we go over what we plan to do today?"

"Sure. I'll start with a run, a shower, then breakfast. After that we need to find a way into the house."

"Good plan. Mind if I join you on your run? The trailer and this place don't come with a gym like the hotel."

"No problem. Let's get ready."

Chapter Three

Who would have expected both of them to travel to the house?

The woman, maybe. She hadn't had a clue about anything before. They had expected her to be more reluctant to pay, perhaps do some digging.

But the writer? His entire family had always paid. Most hadn't even demanded any proof in the past. An important name had to be protected. He had the money, so why wouldn't he just pay?

What did they expect to find in the house?

The old articles stated both women had been found dead there after committing suicide, yes. But why would they think anything of value, any evidence could still be there after a hundred years?

Not that the family hadn't checked. Even right after Cecille's and Mary-Beth's deaths there had been rumors of hidden spaces, hidden letters. Year after year, generation after generation, they had torn the place apart. And nearly all the wonderful money went into the upkeep of the doomed villa, to keep it standing, so it or its ruins wouldn't fall into somebody else's hands. You never knew what people would find accidentally.

So it had become a family tradition, so to speak, to keep the blackmail going — and to receive payments without hesitation.

Now some sick joke of fate had killed his parents and her mother almost at the same time. And instead of drowning in despair or raging from the betrayal of her parents — who could have known they had always told her about the adoption? — those two bastards had decided to play detectives. What was it with people today? Too much information at hand to start with.

Earlier generations might have heard something or found an article or two about the old film stars of the family. But that had been it. Now everything was a mouse click away. Silent film stars – parties – fame and fortune – death and despair – and a house on a hill.

Whatever the writer boy's family had held in their hands over the years, they had never made the trip. And pet girl's blood kin had had basically no information at all. After the end of Barret's career, they had slowly slipped into oblivion, a footnote of history but nothing more.

They both deserved a kick in the ass for making the trip there, and so did the family for getting the update about it to everybody with more than a full day's delay. As if it hadn't been difficult enough to find professions for the family members that kept them close. No, now additional travel was necessary and meant more work to find the places they stayed so a little more pressure could be applied directly.

Chapter Four

Not being able to sleep, July remembered the light that had lit up Scarlette's eyes when Tyler had come back into the bedroom during the call. It seemed this really was different for her friend, so July decided to do her friendship duty and started a search for Tyler O'Brien. Not the rarest name, but his face had been familiar, and by adding his profession, she might get lucky.

She took another sip of wine — and spit it over her screen when the search results came up.

"Shit!" Frantically cleaning her laptop with the sleeve of her pajama, she stared in disbelief at the pictures. It was him, and damn her if he hadn't looked even better with the early-morning scruff and his hair all tousled from sleep than in his official glamour shots. Her friend had bagged herself one of the most sought-after bachelors of the year, and July had talked to him teary-eyed and wearing old comfy pjs. A missed date suddenly wasn't that important anymore.

Things had sounded easy and relaxed between them, as if they had known each other for a long time already. But what was he doing in LA right now? He should be in Europe, probably tying up the details for the Queen's bio deal, interviewing people for it. Now he was helping Scarlette research something that might turn out to be a stupid joke at best, a pathetic attempt at a threat at worst? Strange, very strange.

Scrolling down through some articles, Julia stumbled across his family's charity work and read about the reason for it going back to the 1920s. To a childless couple, a tragic suicide, a friend's death, a house on a hill outside of LA.

What have you both been dragged into? Whatever it is, I have a bad feeling. Getting you involved is one thing, sweetie. But him, that is either incredibly bold or incredibly desperate. Both are dangerous.

Making up her mind, Julia let her boss know she would work remotely for a bit because she had to help a friend. Booking her flights took only a few minutes, and about an hour later she left her apartment.

Once she was sitting in her seat on the plane, she shot a text to Scarlette, then switched her phone to flight mode. Her friend wouldn't persuade her to stay on the other end of the world when she was getting deeper and deeper into a messy situation.

Chapter Five

"Tell me again why I have to go as the half-naked goth girl?" Scarlette demanded while hiking the rest of the way to the villa after they had gotten through the gate at the foot of the hill.

"Because you are very attractive half-naked? Even the goth part works, and it suits the location," Tyler answered while checking out her ass, which was currently wrapped in tight leather hot pants. "Tell me again why you know how to pick a lock, and so quickly at that?"

"If you have ever been in a hoarder apartment in a sweltering summer heat with twenty cats and one overflowing litter box and you must open several crates with other animals, you learn to get a lock open as fast as you can. And don't try to distract me. You can hide under your ball cap, behind your shades. Why can't I play photographer?"

"Because we both know it is much more realistic and less conspicuous to have a female model. You have been pissed ever since you've gotten July's text. She wants to help you, I find that admirable."

"I do, too, it's not that. And yes, I would do the same for her. But she should stay in Australia. She's there because she is helping her father, who was hit by a drunk driver a couple of months ago and had his hips so badly shattered that he needed a replacement."

"Okay, fair point. But do you think she would have left if she wasn't sure he'd be all right for a few days?"

"Stop being so logical."

Patting her butt with a cocky smile, he lifted the camera he wore as much as a disguise as a tool to document the villa so they could study it back at the rented house.

"I'll try. Right now, I'm still wondering how she came to think this would be bigger and riskier and involve my family. I don't figure you for the type who would tell her."

"I didn't, you're right. But you were also right when you said she'd try to find things out about you. She might not contact the FBI, but she knows how to uncover things herself. She works as a Social Media/PR consultant for a global agency. She probably couldn't sleep and looked you up, had half a heart-attack, and then quickly got to the part where your family name leads back to the roaring twenties and a tragic death."

"And you running into me close to the scene of the deaths of our ancestors — two strangely similar stories — and me jumping at the chance to work with you on your case are too big of a coincidence."

Scarlette nodded. "There you have it. She wouldn't have texted it straight like that, but I bet you fifty bucks she's already made up her mind that you and/or your family are involved somehow, too, and to keep me safe, she wants to find out more."

"I think I will like her. Now, why don't you get in the spirit of this and strike a pose, so it looks like we're working here to any nosy neighbors?"

They were standing in front of the old porch now, and Scarlette studied the long-abandoned villa. "It's a shame, she would be a beauty. She has this wonderful Victorian charm, and good bones or she would have collapsed by now. Okay, let's play this up."

Stepping over a broken step, she positioned herself in the doorway, back against the frame, one leg up and the foot pressing against the other side. With her arms stretched overhead, she aimed her gaze directly into the camera. She gave him a moment, then turned around, legs and arms spread in the doorway, leaning a little forward into the house so he got an exceptionally alluring view of her behind.

He nearly choked on the saliva pooling in his mouth, and Scarlette chuckled. "Everything okay there, Link?"

Forcing himself to think of something else, anything else really, multiplication tables perhaps, he did his best to redirect the blood that had shot straight south. "Ah, yeah. Where did you learn to pose like that?"

"Take a guess. No bragging, but I've got tits, I've got an awesome figure, and somewhat unusual eyes. I have friends who have photography as a hobby. You're not the first to ask me to model for him. Only the first to do a fake shooting to get into an old building."

"Oh, I took pictures, believe me. And I vote for a more personal photo shoot at some point too."

"Maybe you'll get it."

Rubbing dust and grime from her hands, she took a step

inside, held out her hand for a flashlight. "Wow, look at all this."

Even under layers of dirt and neglect, one could see the possibilities, the opulence of the lucky ones of an era long gone by. A chandelier was still hanging on the ceiling of the impressive foyer, a wide staircase opened to a gallery leading to two separate wings with their alcoves and towers.

Old picture frames still covered a wall, but the pictures had crumbled to dust or were soaked by rain where a window close to them had been broken.

Studying his surroundings, Tyler got out his own light and shook his head. "You are right, it's a shame. This place must have been amazing back in the day."

"Yeah, absolutely. Whom does it belong to now? You would have checked."

"I did. From what I could find, several old studios and other firms all hold parts of it, so nothing ever gets done because they can't decide what or by whom."

"Too bad."

They strolled through the building, taking pictures of all the rooms, or at least those they could enter without being in danger of falling through the floor.

In the middle of the two wings, they found a room which gave the impression it had been used by both women with its twin set of old chests of drawers and chairs, mirrors and hooks for clothes on two walls. "I bet this was their dressing room where they prepared for the parties, or where they were styled for shooting a movie. Look, here's an old dressing table, and this mirror is almost intact," Scarlette said and reverently ran her hand over old wood and tarnished glass.

"You sound unusually perky about this."

"Oh, I can be girly, don't be fooled. But I don't feel like I need to spruce up every day. Plus, this is a piece of history, that's so cool."

Her finger ran over a flower in the frame and the carving suddenly depressed. Next to Scarlette a hidden door sprang open and revealed a dark passage. She squeaked in excited surprise. "Oh god, how awesome is that? That must be one of the shortcuts around here for the actors during shooting and for the house staff for parties. Let's check..."

But when she wanted to step inside, Tyler took her wrist. "Forget it, it's pitch black in there, the flashlights won't provide enough light to see every inch of that floor."

"Spoilsport." She pouted, but quickly giggled when he poked her ribs.

"Sorry that I want you in one piece back in bed tonight."

"Okay, okay. But take pictures."

"Sure." He leaned carefully into the passageway, snapped a few pictures, then held the camera with one hand and took a few more shots with the flash in both directions.

But hours later, reality sunk in more and more when they found nothing that would help them understand what was going on. Resigned and ready to call it a day, Scarlette walked out to stand on one of the balconies overlooking the overgrown garden behind the house. She let her eyes wander over the yard before turning around and carefully leaning back against the banister.

"Why did we both come here, Ty? What did we expect to find in this place, really? It's been so long, and so much has been taken from here already."

She let out a frustrated huff, and the light of the slowly setting sun played with her hair, made it seem like she wore a fiery crown. Tyler's heart stumbled and, desperate to freeze this image of her, he took her picture, then stepped over to her. His fingers wandered up her sides, then to her face, and from there ran into her hair.

"I don't know, Scarlette. And right at this moment, I don't care. I don't care about the idiots trying to blackmail us, or if our ancestors did or didn't kill their wives. Or I care a little, as I find myself grateful for it all, because it brought me here, and it brought you here, to me. I met you because of all this." His lips closed over hers and he felt her breath escape in a sigh.

"That's definitely a plus in all this, yes."

Back at the Airbnb, Scarlette put some tacos together while Tyler copied the pictures he had taken earlier to his computer. While putting things on the table, she leaned over his shoulder. "You're a pretty decent photographer."

"Thanks. You pick things up with people taking pictures during interviews. And when there was no photographer at hand, I started to sometimes take some pictures myself, mostly when it was for shorter articles or something."

"Nice."

"Hm. Oh yeah, I definitely need to keep this one." When he changed his wallpaper to the picture of her on the balcony with the sunlight hitting her hair, she laughed.

"Not my sexiest smile."

"No, but so completely you. Not trying to impress or to pose, and still overwhelmingly intense. Very compelling."

"That's the writer in you."

"It is, but he tells the truth. Dinner for now?"

"Yes, let's put this aside for a few minutes."

And for a bit, they did. They talked about simple things – movies, the music they liked, games they played.

"I'll make you cry when you lose at *Mario Kart*."

"As if you could beat me, Sparks."

"Can and will. I have played every game, starting with the SNES version."

"Seriously? That came out, what, the year before you were born?"

"Yep. And as soon as my hands could hold a controller, I started playing. One of my uncles is obsessed with games; I love him."

"Okay. Future relationship defining question, then." Ty rested his forearms on the table, leaned over closely.

"Should I be afraid?" Scarlette gave a pretend shudder.

"Maybe. *Breath of the Wild.*"

She narrowed her eyes, kept them on him while she took a sip from her beer, considering.

"Excellent question. I will admit that it misses the classic *Legend of Zelda* feeling, therefore it feels different and somewhat distant from the series as we all know it. As a game itself, I loved it. It's well done, the world has been created carefully, you feel that there's lots of love and hard work in there. I'm a fan of the classic feel, but I don't feel, even with a different approach, that it trampled on the legacy." She drank some more beer, watched his smile spread.

"Nicely put."

Grinning, she leaned on the table as well. "My time to ask. *Star Wars.*"

"Episode four, five, six. The old version, naturally. And is there really another answer?"

"You'd be surprised. I guess that means we're destined to be together."

"Agreed. Wanna marry me?"

Laughing, Scarlette shook her head. "Ask me again in a week, then I should know you well enough."

"All right." He took a slow swallow of beer, watched her with gleaming eyes and curved lips.

Her stomach twisted in a mix of utter joy and rising panic. "You meant that."

"Oh yes, I did." He hadn't known he had, not before the words had just come out of his mouth. But the second they had been out, he had been sure that she was the woman he wanted for the rest of his life.

"Ah, wow. I think, I did, too. A week, then I can tell you."

"All right," he answered again and gave her a hard kiss.

After dinner, conversation drifted back to the past.

"Have you asked for any proof, yet, Ty?"

"No. I wouldn't even know how. The letter was slipped under my door at the hotel I was staying in for an interview. Nobody could tell me by whom or when. Seeing as they knew where I was, I must assume they keep tabs on me. They can find me, but so far I have no idea how to find them. What about you?"

"No idea, either. I found the envelope with the letter in my mailbox one day. A blank envelope, no address or anything else. But still, I think we should both demand proof. We won't pay, but whatever they give to us, we can use as further evidence with the cops."

"You're right. And it might be more useful than this." Ty

shoved at the photos from his family's collection on the table, cursed.

"Sucks, doesn't it? Leave it for tonight and come to bed with..." She stopped mid-sentence and her gaze shifted from table to laptop and back.

"Scarlette?"

"Weird. You managed to take close to the same picture as this old one of Cecille."

"You're right. It must have been in one of the old albums. It's a decent spot for pictures. Light, excellent framing, view across the garden."

"Yeah. And did you see this?"

"What?"

"In the background, down in the garden. Doesn't it look like somebody is hiding something under the gazebo?"

"Wait. I have them all on the computer, too."

He scrolled through the folder, finally found the picture, and zoomed in.

"Admittedly not the best quality, but yes, it appears like there's a hidden compartment beneath the gazebo. And that looks a lot like Mary-Beth stashing something there."

"It does. And that gazebo is completely overgrown now. I don't think anybody has done anything with it in a very long time."

Judging the light outside, Tyler walked his fingers up her arm. "Scarlette, darling, how do you feel about a stroll through a historic garden at sunrise? Perhaps some landscaping, very likely some light demolition work?"

"I thought you'd never ask." Giggling, she slid onto his lap and pecked a kiss on his lips, squeaked when he got up with her in his arms and strode towards the bedroom.

Chapter Six

W hile Julia fought her way through customs after an exhausting flight the next morning, Scarlette and Tyler knelt beside the base of the old gazebo.

"You were right; now is the perfect time: there's enough light without flashlight beams drawing attention. And listen, this sounds strange." With a bright grin Scarlette tapped against a side panel and compared the sound to the planks on each side.

"I believe you are right. Do you want to do the honors?"

"Happy to." Scarlette eagerly jammed the crowbar they had bought earlier between two of the boards, levered against it. The panel fell out easily and she rubbed her hands. "Open sesame."

"Awesome. Let's see what's in there." Thinking of rats and other vermin, Tyler shone a light into the opening and found the small space empty. "We are sure that's the correct spot, right?"

"Yeah, of course. Hm... Let me see. Wait." She bellied down in front of the opening, tapped the floor carefully with the crowbar until she heard a metallic ping. "And there you go."

"Again, marry me, I mean it."

She rolled on her back with a laugh. "I know. I still would like to have a few days more to get to know you before I make a life-altering decision."

"Okay. Six days." He leaned down, pinned her on the ground for a deep kiss, then let her sit up again.

"Okay, yeah, six days. Now let's work to get that out of there."

They dug out a small metal lockbox, and Scarlette studied the lock. "Want me to try to pick it?"

"No, I don't think that's necessary. I think I have seen a key that could fit, but we will have to get to my family's estate for it." He put the box into the satchel he carried across his body and got up with Scarlette after setting the board back in its place. "So, are you coming back home with me?"

"Well, we haven't found anything else of any use here, have we? And in case they really keep an eye on us, I'd prefer to be on our own turf, so yes, let's pack up and leave."

"Good. Very good, to be honest. I had hoped to be home soon, so I'll be there when my brother comes back."

"I can understand that. How is he dealing with everything? How are *you* dealing with it? With losing your parents, I mean? I didn't want to pry before, but..."

Taking her hand to find some comfort, Tyler was silent for a moment, sighed deeply.

"It's hard, I won't lie about that. We lost them without any warning, no sickness with time to prepare. Wouldn't make it easier, but different. But like this? I had dark moments, still have them. But mostly I buried it under my own work, under the funeral preparations, under the things I had to take over with the family business, at least temporarily. For Josh it's hard. He is seventeen; he was a surprise, but a happy one, and he was always the baby of the family. He's kind, he's sweet. He tries to pretend he's okay because he doesn't want to burden me, but I know it's terribly hard for him. He insisted on going on this class trip, and that meant I could come here. But it's better that I'll be home when he's scheduled to be back. I just hope I'll know what to do for him."

On the street, she turned to him and rose to her toes. Her gentle hands captured his face and her lips floated softly to his, working like a soothing balm on a fresh wound. Her eyes looked directly into his, into him. "I think you are a wonderful brother."

When he dragged her close, when his arms came around her, she felt him shudder. "God Scarlette, I need you. I need you so much already."

"I know." She kissed him again, sweetly smiled at him. "Yes."

"Yes wha... Yes?"

"Yes. Screw six days, I know what I feel. There's a lot of lusting going on, but I know underneath it is more. I have never felt for anybody what I feel for you."

"I love you."

"I know." When he burst into laughter, she threw herself into his arms and was twirled around. Ty set her down, took her face. "Tell me."

"I love you, Tyler."

Stumbling through the backyard, they lost the first clothes in the kitchen.

Chapter Seven

Julia was about to ring the doorbell when she heard a cry from inside. Finding the front door locked, she ran around the back and into the house. In her rush to help her friend she didn't see the clothes.

"Scarlette, where are you? Are you okay?"

July pushed open a door and stumbled out backward when she saw Scarlette's naked back, saw that Tyler was sitting under her on a chair, his face buried between her breasts and his hands kneading her butt.

"Sorry, sorry, sorry!"

Scarlette sighed, then dropped her head on Ty's shoulder with a chuckle. "Good thing we were finished."

"And here I was hoping for a second round under the shower."

"You have a whole life of shower sex and second rounds coming up."

His hand ran possessively up and down her back. "I'm a lucky man."

"You are. I think I should check on July."

"Yeah, maybe. I'm taking a quick shower."

"Okay."

Wrapped in a robe, Scarlette found a still-flushed Julia in the kitchen searching for things to prepare some tea. She nearly dropped the mug in her hand when she heard somebody behind her.

"July, sweetie, hi!"

Scarlette took the mug and set it on the counter, then threw her arms around her friend and swayed with her. "I missed you."

"I missed you, too. And I'm really, really sorry. I heard a cry and... well... seriously incredible, I guess?"

"Yes. And so much more. We'll tell you later. I didn't know you'd be here so early."

"I got lucky in a strange way. One of my connections was canceled and I was booked on another, faster one."

"Great. Because we were talking about packing up. Then we got distracted. But we need to go to Tyler's family home."

Julia ran a hand through her hair. "There's a lot going on, it seems."

"And then some. I'm gonna take a quick shower, too, then we'll talk while we pack."

"Sure. You get ready, I'm plundering the kitchen; plane food is the one thing getting worse and worse every year."

"True. I'm so happy you are here," Scarlette said with a kiss on the cheek for July, then ran back into the bedroom.

Tyler was already out of the shower again and was searching for some clean clothes with a towel slung around his hips. On her way to the bathroom, Scarlette tugged the towel away with a laugh. "Mine. I need one for my hair."

"You gonna pay for that."

"Oh my, I hope so."

Ten minutes later, Scarlette heard Tyler and Julia talking in the kitchen and joined them.

"I updated Julia on the past of my family in this whole situation." He wrapped his arm around Scarlette's waist when she leaned against him.

"That's all?" Scarlette asked.

"I didn't want to take the future away from you."

"Thanks. So, July, more to tell you about the blackmail stuff, but this is important, too. Ty and I are getting married."

Completely dumbfounded, Julia gaped at them, then blinked. "I'm sorry, what? I think I heard you say you were getting married."

"You heard right. We got engaged this morning, hence the distraction from packing."

July took a deep breath. There was no kind way to do this, so she took a page from Scarlette's book and went with the blunt approach. "Have you lost your mind? Both of you? You've known each other for what, three days?"

"And other people have known each other for years before getting married and still end up with a divorce," Scarlette answered calmly and took her best friend's hand before she went on. "July, sweetheart, I know how this must sound. But we know the important things about each other, we want the same things from life.

"More importantly, I know myself. I know when I'm hot

for a guy, when it's one night or two of fun. I know how it is to be sweet on someone, to feel something to cruise along on for a while. But I have never been in love, not truly all the way in love. I love Tyler."

Reason had no chance against the happiness in Scarlette's eyes. Worse, reason told Julia that Scarlette indeed knew herself that well. She huffed out a breath, then dragged Scarlette into her arms. "Congratulations. I'm happy for you. I think. For you, too," she said with a grin in Tyler's direction.

"Thanks, sweetie," Scarlette answered with a grin.

"Thanks, Julia."

"Sure. No ugly bridesmaid dress or I'll have to kill you." She shot a finger at Scarlette, who giggled and drew one of her friend's curls long to watch it spring back into place.

"No ugly bridesmaid dress, I promise."

"Okay. Have you told your mother?"

"Not yet. You basically ran in on our private celebration."

"And it's forever burned into my brain. She'll be okay with Tyler, I think. Oh, I'm supposed to say hello from Dr. Branson by the way. I ran into him when I arrived at the airport."

"Hm, interesting. I wasn't aware of any conference or something here at the moment. But thanks."

"Who is he?" Ty wanted to know.

"Oh, he was July's and my pediatrician, and my mom has still been referring patients to him until recently, as far as I know. I think he's close to retirement by now or has retired, I'm not sure, but he's always kept himself up to date."

For a few minutes they all put the rest out of their minds and started on some first wedding plans, until Scarlette frowned.

"We need to stop talking about it. We have to pack, and more importantly, I have to tell my parents. My mom will want to plan with us."

Tyler nodded in agreement. "You are right, Sparks. Then let's do that."

July observed them together and saw real affection, care-free gestures, trust, and warmth.

"You two look good together. Go packing, I'll take care of the kitchen. We have time to talk about all the rest on the way to the airport."

The women returned the rental car and Scarlette waited with Julia for Tyler at one of the coffee shops.

"You still think that I'm crazy, that we are crazy, don't you, July?"

"I wish. But no, not after seeing you together. And my brain has no room for that kind of thought right now because it is focused on thinking how crazy *I* am for getting on a plane again after the trip earlier."

From behind her, Tyler stepped up and slung a friendly arm around her shoulders. "Fear not, this trip should be more comfortable than the last. Are you two coming?"

Whatever she had expected — an upgrade, sure, maybe even first class — July hadn't expected he'd guide them to a smaller terminal with a private plane waiting for them. Seeing the women gape at the plane, he laid his arm around Scarlette's shoulders. "I know, a little over the top, but we have it and had it customized because we use it to transport our horses personally."

Scarlette slanted her eyes at him. "We'll definitely talk

about your family business later in more detail. Right now, let me say, that's an impressive way to travel."

Beside her, July nodded. "Uh-huh. Okay, you are officially not crazy for hooking up with him and planning a future."

Scarlette chuckled. "Ah, we're lucky. My best friend approves of your money, babe."

"I'm relieved. Why else would you be with me and marry me? And to think she might ask me to give it all up so I could have you."

July stuck out her tongue at both of them. "Shut up."

Scarlette laughed, hooked her arm under July's, and grinned at Tyler. "I'm the last to complain about this, but to be fair, I would have also fallen for you if you hadn't had any money."

"I know." He gave her a quick kiss, then greeted the waiting cabin crew.

After take-off, Tyler took some coffee from the flight attendant and smiled at Julia. "Better than the last flight?"

She glanced around the cabin with its leather seats and tables in gleaming wood. "Serious upgrade, yeah."

"You still look tired, though. There's a sleeping compartment. We'll be in the air for a few hours to get back east. Why don't you get some sleep?"

With Julia snuggled into the small, separated sleeping area, Tyler sat beside Scarlette and with his fingers under her chin gently turned her head so his lips could brush hers. "And what about you? You've been quiet since we've boarded. Everything all right?"

Look at him, she thought, *only a few days and he knows me so well.* She had become nervous when she had seen this part of his world. But now he watched her with those quiet blue eyes, his fingers softly caressing her skin, and everything settled again.

"Yes, I'm fine. For a minute I thought I couldn't do this, couldn't really marry you. July is right, we've just met, and you have all this," she explained, gesturing around her at the plane. "I haven't had a chance to see that side of you, yet. To take it in. Whatever I said a little earlier, it didn't really hit me until we boarded."

"Scarlette." For the first time she saw a hint of impatience flicker in his eyes, heard the edge of it in his voice; but it was more than that for him. Fear was a keen blade pushing its tip into his gut. She would not back off. He still didn't know why, might never completely fathom it, but she was what he needed.

"Let me finish." She wrapped her fingers around his wrist, felt his pulse beat there, fast and strong, and a little unsteady. "I got scared for a moment. I'm good at what I do, I'm good at being me. I got scared, because I wasn't sure how good I would be as a wife. As *your* wife, your partner. All this comes with a lot of responsibility, and parts of our life together with more publicity than I'm used to." She brought both hands to his cheeks, gazed deeply into his eyes. "Then you touched me, looked at me. And everything fell into place. There'll be so many changes, for both of us, but we'll deal with them. We'll make it work – together. And that's a lot coming from someone who's used to handle things alone because I like it that way."

He huffed out a sigh of relief, rested his forehead against hers. "You scared the hell out of me there for a second, Sparks. It's crazy that we should feel all we feel after only a few days, but we do. And we'll figure things out together. I think I never paid enough attention to those words. We. Together. They sound damn fine to me now."

"Same for me. So let me ask you, how long until news of our engagement hits the press? Because I know we don't have a lot of time when we should be figuring out the blackmail deal, but I don't want my parents to read in a tabloid about her daughter marrying some semi-famous writer. So I would like to tell them soon, would like them to meet you."

Tyler teasingly nipped at her bottom lip, drew her closer. "The semi-famous writer would like to meet them, too. But sadly it's true that we have other things to focus on as well. Do you want to tell them in person, or would video be okay for now, too? We have an excellent system on board; beats a normal call with your mobile. And unfortunately you're right, the news might hit the press soon enough. The crew here is discreet, I know them all personally. But people on the ground might have heard us talking."

"Right. Hm, video would be okay for now. We'll get to the in-person part soon enough. Let me check where they are."

Two minutes later, Scarlette was sitting in front of a big screen with a fresh coffee in hand. "I admit, that's a superior setup. My mom upgraded her home office during the pandemic, too, but this tops it. I got lucky to reach them both at home together. Mom was preparing something for a charity function and working from home today, but dad was almost on the way out to get to the restaurant."

"Perfect, I think they should both hear this together."
"Yep."
The call brought the screen alive with two cheerful faces.

Tyler saw a lean woman with calm blue eyes and a narrow but open face topped with short blond hair. A quick flash of her hand showed short, well-manicured nails. She was a picture of competence and efficiency complemented with charm and a loving, warm smile when her eyes rested on her daughter.

Her husband stood behind her, his hands resting on his wife's shoulders. Working hands, Ty thought. Scrapes and scars from working in the kitchen, but the same short and cared for nails. His face radiated happiness when he faced the camera. It showed no sign of a man being pressed for time to open his business. Shining dark eyes, nearly as dark as his hair, which showed only the slightest threads of gray, and a mouth curved in a smile were all inviting for a casual chat.

Tyler had never met them before, but he saw the unity, the love between them right away. And he saw clearly they felt the same for their daughter. She was part of them, blood relation or not; she was completely and entirely theirs. And now he wanted to take her, or part of her, away from them. It left his mouth dry with his own spurt of panic, and he could suddenly understand Scarlette's earlier fear about what a marriage would mean. Then she shifted beside him, and her scent flowed over to him. It coated his fear as effectively as his eyes had done for her.

"Mom, dad. Hi!"

"Scarlette, sweetheart. It's so good to hear from you. Is something wrong? You said it was important," her mother began, and was interrupted by her husband.

"Bella, hello. Where are you? On a plane? And who is..."

"Wait, is that Tyler O'Brien?" Her mother's focus had shifted to the man beside her daughter as well.

"Yeah, that's him."

"Tell me you convinced him to join us at the charity gala next week and contribute generously." Giggling, Scarlette's mother gestured to the back of her office. "Your dress arrived today with mine, by the way. And I am sorry for my manners, Mr. O'Brien. We're an incredibly direct family, and the gala is mostly all that's been on my mind for weeks. It's very nice to meet you. I'm Cynthia Langella, this is my husband Marco."

"It's nice to meet you, indeed, Mr. O'Brien," Marco agreed with his wife.

Any remaining uneasiness slipped away from Tyler, and he smiled broadly at the camera. "It's a pleasure to meet you, Dr. Langella, Mr. Langella. No, Scarlette hasn't mentioned the gala, yet, but I would be thrilled to join you. My family's charity is involved already, I'd be happy to see the results of it all personally."

"Wonderful. Scarlette, be so kind to share the details. I hope we won't interrupt your plans too much, Mr. O'Brien. Feel free to bring somebody along, we'll make sure there's room for two."

Out of range of the camera, Tyler ran his fingers along Scarlette's hip. "That's very thoughtful. I think I already have the perfect woman in mind."

Scarlette could only shake her head and tried to hide her grin. "Mom, didn't you want to know why I wanted to talk to you?"

"Oh, yes, of course. I'm sorry, I got carried away."

"Really? I hadn't noticed. Anyway, I called because, uh..." She needed to take a bracing breath. "... because I wanted to tell you Tyler and I met, and well, we are together."

If possible, an even brighter smile spread on Cynthia's face.

Marco gleamed with joy. "Well, Bella, that explains the shine in your eyes," he concluded.

"Yes. You look happy, sweetheart."

"Yeah, I am. Um, that's not all. We are getting married."

For a full five seconds there was no movement or reaction at all on screen.

"Are you still there or did we lose the connection for a moment?"

Cynthia covered her mouth with her hand and nodded. Marco's fingers dug into his wife's shoulders a little. "No, we're still here, Bella. Did you say what I think you did?"

"Yes. Ty and I are engaged."

Cynthia left out an explosive breath. "Holy shit. Really? You're sure about this, honey?"

"Really. And yes, absolutely."

"Damn, that's fucking amazing. Sorry, Tyler, as you're part of the family now, you'll have to live with the normal part of us, too, without the veneer of polished manners for fundraisers and the rest of the work."

Beside Scarlette, Tyler broke into a laugh and easily slung his arm around her shoulders. "I like the normal part of you very much already, Dr. Langella."

"Cynthia. And Marco. Family, Tyler. Scarlette wouldn't have told us this, or gotten engaged to you, if she wasn't a hundred percent sure you're the one. She told us, and she'll marry you, so you are family."

"Thank you. I couldn't wish for a better one, I would say."

"We'll get along fine. As family, let me say I'm sorry about your parents. We heard about the accident. If there's anything you or your brother need, anything at all, let us know."

It touched him deeply, because he could feel she meant it. These weren't empty condolences, and god knew he had heard enough of those. Not only didn't she blame him for ripping part of her heart out by stealing her daughter, instead she just opened it to make room for him. "Thank you, Cynthia. I wish we could come by tonight, I would love to meet you face to face."

"Our door is always open, but from the texts Scarlette has been sending, it sounds like you have a lot on your hands."

"Yes. We're on our way to the family home to find out more."

Tyler gave Scarlette's parents the quick version of what had been happening the last few days, and Marco nodded. "For all the mess it is, and I am sorry for the added stress to your family, I am still glad our daughter doesn't have to face this alone. And if there is a connection in the past, maybe it will stop this from going on in the future, when you figure it out together."

"That's what we're hoping for."

"I would feel more comfortable knowing you would involve the police, but I understand your concern about any leaks. Even more so now, as I see Cynthia is getting the first questions on her messenger here as news of your engagement has apparently found its way online."

Tyler sighed. "Well, that was fast."

Cynthia nodded. "Yes. Scarlette, thank you so much for letting us know, and so quickly. But I think you should contact your brother now, Tyler. He needs to hear it from you, too."

"You're a treasure, Cynthia. I can't wait to come by together with Scarlette."

"We're looking forward to see you," Marco finished and waved goodbye to the camera together with his wife.

Tyler had his phone in hand already, knowing that with Josh on the class trip, the mobile would have to do, when it started ringing.

"Josh, hey. I was about to call, you beat me by a few seconds."

"Hi, Ty. So, what did I read on Twitter? Engaged?"

"Ah, yeah. Wait, here, that's her."

He adjusted the phone, and Scarlette gave the boy a friendly smile. "Hello, Josh. I'm Scarlette. I'm sorry you heard it online first. We really tried to be faster, we were just telling my parents and then the news already spread."

She saw the careful consideration in his eyes and couldn't blame him. He had been through a nightmare, and now this news was dropped into his lap without any warning.

"Aha."

Tyler suppressed a frustrated sigh and changed the angle to include both him and Scarlette on screen. "Josh, I know this is a lot, and like Scarlette said, we're sorry we were a few minutes too late to tell you first. But I still would appreciate it if you could give her a chance."

"Yeah, sure, the woman who conveniently runs into you when everything is this huge mess."

"Josh, she isn't involved, not in the way you think. Her

great-great-grandfather was friends with ours. There's something connecting our families, but she isn't involved in blackmailing us. She's being targeted herself, and instead of doing the sensible thing and going to the cops, she wants to help me.

"We fell for each other, hard. I can't tell you any more than that I know she's the one, and after losing mom and dad, I realized how precious that is and how devastatingly short life can be. I don't want to waste any time I can have with her, so I asked her to marry me.

"We are on our way home, so if nothing comes up dragging us away again, you can meet her tomorrow. Okay?"

"Yeah, yeah, whatever." Josh mumbled something unintelligible for his brother, but Scarlette perked a brow.

"Josh, I don't know you yet, but I don't think your brother deserved to be called that."

"How would you know what I said?"

"You think you're the only one with some basic knowledge of Goa'uld curses?"

"You... you know *Stargate?*" Surprise and amazement bloomed on the boy's face.

"Well, yeah, who doesn't? Scratch that, I actually know too many people who don't. We can get into those details later. But Ty wants to do the right thing, he's worried about you. Terribly worried. He loves you, Josh. The way he does, the way he cares about you is one of the reasons why I fell for him. We wanted to tell you differently, but things just happened. Let's get to know each other before you decide to throw me in the vortex of an opening wormhole, okay?"

Tyler squeezed her thigh in a soundless gesture of gratitude – not for the defense, but for the first steps of connecting with his younger brother. "I forgot to mention she's an even bigger nerd than I am, I guess."

"Aha." But this time the sound carried admiration with it. "Yeah, okay, I guess we can talk tomorrow. I gotta go, group project and all. See ya."

After hanging up, Tyler grinned at Scarlette. "Some high praise from him when he's in a mood."

"I figure on a *Stargate* marathon once all this mess is over. We should bond just fine over that."

"I love you, Sparks."

"I love you, too, Link."

He gently pushed her down on the seat, had her on her back and was nibbling on her ear. "Then let me make love to you later."

"I already planned on ending up in the same bed with you and having fun."

"And that's a great plan. But I want more from you tonight than fun."

"Really? And what would that be?"

His hands ran through her hair, his lips skimmed over her neck, leaving her with goosebumps all over, and he whispered into her ear. "Love. Trust. Absolutely all of you. I want to take you slowly this time, find all your secrets. I want to make you tremble, make you go all soft and sweet. I want to hear you sigh when I touch you, when I taste you. I want to feel you go up so slowly that it's almost torture. And when you come, I want to look into your eyes, I want to see them go dark with desire."

He was lying on top of her, his firm body pressing into hers, and his words alone had her very nearly begging him to take her like that. Slowly, thoroughly, endlessly. Her breath hitched when he ran his hand to her breast, caressing her nipple through her shirt.

"I love the way you look when it takes you over. I want to see that again and again tonight. Until we both can't wait any longer, until I'm inside you. It makes me crazy, when you surround me, when I feel you shudder around me."

He was hard as rock, she could feel it, and he had her wet and throbbing. When he took her mouth, she moaned quietly, and it was she who deepened the kiss until he gently let her go.

She stayed on her back, stared mindlessly at the ceiling. It seemed to take forever until her brain found its way back into her body. "Oh god, you're good. I mean, really good. You better get us something cold to drink."

"Okay." Leaning over her once again, he couldn't refrain from giving them both a preview and pressed his hand between her thighs, covered her mouth again to muffle her low cry of release. "Any wishes? Water, Coke, Champagne?"

"What?"

Grinning, he pushed himself up, took one of her hands and kissed her palm. "I'll find us something."

Chapter Eight

"Estate" was definitely the right word to describe Tyler's family home, Scarlette decided when they drove through large iron gates onto a long driveway just outside of Hope. "New Jersey, hm?"

"Well, I have my own place in New York. But it's not too far for a weekly visit, and we're a mixed bag anyway. My dad came over here as a kid from Ireland, mom lived in Maine most of her childhood, so we're not too focused on what state we live in as long as it's convenient. And the family business needs enough land."

"I can imagine. Tell me, how did it happen that your family has a vineyard, and breeds some of the world's best racehorses? It sounds like an odd combination."

"Not with the story behind it. A long time ago..."

With a wide grin Scarlette interrupted him. "In a galaxy far, far away?"

"Maybe there as well. But this happened in this one," he said and poked her in the side. "Now, as these stories go, a long time ago, some great-uncle or cousin, I would have to check on the exact relation, he was a successful horse breeder. And one of his horses made headlines when it won every race. The breeding focus shifted specifically to racehorses, and he visited the racetrack, naturally. He met a woman and they fell in love. Her family always had been working in the wine business, but they had a fairly small winery. Due to some family tragedy on her side, the business came into her hands. She turned out to be a canny entrepreneur and discussed with her new husband the fact that at the races people gather for socializing as much as for the sport, and with the socializing comes the drinking. Why not provide a wine bar with their own wine, sold with the love story of them and the connection to many of the horses down on the track? Every year they named a bottle in honor of the most successful of their horses. The basics haven't changed on that, people still attend races, people still drink, thus we still have both enterprises. We only shifted a little and hired more outside specialists, because my parents believed we should do what makes us happy. I have always been somewhat involved, but my passion is writing, so I focus there. My mother mostly worked with the breeding branch, but she also put a lot of effort into charity work, as you know."

"Yes. I think I even met her once, for a minute or so. We don't have your kind of money, but we're doing okay, and with my mom pushing the charity work, she often takes me to events for some sweet-talking and palm greasing."

"I can see why. It's hard to say no to you," Tyler said with a wink and stopped the car in front of a huge stone house. "My father, he kept to the wine business. But it was more of an advisory role. He practiced corporate law very successfully, and it sure helped to set things up even better for us.

Josh has always had dad's interest there, and I think he might decide to study law as well, but we'll see. It was unusual for the time, but dad took mom's name when they married, to keep the legacy alive, you could say. He branded our name into law circles here, too. It might help Josh, should he follow dad in that direction."

After getting out of the car, Tyler took Scarlette's hand and led her and Julia around the house instead to the main entrance.

"Down there is a small part of our winery. More for experimental bottlings, you could say." He gestured to a good-sized wooden house at the bottom of a gently falling hill.

"On the other side, there are stables for our own horses, for some of our mares too old for breeding. When it's time for them to retire, we usually try to give them a home here, or with friends. They are more than income for us, they are part of the family in a way."

Seeing the stables in the distance, the adjoining large paddocks, and several horses running and obviously playing on a large meadow, Scarlette's heart melted. "I'm not a typical girl who always wanted a pony, but this is wonderful. You care for them, you love them, and you do it properly from what I can see from here. No wonder I fell in love with you." She leaned into him with a content sigh, rested her head on his shoulder when he put his arm around her.

Julia nodded. "It's hard to argue with Scarlette there. I was prepared to scrutinize everything about you, to find some pompous, narcissistic writer who likes to read his own words everywhere, but that's not you, and that's not this. This place, and what your family has built for generations, is impressive.

I feel better knowing that, and seeing my best friend happily in love with a good man."

Tyler let go of Scarlette and laid his hands gently on Julia's arms. "Thank you." He kissed both her cheeks. "It means a lot to me that one of the most important people in Scarlette's life accepts me for her."

"You're welcome. Even though it wouldn't matter, she always does what she wants."

"It matters a great deal, you matter a great deal to her. She either wouldn't let me in completely without you being okay with me, or it would cause a rift between you both. I would want neither of those."

Sighing, Julia looked over his shoulder at her friend. "Damn, you know how to pick the right one, girl."

"Yeah, I do."

With his arm around Scarlette again, Tyler turned towards the house and unlocked the door leading into a mudroom that opened into a huge, spit-clean kitchen with gleaming appliances. White painted wood stood in contrast to shining metal, and the dark granite counter and kitchen island practically begged to be used to cut vegetables or roll out dough.

"Oh my... My dad can never see this. Or my grandma. They'd never leave."

"As long as I get some food out of it, I'd be okay with that. It's a big house, and I got along swell with your dad on our call earlier."

"True enough."

They were interrupted when the kitchen door swung open and a middle-aged woman came in with a smile on her face. She wore an apron in bright pink which matched the one pink streak in her still-dark hair. Brown eyes shimmered with amusement and joy in a slender face. She was maybe 5 feet tall and thin as a young tree, but her voice was as rough and loud as a foghorn.

"Come here, boy! I let you out of the house for five minutes and you come back with a fiancée. For what it's worth, you seem happy." He had to lean down, but she hugged him with a force that almost crushed his ribs.

"Lorraine. I missed you dearly."

"Better for you. Now, where are your manners, introduce me to your girl and her friend."

He lifted her off her feet for a second, before setting her down with a laugh. "I'm sorry, ma'am. This is Scarlette Langella, my fiancée and the love of my life. And this is her wonderful friend Julia Stone. Scarlette, July, this is Lorraine O'Donnell. She helped raise Josh and me, she's our cook and oversees housekeeping. But above all, she's the heart and soul of this home. She lives with her husband in the house over by the pond." Through the window he pointed to a house about a hundred yards over to the left, nestled close to a small body of water covered with water lilies.

"Like I'm ever done raising you boys."

Grinning, Scarlette held out a hand. "Hello, Mrs. O'Donnell. It's a pleasure to meet you."

The cook spread her arms, hugged Scarlette tightly. "That's Lorraine to you, we're practically family. I hear your pa cooks. Have you picked up on that?"

"I can hold my own in a kitchen, but he and grandma do it better."

"We'll have to spend some time here together, then. Whatever Tyler might have told you, he's always been a failure at the stove, and Josh isn't much better. Their mother and I tried everything we could think of, and nothing helped. It'll be nice to have someone around who knows parsley from cilantro."

"I think we'll be friends."

"I think so, too. Hello to you as well, Ms. Stone," Lorraine said and offered her hand to Julia.

"Hello. Nice to meet you. And please, make it Julia."

"Very well. Why don't you freshen up while I make some coffee. You'll be busy enough later, I'd think. Your bags are in your rooms already. Ty, I put Julia in the second-floor guest suite in case she needs some office space."

"That sounds good, thanks, Lorraine."

Tyler led them out of the kitchen and Scarlette took in the first details of the house. It was big for sure, and on the main floor she found a parlor and a formal dining room along with a smaller family dining room, and a beautiful library. Everything radiated a cozy charm, and even though the walls were mostly painted in light pastels, just about every room had some color splashes, either in the form of dark, inviting wood or leather, or some strong blue or dark red pillows and rugs.

But what captured Scarlette most was a family portrait of Tyler and Josh with their parents. Far from the usual formal staging, this picture showed a real connection. Tyler stood next to his father and had his arm comfortably draped over the man's shoulder. The parents stood hip to hip, arms around each other's waists, and Josh stood in front of his mother, her other arm running over his shoulder and across his chest. They all grinned. No forced, frozen-in-place smile, no stiff, straight back, but a normal, honest family moment.

"I love this. They must have been great parents."

"They were. We miss them every day."

"I can only imagine. Your mom was beautiful. You have her eyes, and Josh has your dad's nose and chin. There'll always be part of them in you."

Sighing, Tyler ran his arms around Scarlette from behind, rested his chin on her shoulder and laid his lips on her cheek. "Thank you for that, baby."

"Always." Scarlette laid her hands over Ty's, gently returned the kiss.

Watching them, Julia's throat closed, and she had to fight hard to keep her eyes from tearing up. In spite of only knowing each other for a few days, they already shared the intimacy of long-time lovers and weren't afraid to let it show. They seemed to complete each other, even though none of them had known there had been something missing before. She couldn't help but sigh.

"Are you okay, Julia?"

"Yes. Sorry, I didn't want to ruin your moment, Tyler."

"You didn't," he assured her.

"Sweetie, you know you'll find someone, too, right?"

"Sure. I just thought if I didn't love you, I'd hate you for finding him and finding what you have with him. I'm honest enough to admit that I envy you right now."

"That's kind of sweet, I think."

"Yeah, yeah."

Tyler let go of Scarlette, put his arm around Julia's shoulders in a companionable gesture. "I have this friend..." he said with a laugh.

"Oh god, no, I haven't fallen so far yet. I still hope I don't need any matchmaking to get me a guy."

"Okay. Now, do you both want to see more of the house?"

He showed them a second floor with a family room, offices, and a larger guest suite, where Julia's bag was waiting for her on a bench at the foot of a big bed. "This will be your realm, if you like it. There's a bath, and you have an adjoining guest office and a small living room for yourself. If there's anything you need in addition to what's there, let us know anytime. The guest living room has a small kitchenette, but I think you'll be happier to join us downstairs."

Julia turned around and stared at Tyler. "Wow. Just wow. Thank you, this is awesome. I'll totally be fine."

"Happy to hear that. If you want to, you can come upstairs with us, but there isn't that much to see. Two smaller guest rooms, and Josh's room, my old room, and the master. Not that interesting. Scarlette and I will probably spend most of the time after coffee and before dinner even further up in the attic, where I hope to find the key to the lockbox we brought along."

"Ah, no, you two freshen up, and I will, too. I'll find my way down to the kitchen in a few minutes, but I need to do a quick check on my work emails."

"Okay. Oh, and there's a list on the desk in the office with voice commands because Josh and I have been updating the house more and more with smart tech over the years."

Beside her fiancé, Scarlette shimmied her hips. "Epic! You are seriously great, Ty."

"I knew the nerd would approve."

"Hell, yeah."

"Come along, I want to show you our room."

"Sure."

The third floor had the advertised guestrooms, and Scarlette had no problem finding Josh's room when she saw the door painted in a Tardis design.

"The one thing I'm not hooked on. But I already like your brother."

"I'm glad to hear that. So... I couldn't bring myself to move into the master, yet. I haven't been here so often, and Josh was either in New York for a bit, or gone for school. And..."

"It didn't feel right?"

Pure relief washed over him for her understanding. "Yes, exactly. Lorraine and I, we put my parents' things away, but it was too strange and sad to sleep there. I know we haven't discussed any living arrangements or anything yet, but I think I will have to move here. I don't want kids, but Josh is still family. I can't uproot him from here after what we've been through."

A little confused, she tilted her head. "Ty, what is there to discuss? Your brother lives here. You can write here. I have my business, yes, but since the pandemic, we've restructured to a lot of remote work anyway. On-site consultations have always meant driving in any case. I'll just start organizing my appointments to have most of them on the same day, then do the office part of my job for the rest of the week from here, too. If I have too many meetings for one day, I can always stay at my parents' for a night."

A flood of emotions rushed through him, and his only defense was dragging her in for a desperate, hungry kiss. Clinging to her, he devoured her, poured his heart and soul into her. "I love you, I need you. God, I want to marry you right now, I want you to be mine."

She gentled the next kiss, then framed his face. "I already am. We'll arrange for everything, and we'll get married as soon as we can, so it will be something small, just for us. And then we'll probably have to throw a huge party later, but who cares. I don't want to take over here, but I want a life with you. This has always been your home, let's make it ours. I love this house already. I don't care which room we sleep in, as long as we share the bed with each other."

He looked at her for a long moment, then brushed his knuckles over her cheek. "With you, everything feels right again in my life. It's our home now, and we'll take the master, make it ours." And because he needed to lighten the mood a little or he'd drag her to the nearest bed, he glanced at the door at the end of the hallway leading up to the attic. "We'll most likely start with making the master bath ours first, because after spending time up there we'll need a long shower. But then we'll have the whole night to make love, to enjoy each other."

"I'm all in for that."

Chapter Nine

They were gone again.

It had taken some acting, some inventive truths, even some bribes, but in the end, the trailer and the house had been found. And it was all for nothing. They hadn't left anything behind.

Talking with some of the neighbors confirmed some photographer and a model had been up at the mansion. Admittedly nothing new, even though the family tried to prevent it. You never knew what people might see in a picture. Better not risk it, even if some people offered a hefty sum to rent the location for a day or two.

But this time it had certainly been O'Brien and Langella. Inventive truths here as well, it seemed.

A thorough search of the house revealed hardly any disturbance, but they had apparently found an old passageway. Nothing in there, and the floor was too rotten to tread on it, so nothing had been taken from there. Nothing to worry about.

Had they left again without anything? One could hope, but it didn't feel like it.

The news of the engagement hit right before leaving again. Riding on fury, a family meeting was called.

How could nobody have known the writer and the woman had been together? Obviously, they couldn't first have met in LA only days before. Why were they throwing so much money away for education and false identities? Why were they putting in the effort to have people close, when nobody even realized their targets had been together long enough to get engaged?

The family had been warned those two were different. A man who had learned to guide a story, a woman with hardly anything to lose except the trust in her family – and how well had that penned out? – it had been an unlucky situation to begin with.

But they didn't have anything, and the family could still find a way to make them pay.

In the hurry to leave and organize everything for the family meeting, a heap of freshly cut vines outside didn't draw attention.

Chapter Ten

1928

She shouldn't keep the letters; Mary-Beth knew better. But she couldn't bring herself to destroy them. So, she had taken them and all other notes that might be incriminating out of the safe and would keep them hidden where nobody would find them. The gardens were hers. They had somebody for cutting the grass and pruning the trees, but all the flowers were her doing.

That meant nobody questioned it when she went outside with some tools and a big basket to cut some flowers for the party later that evening. Nobody saw the small lockbox under a damp towel. And nobody paid attention when Mary-Beth knelt close to the gazebo – where she had planted the most beautiful roses she often used for a centerpiece.

The parties had always been a blessing.

Ever since Charles and she both had become famous, she felt like she was under constant observation. Prying eyes everywhere, looking for a scandal. When they had gotten married, she had pushed for a new project instead of their honeymoon – she knew she wouldn't have enjoyed it.

But the parties meant an evening away from the city. Often more than that when she arrived earlier to prepare everything, to oversee deliveries and decorations.

The people they invited here were their friends, or crews when they were shooting something at the most, but no reporters were allowed on the grounds except for special occasions.

She had always felt like the mansion up on the hill was her sanctuary, the place where she could always find her peace of mind, or on the evening of a party simply forget the world outside for a while.

Oh, what wonderful parties they had given. She still remembered last New Year's. Music had echoed through all the rooms, people had danced and cheered, had chattered and sung along with the band. It had been a rush to be swinging on the dance floor, sequins catching the light from the candles and the huge chandelier, the fringes of her dress tickling her legs. Her feet had killed her after an hour, but the bathtub gin Eton sometimes distilled for special occasions had numbed the pain, and laughter had kept her going until the early morning hours.

She loved the parties, and with them the stolen glances, the brush of a hand, an innocent hug.

This was the life she had always associated with fame and fortune.

Then she had found the first note on her bed the day before, and she had seen the other side of it – the vulnerability to rumors, the need to protect the status quo. And she had followed the demand.

Tonight, she would go on with the party, show a brave face. After the party she would need to talk to some people again. For now, she would lock the note away with everything else.

Chapter Eleven

It was getting late in the afternoon when Scarlette and Tyler made their way up to the attic, and yet it was still brutally hot.

"It's the only part of the house without an AC, sorry."

In an attempt to keep herself a bit cooler, Scarlette tied her hair up in a high knot. "It's okay, I kind of expected it. Do you have any idea where to start?"

She glanced around and sincerely hoped he did, because the attic covered roughly all of the floor below, and boxes and old trunks, suitcases and crates, bags and covered furniture were filling up most of the space. It would probably be fun and bring many interesting things to light if they had time to go through it all. But when you had some crazy blackmailer giving you a deadline of a week to gather a lot of money and that week was halfway over, you sincerely wished somebody in the past would have had the good sense to keep some sort of order.

"Ah, somewhat. We tried to keep things separated by generations; so right here," Tyler said and pointed into a corner close to the door, "that's the newest stuff. Things from back when Josh and I were kids, our Christmas decorations, things like that. The farther you go in, the older the boxes get, in theory, and mostly it's correct. I went through lots of things when I received the note. So I know where to start."

She followed him through a maze of family heirlooms and keepsakes, smiled at some old dresses from the seventies hung in protective bags on a rag. "Give it a few more years and those will be back in style."

"Feel free to try them on, babe."

"What, to feed your horny fantasies?"

"They're always hungry."

She bumped him with her hip and her laughter carried through the whole attic. "Later."

They found the corner Tyler had searched days before, and Scarlette found everything back in its place. He took care, and he had a mind for the order of things, she much appreciated that.

Reaching out, he lifted the cover of an old *recamier*, nodded. "It's not perfect, but a better place to sit than the dusty floor. I hope you don't mind the spiders around here."

"Thanks. No, spiders and I get along. July is more careful, given she currently lives in a place where everything wants to kill you. But I've survived excursions into the rainforest, this is harmless."

"Cool. Okay, so maybe you can go through this. It's an old trinket box and somebody collected all kinds of keys in it. I'll go through some of these old clothes. I've found coins and other things in there before, could be I missed a key."

She studied the mother-of-pearl box he passed her, ran a careful hand over it. "Sure. You could open a museum with all this stuff."

"I thought about it. It deserves better than being locked away up here without the proper conditions. But I want to know what and whose things I would exhibit, first."

"Understandable."

She set the lockbox she had carried up next to her on a small table and opened the trinket box. And gaped at easily a hundred keys. "Somebody was a little obsessed."

"Yeah. But hey, all in one place."

"True, that's handy."

Settling into the work, Scarlette went through the first keys, while Tyler opened an old wardrobe trunk. His hands ran over a carefully sewn flapper dress in dark green covered with shining sequins and finished with fringes. "This would look amazing on you, Sparks."

She shifted her attention to him and her eyes widened. "Oh, wow, that's gorgeous."

"It is. When this is over, I want to see you in it. I mean it."

She chuckled and rolled her eyes, but nodded. "Okay, yes."

They worked in silence for a while, but then Tyler examined another garment bag, found a note attached to it. "Hey, I think I found something that belonged to your great-great-grandfather. It's a suit, there's a letter:

'Dear Eton, Thank you for standing up as my best man once more. Elizabeth sends her sincere apologies again for her aunt's mishap with the gravy. We had your suit cleaned. We are looking forward to more occasions to celebrate together again. Your friend, Charles.'

"This must have been about three years after Mary-Beth's death. That's when Charles remarried. I think they planned to send this to Eton, but soon after the wedding Elizabeth was pregnant and there were complications. They packed everything up and moved close to her parents so her mother could support her. I suppose they forgot about the suit."

"Crazy, isn't it, how life just goes on and our ancestors could write such simple, affectuous notes. Then our families lose contact, and now here we are, planning to get married."

"Fateful, I would call it."

"You know, for once I'll buy into that."

Tyler ran his hands over the suit more out of routine than in hopes to feel a key. He didn't come up with one, but instead found a folded paper, which had dropped in between the lining through a hole in the inside pocket. He put it aside on a small table to read it, but first replaced the garment.

His phone rang, and when he checked the caller ID, he frowned. "That's my agent. It's the fourth time she's called me since the news leaked. I should take this."

"Yeah, of course. I'll keep trying my luck here."

Tyler walked closer to one of the windows to have better reception, and she heard the exasperated tone of a man who was getting a verbal kick in the balls. His hand ran through his hair, and she could make out an apology on his side. Perhaps he deserved a little mood lift after the call. She raised a hand to open a button or two on her blouse, while her other hand already automatically tested another key in the box – and the lock turned.

She nearly jumped up from the surprise, then carefully opened the lock and lifted the lid.

Tyler came over, the phone back in his pocket, and laid his hands on Scarlette's shoulders. "We may live, as long as we meet her tomorrow for a strategy meeting. The timing sucks, I know."

"That's life. We'll manage. But check out what I have here," she told him and held up the open box with a huge grin spreading on her face.

Annoyance was forgotten in the excitement, and Tyler pressed his lips to hers. "You are seriously awesome."

"Sometimes I am. We should take these downstairs with us. Better light, and I don't want to spread them out in the dust here."

"Okay."

Scarlette helped Tyler to clean up most of what they had taken out of boxes, replaced the unused keys and, for now, put the trinket box on a side table before picking up the lockbox.

An office on the second floor should work well enough, Tyler thought, and he had just stepped on the landing with Scarlette when Lorraine came upstairs. "Good, I wasn't excited about climbing into the sauna up there. You need a damn smart speaker there, too."

"I'll put it on the list. What's up? It's still early for dinner."

"It is, and I'm not here because of that. Scarlette, you've got a visitor."

"I... what?"

"Down you go, girl. In the parlor."

A confused Scarlette handed the box to Tyler, then went

another flight of stairs down. But when Tyler wanted to follow, Lorraine stopped him with a hand on his chest. "Give her a minute."

"Who is..."

He was cut short by a squeal and heard his fiancée exclaim a euphoric, "Granny!"

"Thank you, Lorraine."

"Don't thank me; the lady is something. She told me she heard the news, confirmed it with her son, and when he told her where Scarlette would be, she apparently jumped into her car and drove here."

"Jesus, she came here by car, alone?"

"Seems like it. I'll get a guest room ready."

"Thanks. Oh, and would you move our things into the master suite?"

Lorraine became still for a second, then gently laid a hand against his cheek. Tears shimmered in her eyes but didn't fall. "She is very good for you, boy."

Moved deeply, he put an arm around her, kissed her cheek. "She is. Thank you for welcoming her into the family."

"She makes you so obviously happy, not much to think about there. I'll see to the rest. You go..."

But she was interrupted by a yell from downstairs.

"O'Brien, move your butt down here! I want to meet the man who steals my little girl from me. Or are you afraid of an old woman?"

"Coming!"

He quickly put the box away, then decided to follow an old childhood tradition and took the fast way down by sliding on the railing.

Scarlette's grandmother caught the move and his easily balanced landing, and nudged her granddaughter. "He can move, built well, too. I'd say you're lucky when it comes to the bedroom."

Scarlette buried her face in her hands. "Granny…"

"Stop pretending you don't have sex. And I have enough children, pretty sure I still know how they're made. Doesn't matter if you have fun to plant something or not, does it?"

Tyler had never seen Scarlette even remotely embarrassed. He made sure to take in every second. "Hi there."

He studied the woman standing next to his fiancée. She had gotten smaller with age, but it didn't diminish the picture she made. Her dark-gray hair was neatly pinned at the back, and despite a few wrinkles clearly coming from a long life full of laughter, she had clear, dark eyes. Hadn't he known Scarlette had been adopted, Tyler would have sworn she had inherited the curves from her grandmother. She must have been approaching eighty, but she had kept herself in shape, and the dress she wore spoke of the innate talent of Italian women and style.

He had the feeling she was as much a force as Lorraine. He was sure he'd like her.

"Hello. So, you're Tyler O'Brien, hm?"

"That would be me, yes."

They both grinned broadly at each other while Scarlette tried to vanish, maybe melt into the floor.

"Good. I'm Beatrice Langella."

"I'm very excited to meet you, Mrs. Langella."

"What's that? That's *Beatrice*, Tyler. Her parents already approved, but I wanted to make up my own mind. Looking good, even with that long hair, that's a bonus. Sharp, too. And not after her for any money. I can approve of all that. Are you of any use in the kitchen?"

"As I was informed just today, it seems I'm a failure there. Sorry to disappoint you."

"Ah, nobody is perfect. Met your cook. She sounds capable, and my girl isn't too shabby either. I don't think you two will starve."

"Oh, thanks Granny, thanks so much," Scarlette mumbled.

"Be quiet while I talk to your man here."

Tyler walked over, took her hand to kiss it. "I didn't think I'd ever meet someone who could talk to her like that and live. You have my deepest respect, Beatrice. Can I get you a drink?"

"Manners, too. Very nice. Well, you're bringing in money with wine, so give me some of that to try."

"Of course. Sparks, something for you, too?"

She didn't even have to see his face to hear the amusement in his voice. "You got any whisky? No bourbon. Neat."

"Sure."

Tyler poured the drinks, handed the wine to Beatrice with a wink, then turned to Scarlette, who was currently studying her nails and pretending to ignore them both. He lifted her face with his fingers, gave her a hard kiss. "Your drink, babe." And pushed the glass into her hand.

Beatrice exploded with laughter. "Oh, I like him a lot."

God, she could never hold out against that woman – and apparently not against the man in front of her either. She took a quick sip, and let the smile bloom on her face. "Yeah, I like him, too."

Scarlette shuffled closer, snuggled against Tyler.

Watching them, Beatrice narrowed her eyes. "And are you good with her not planning on having children? There's a lot of compromise involved in a marriage, but some things you can't compromise about."

"You are absolutely right. There are things you either agree on or you don't, and if you don't, things won't work out in the end. Lucky for both of us, I never wanted kids, either."

"All right. Shame for the gene pool, yours would probably come out all right, but it's a solid foundation that you already talked about it, that you see eye to eye on it. And our family is legion already, we will survive. For yours there's still a brother, right?"

"Yes, but please don't give me a heart attack by making me think about him fathering a child. He's seventeen. My main goal right now is seeing him survive until he's twenty. That's one milestone, we'll go from there."

"Smart man, I have to repeat myself there. Now that we all get along so well, update me on the rest." Beatrice settled into an armchair, gestured with her glass.

They sat down on the couch and did just that.

"Julia is upstairs?"

Scarlette nodded. "Yes. I think she has some meetings, but she'll be down for dinner."

"Good. Haven't seen her in a while. How's her father? You would have asked."

"Sure. I talked to her on the way to the airport, trying to figure out if I needed to put her on the next plane back. She says he's doing a lot better, the PT is going well, and while she's here a neighbor will help out."

"Glad to hear that. What did she say to the both of you?"

"Asked if we had lost our minds."

"I love that girl. An honest friend is important. An honest family, too. You have enough on your plate, but you should know Patrick showed up at the restaurant after the news broke."

Scarlette set her glass down sharply, balled her hands into fists. "What? Oh for fuck's sake, that idiot. Two years we've been fine. I'll call the lawyer first thing in the morning, have him widening the RO to protect you all, too."

"You do that, and I didn't bring it up to upset you, but you should know. You both will generate some press for a bit, he might find brain cells enough to put it together that you're living here now. And the place isn't that hard to find. I know Lorraine is careful; she double-checked everything before letting me in. But you should inform everybody who needs to know, so nobody accidentally lets him onto the property."

"Yeah, I know. Thanks, Granny," Scarlette sighed, and Tyler took her hand.

"Indeed, thank you. We will make sure to take the necessary precautions."

"All right. And I hope you know I want to see those letters, too. For all the mess it is, it is also highly entertaining."

"Sure. I think we will have dinner first, but after, we can all read them together. I took the liberty of asking Lorraine to get a room ready for you, Beatrice. I hope that was all right."

"Sure thing. I'm glad if I don't have to drive back all the way tonight. It's too hot, people drive like morons. And once it gets dark, they still drive like morons because they try to make up for the heat and enjoy the cool breeze while racing each other."

"If you don't mind, we'll drive to New York with you tomorrow. My agent made me swear to come by; she insisted on pictures. But as I've learned how well your granddaughter can pose for a camera, I'm sure we will be fine."

Humor swam into Beatrice's eyes, and Scarlette playfully punched Tyler. "Be careful or you can forget about that private photo shoot."

"Why don't you both go grab a shower? You have cobwebs in your hair and dust all over. I will find my way into the kitchen, see what Lorraine is putting together, and later we won't have to send you away from the table for sitting down like you're preparing for Halloween already."

Tyler got up from the sofa and kissed Beatrice's cheek. "I think I love you."

"You're a good man. Have fun upstairs," she told him with a grin and took her wine with her to leave them for the kitchen.

Scarlette stared after her with an open mouth. "What the hell just happened here?"

"Family bonding? I don't care. She said I should have fun. I intend to follow her advice."

Since he had found a sweet and unobtrusive way to make sure that her grandmother would get back to New York safely, she didn't care either. And when he picked her up and threw her over her shoulder, she squeaked.

On the stairs, she poked him in the ribs. "You know, sometimes you have a real caveman thing going."

"Is that a complaint?"

"Nope," she answered and laughed all the way upstairs.

Chapter Twelve

With the temperatures still up and the last of the evening sun glistening, Scarlette had chosen a sundress with thin straps from her suitcase, and Tyler had grabbed some light clothes as well. They both knew they had a long list of things to do, but when they ambled downstairs hand in hand, for a little while they only enjoyed the moment; all the more so, when they found Lorraine and Beatrice had worked together to make homemade ravioli.

Dinner revolved less around letters and blackmail than around childhood stories of Scarlette and Tyler brought on by her grandmother and Lorraine, and updates about several aunts, uncles, and cousins on Scarlette's side of the family.

"You really are legion," Tyler decided when he was trying to keep track of who was who.

"Oh yeah. And this is what happened last week alone. And damn, I still need to find a graduation gift for Cora," Scarlette remembered.

Beatrice toasted with her wine. "You really want to do her a favor, you talk to your landlord and make sure he keeps your apartment for her and her friend, so once you've moved here, they can move in."

"Hm. Yes, that's not a bad idea. Sorry, I think tomorrow will be packed," Scarlette said to Tyler with an apology in her eyes.

"It's no problem for me. Josh won't be here before late afternoon, we should manage most of it by then."

"Okay. Oh, and I need to get more stuff from my place, I didn't pack for more than a few days."

"I have a pick-up in the garage in New York, we can take that one for the trip back here and already bring along the most important things."

"You come in handy."

"I do my best. Lorraine, Beatrice, this was delicious."

"We had a fun time throwing it together, didn't we, Bea?"

"Absolutely. Fair warning, I will invade your kitchen more often in the future. And once your papa has been here, so will he, Scarlette."

"Oh, I know. I doubt we will complain. As long as Lorraine is okay with it, I don't mind. It's her kitchen after all."

The cook stood up, wrapped an arm around Scarlette, and gave her hair a kiss. "I knew I liked you, girl. You all go study these letters now, I will clean up here."

"We can help you first."

"No need, I have my own system, it works just fine."

The office had belonged to Tyler's dad, and he admitted it felt strange to sit in his father's chair like this. But when Scarlette rested a hand on his shoulder from behind him in a gesture of sympathy and understanding, he felt more at peace than he had hoped for.

Julia and Beatrice had each grabbed a chair on the other side of the desk and peered at the box in anticipation. "About a hundred years buried in the dirt, and it held. We won't look that good after such a long time in the ground."

"Bea!" With the comfort of an unofficial family member, Julia gently nudged the woman beside her and laughed.

"What? It's pure waste. See, this was buried to be preserved, to last. We get boxed up and dumped in a hole in the ground to rot along with the box around us. And then half of that box won't even do that properly. Scarlette, I read about those compostable coffins online. I want something like that. Least we can do."

Resigned, Scarlette shook her head with an eye roll. "Sure, I'll discuss it with mom and dad when you die in fifty years."

Beatrice roared with laughter. "That's the spirit. Now boy, open this damn thing, we aren't getting any younger."

"Yes, ma'am."

He opened the lid and saw again what he and Scarlette had already peeked at earlier that evening. A neat pile of envelopes and accurately folded notes.

Carefully, they unfolded the notes at first but found most of the ink had faded over the years. They could make out some letters, and Tyler set the papers aside to be examined later and possibly be restored.

The letters within the envelopes seemed more promising, and after lining them up Scarlette considered the dates in the upper corner.

"These span about five years, possibly longer. I can't

make out the date on this one, but it reads like it's the first."
She laid it out for all to read.

XXXX

Sweet Mary-Beth,

What happened last night? I cannot explain it to myself, nor to you.

I want to pretend it was just a dream, but I still remember how the mood changed when we were alone. So easy at first, then I saw something fierce in your eyes. And when I touched you, you did not retreat. When I tried your lips, you sighed. When I drew the dress away from you, you quivered. And your hands began to wander.

What will we do now? How can I say it was a mistake, when all I can think about is you, seeing you again, kissing you again, running my hands over the skin under your skirts again?

Everything has changed for me, and I fear, and I hope it is the same for you.

We will talk.

After screening several others, Julia could have sworn she was blushing. "Well, they don't get any tamer, do they? Weren't they supposed to be all decent and prudish back then?"

"July, if mankind had ever been decent and prudish, we would be extinct by now," Beatrice chuckled.

"Maybe, but I'm pretty sure there's less graphic porn nowadays," July mumbled.

Tyler scanned the letter she had been reading. "But also bolder. Think about how many famous art pieces are nude studies. We've always liked boobs and sex. It's a weakness, but it's almost charming."

Frowning, July shifted her eyes from Ty to her best friend. "Are you sure you want to marry that guy?"

All Scarlette did was laugh. "Sure. He's right, a fine pair of boobs can be pretty to look at."

"Good to know you two agree on that."

Tyler thought for a split second about Bea, then shrugged. "Of course we do. And Sparks has great tits to look at, and to touch," he finished and put his hands on them for a quick squeeze.

It lightened the mood for a moment, but in the end, they all focused on the letters again.

"I don't like saying it, but it appears like Mary-Beth has had a very long, very steamy affair with somebody. She married Charles in 1923, right?"

"Yes. And you're right. These letters cover basically all their marriage."

"There's a small chance those were from her husband," Julia said, then shrugged when three pairs of eyes gazed at her with eyebrows drawn up. "I'm not saying it's likely, just possible. They were famous by then, weren't they? I would assume they'd try to keep something like that private, even if it was between the two of them."

"They were, and I agree they wouldn't like this to be

public. But still. None of those are signed, they read too much like secrecy. If they had been from Charles, she might have hidden them, but I doubt she would have buried them like this. And aside from all that, why would he allegedly have killed her, if he had been the author? This rather seems like he found out about the affair and ended it in a terrible way."

Feeling for him, Scarlette massaged Ty's shoulders, laid her cheek on his hair. "And then staged it like a suicide with the fertility problems as a reason to cover it all?"

"Possibly. Associated with the depression, he managed to pressure the insurance into paying the life insurance policy for Mary-Beth. Nice and tidy, isn't it?"

It was all the more depressing to consider it with the distance of time and with a different mindset.

"Ty, we don't know if that's really what happened, yet. I feel like there's more."

"Yeah, so do I. But we won't find that more tonight with these letters alone. Maybe more with the other notes, if there can be anything recovered. You know, I think after this we all should take a little break, talk about something positive."

He got up, ran an arm around Scarlette's waist. "Plus, I meant it, I want to marry you very soon. Let's go make some wedding plans."

Thrilled about the idea, they all settled into the family room up here, called Cynthia to participate, and naturally invited Lorraine to join them.

With a bottle of champagne and ice cream for everybody, they talked about licenses, food, and locations. When the talk drifted toward her wedding dress, Ty felt he should not hear too much about it. So, he had left Scarlette with a kiss to give her some girl time with her mother and grandmother, her best friend, and Lorraine, who had become part of the group in a heartbeat. He hadn't lied when he had told her he wanted to go over some things for Josh's return tomorrow.

But he also wanted some time to prepare everything for their first night together in what was now *their* home.

Later, Scarlette took her time strolling to the master suite after saying goodnight to the others. She had already fallen in love with hers and Ty's new private haven earlier when she had been able to think and notice things again after the shower.

The separate dressing room had given her a jolt, and the bathroom with its huge shower and the freestanding bathtub spoke of a timeless elegance without fuss. But the bedroom itself she would treasure especially. The big bed with its high headboard was inviting you to spend whole weekends cozied up in it, the fireplace with its quietly dark sage-colored mantle across from it would be perfect for the winter. And she knew the cozy sitting area with its small table and deeply cushioned armchairs arranged in front of a small balcony would be one of her favorite spots to watch the sunset.

Now she took in more of the house while she walked it by herself, late in the evening with everything peaceful and quiet around her.

It carried the style of the New England heritage of Tyler's mother, with details hinting at Ireland, likely chosen by her thinking of her husband.

The dark hardwood floor felt smooth under Scarlette's feet, and she could see it was as well cared for as the matching banister of the stairs. Soft rugs with subtle Celtic designs covered the floor, adding comfort and, in the winter, she supposed also extra warmth.

Tyler hadn't lied when he had talked about outfitting the house with smart tech, either. Motion sensors turned on lights for her, then changed them to a dim, warm white for the evening. It would be fun to check out the system. She saw a smart speaker on an old sideboard close to Josh's room, its display set to show a slideshow of retro comic book covers.

This had always been a home for all of them, not a place created for presentation purposes. Their parents had started to change it when they had taken it over from the generation before, and later had wanted the boys, then the men, to take part in the design, in making it home, too.

More family pictures decorated the hallway walls up here as well. Pictures of a picnic, of a trip to the beach. Tyler was younger there, in his late teens probably, and with his hair surprisingly shorter than he wore it now. He was sitting in the sand and building a sandcastle. Next to him was a small boy, his huge eyes adoring the teenager, his grin radiating utter joy and love for his older brother.

Scarlette could understand it. Not every teenager would play happily with his thirteen years younger brother, but their bond had apparently always been strong.

No, she never could and never would want to disrupt that and ask Tyler to move somewhere else. He belonged here, to his brother. She hoped with all her heart she would find a way to bond with the boy, and she felt unbelievably grateful Lorraine had accepted her so open-heartedly, had let her

know she belonged here now, too. Floating on the contentment of that feeling of belonging, she yearned for Tyler and
the demands he had whispered to her on the plane.

They had enjoyed the shower and quick bout of fun
under the sprays earlier, sure, but as much as he did, she, too,
wanted to feel the intimacy of what was growing between
them.

He had told her he wanted the slow and sweet, but when
she stepped into their bedroom, she hadn't expected to find it
illuminated by the light of dozens of candles, or to hear Miles
Davis playing quietly on the stereo.

"Wow."

Tyler turned around from a table in the sitting area
where he had been pouring some wine for them. He still
wore the comfortable dark linen trousers he had put on after
the shower, and his white shirt was carelessly unbuttoned
against the warmth of the candles. She felt her heart stumble
in a storm of love and lust. He was gorgeous with his lean
body showing. The firm muscles defining his chest and his
flat stomach made her insides curl in delight. He had tied his
hair back in a loose tail, and one streak had escaped it and fell
around his face. She felt her fingers itch to play with it.

Smiling, he stepped over to her, whispered his lips over
hers, and handed her the wine. "Everybody all right and okay
with their bedrooms?"

"Yeah, everything's fine." She took a small sip, gaped at
the room again. "Tyler, I don't even know what to say."

"Try, 'thank you for the wine, it's delicious.'"

"It really is, thank you."

"You are welcome. So, I planned this to be particularly
romantic and memorable..."

"It already is."

The slow smile that could make her knees weak spread on his face again. "Wonderful. I just want to talk about one last thing with you first, before I lose myself in you and have to ruin a moment later."

"I'm all ears."

"I had my annual check-up about two weeks ago with my doc. The final results came in today, and everything is all right. I haven't been with anybody but you since the exam."

When he brushed her hair behind her ear, she smiled up at him from under her lashes with humor shining in her eyes.

"Is that a subtle question to skip the condoms from now on?"

"Since I suppose you have been as careful as with me when you had sex with somebody else before, and since I figure we have established this as a serious, monogamous relationship, and you told me you've had a sterilization, yes it is. Even though I would have asked directly in a moment, too. I would say we're both open enough to talk frankly about sex."

"We are. And you're right, I've always been that careful. So, thinking back to earlier, condoms in the shower work, but it's tricky. Also, adding to the we're-fated-for-each-other part, I can tell you, I had my own check-up about five weeks ago, came out clear, too, and didn't have sex again with anybody before I ran into you, either. So yeah, I'd say we're okay without them from now on."

"Perfect."

Teasing him, she nipped at his bottom lip. "You know you went down on me on our first night without protection."

"I did. I admit I weighed my chances there, seeing you were prepared enough to have your own condom. I usually skipped that part before, when I was with a woman I wasn't a hundred percent sure about."

"Hm, lucky me, then. You have a superior technique there."

"I'll happily give you another demonstration later."

"I'd like that."

"Me, too. But right now, I want to dance with my beautiful fiancée."

He took her glass and, together with his own, set it on the mantle of the fireplace next to them, then let his hands wander to Scarlette's hips. Tasting her lips again, he began guiding her into a slow dance and drew her closer inch by inch, until her body rested against his.

With his arms circled around her, his hands wandered up and down her back, up and down again, relaxing her every muscle. He laid his cheek on her hair, drew in her scent. "Your smell is enough to make me crave you, even when you aren't right beside me. When you left after our first night, I could smell you on my pillow. It made me crazy. I dreamed of you that night."

"Mhm. I tried really hard to get you out of my head. In the end, I stood under the shower in the morning cursing you because as well as I know my body and how to please myself, I realized I'd never feel that kind of pleasure again."

"Good thing we found each other again."

"Oh, yes."

She shifted a little, lifted her face, and found his lips with hers.

"I love your taste. Everywhere. But even only a kiss tastes so delicious. All you. All mine."

"All mine," Tyler echoed her and lowered his mouth to

hers for another sample.

They swayed in each other's arms, slowly made their way to the big, soft bed. His lips feathered along her jaw to her neck, awoke nerves she had barely known existed. He ran the tip of his tongue over her collarbone, lazily opened the zipper at the back of her dress. His fingertips followed the lines of subtle muscles under soft skin, and when she gently shoved his open shirt from his shoulders, he murmured something sweet against her skin.

Oh yes, he tasted delicious, Scarlette thought once again, when her mouth roamed dreamily over his chest, when she gently used her teeth on him.

His hands worked their way up and carefully pushed the straps from her shoulders. Her dress slid down her body with a whisper of fabric against skin and pooled at her feet.

He gasped when she suddenly stood naked in front of him. "Good god, you kill me."

"Let's hope not, I still have a lot of ideas on how to use you."

When he took a step back, when he studied her pale skin gleaming in the candlelight, it was her time to slowly curve her lips. He didn't touch her now, and she knew he needed the distance to regain enough control not to simply ravish her on the spot.

"You wanted sweet and slow. I didn't pack any lingerie fitting that, so..."

"So..."

She had taken him by surprise, but the way she stood there, naked with bare feet, excitement and expectation shimmering in her eyes, she looked so pure that tenderness came back to him. She was far from innocent, he knew, but this was another first for them. The first time in the bed they would now share forever, the first time not just following the drag of passion but taking time, cherishing the other. He had wanted that the first night, too, but then greed had taken over.

Now he reached out, caressed her cheek, then traced her mouth with his thumb.

She closed her lips over his finger and sucked luxuriously on it with her eyes on his, while her hands unknotted the tie of his trousers, so they fell to the floor.

"Take me to bed." Her voice was already heavy with desire, but she kept her touch light when she ran a finger down his belly.

So he did. He took her waist, gently lifted her, and set her down on the side of the bed. Stepping in between her thighs, he let his fingers comb through her hair. "You're so damn beautiful."

Lightly tugging on her hair, he angled her face up so he could indulge them both in a long, deep kiss.

Her hands traced his shoulders, his spine, and her lips opened to his. Her mind began to float.

Soft, she was so soft. Her hair, her lips, her skin. He could spend days wallowing in that softness.

When his lips left her mouth, he felt a sigh escape, felt her breath on his face. "I never wanted anybody as I want you. I love you, Scarlette."

"I love you, Tyler."

He pushed her gently down onto the bed, braced over her, so his lips could travel over her body. Her pulse beat thickly under her skin, and he could still taste a last shadow of her body lotion. Sweet, but now with a first hint of salt underneath from her skin going damp with longing.

Her shoulders, narrow but strong. Her arms, long and limber, the skin in the crook of her elbow so sensitive. His gliding tongue made her shudder, and he lingered there for a moment.

Her fingers, so delicate but nimble. She could seduce him with just the slightest touch. Now he would seduce her. He took her hand, kissed every finger, nibbled on her knuckles, then pressed his lips against her wrist.

Her fluttering pulse made him smile.

He slowly wandered back up her arm, laid a line of kisses down her ribs, before he let first his fingers then his lips feather over her breasts.

Her moan clouded his senses, but he leashed his own needs.

Lips and teeth and tongue played over her, advanced to the point of pleasure, then retreated again, over and over. Until he finally sucked her hardened nipple between his lips, until his teeth scraped over her.

She came with a low groan, shivering from it.

She hadn't believed it was really possible to peak from that simple contact alone, but what he did to her focused all sensations of her body on this single point. And when he took her other breast, it took hardly more than a flick of his tongue to nudge her over once more.

Still slowly, still awfully gently, Tyler moved down her body, played his fingertips along the skin between thigh and crotch, then kept exploring.

Long legs, tough with muscles from her runs. He caressed the back of her knee and drew a sigh from her, felt her yield yet a little more to what he was giving her.

Kneeling in front of her now, his finger traced the arch of

her foot while his teeth lightly nipped on her toes, and she shuddered.

He had wanted her like this, too steeped in her own desire to do anything but feel, and he knew when he shifted, when he made his way back up, she would give herself to him completely.

With only his tongue at first, he played her. She was already swollen, and with the touch, a new climax rolled through her.

When his fingers followed his tongue and he smoothly buried them in her, she clawed her nails into the sheets and moaned deeply.

"Oh god, Ty." It escaped her in a breathless whisper, and it took all his willpower to ignore the almost painful pounding in his loins to go on pleasing her.

"More, take more, baby."

She did. More and more, until in the end she was so overwhelmed with sensation and pleasure that tears ran down her cheeks.

"Take me, please. I want to feel you inside me."

They shifted both completely onto the bed, and he rolled on top of her, cupped her face with tender hands. "Be mine."

"I'm yours." She lifted her hips to meet him, felt the tremor run through him when he so terribly slowly slipped inside her. Just him, absolutely no barrier between them, however thin. He was the first she had ever allowed this.

She came again with that knowledge and the sensation of him filling her, and when her eyes clouded with the orgasm, he kissed her.

They moved together, hands roaming over skin, lips finding each other again and again.

And when desire became urgency, their hands linked, and when Tyler spilled himself into her, Scarlette came with a cry.

Filled with him, overfilled with happiness, she felt another tear roll down her cheek.

"Are you okay?"

"Yeah. Yeah, better than I've ever been. Thank you, Ty. This was wonderful."

"It was."

Playing with the loose strand of his hair, wrapping it around her finger, she seemed to consider something. "Hm."

"Hm?"

"It feels different. Only a bit, but there's a difference. A little weird, but somehow really nice."

"What's that?"

"To feel only you inside me like that. I never had that."

"You never..."

"No, everybody else I made sure they'd suit up, even when I was safe contraception-wise."

And he understood that even before he had touched her, with her agreement she had given him that absolute trust he had asked of her earlier that day. That she had given him all of her and let him be the only one who would ever feel her so intimately without any shield.

And when she felt warm drops of liquid on her thigh, she giggled. "Okay, and not always practical. I gotta get up."

After a quick dash into the bathroom, they cozied together in bed for the night.

Chapter Thirteen

Tyler knew it was pointless, but he nonetheless wished they could sleep in, spend the day in bed making love, only leaving the bedroom to hunt up some food, then stumble back into the sheets. Knowing that couldn't happen, he found it only fair to have at least one round of fun before getting on with the rest of the day.

Scarlette was lying beside him, all naked and warm and soft from sleep, how could he possibly resist her?

He rolled on top of her, woke her with a slow kiss, and swallowed her sigh when he slipped inside her.

New York was the typical madness, but Scarlette found Tyler well-equipped to deal with it. He only threatened to kill three people on his way to bring Beatrice and her car home. *He must have superior anger management skills*, she thought, given that by now she probably would have physically assaulted five people. Trusting him with the driving, she left her grandmother to plan the daily menu for the next few days and instead gave her lawyer a call about the RO.

Tyler studied the neighborhood when he stepped out of the garage with Scarlette and Beatrice. Brooklyn Heights wouldn't be his first choice, but he could see how it would work well for a family restaurant. He was happy to learn Scarlette's parents only lived a few houses down, with the restaurant settled in the middle of their and Beatrice's home.

"We could go by, couldn't we?"

Scarlette checked the time, shrugged. "Your agent will hate us for being late, but yeah, sure. Mom should be home being buried under papers for the gala preparations. Dad is usually at the market or on his way back this time of day, though, so we'll probably miss him."

"I'll start with your mother, then." He turned around to Beatrice and enfolded her in a comfortable hug. "Bea, it was great to meet you."

"I can say the same. You two come to dinner sometime, there's always a table reserved for family."

"We will." He let her go with a kiss on her cheek, so she could say goodbye to her granddaughter. And once she was safely inside, Tyler took Scarlette's hand to walk down the street with his fiancée.

It was a corner of New York he didn't visit that often, though he had some friends living close by, too. "It's a good place for them here. And I'd say you do better than okay."

Scarlette studied the street, shaded by trees from the already bright sunlight, and bustling with dog walkers. "Yes, it is. And yes, we're doing fine. But we've also had roots here for decades, that helped a lot. Also — and that is something Patrick's visit here has me thinking about — those blackmailers, why didn't they go to my parents? They do even better financially than I do. Or to some other part of your family, say, your dad's siblings? Easier than you, who first has to find a way to get to the money with everything going on. We've studied the family history. From all we could find, they've always used the most direct blood relation to Eton and Charles."

"Perhaps they try to be morally superior, not involving other families. Who knows? And with us, my dad's siblings, they do okay, but they chose to tap the biggest well with me, and probably hoped I'd pay without talking to anybody. Had they asked too much from my other family members, they might have come to me, and things would have come out."

"They will now, too."

"Yes, and I think they won't like it."

"No, most likely not." But for now, she turned at the entrance of a two-story townhouse and dropped the subject.

Twenty minutes later, they stepped out again, and a perplexed Tyler stared at Scarlette. "How the hell did that happen?"

"What? You agreeing to give a speech at the gala? That's my mom for you. Be glad she didn't use our engagement to sell more tickets."

"Only because we agreed to this monster of a wedding party later in the year."

"True. But hey, she's okay with us having the wedding in a couple of weeks, privately at home, as long as she'll be there."

"And I'm eternally grateful for that. Very simple: just us,

your parents, your grandma, Josh and Lorraine, and Julia, if she can stay that long."

"I hope so. But yes, that sounds perfect to me, too."

They took a cab to get to his agent's firm and were escorted into a sleek office with a severe-looking woman around forty ruling a large desk. Cool blue eyes ran Scarlette up and down; a quick, hardly perceptible nod followed. "She looks more impressive in real life than what I could find online, which wasn't that much. We can work with that. You have a good eye, Tyler."

It felt like the temperature in the room dropped to freezing without any warning.

He opened his mouth but didn't manage to get a word in before Scarlette got started. For a second, a primal fear of being in the same room with them shook him. Then, taking a step to the side, he decided to simply enjoy the show – from a safe distance.

"*She* has a name and is not a damn fashion accessory. I'm aware I'm not your priority, but I advise you to be careful about what you plan to do here about me and our engagement. I have a business of my own to think of, and I have a PR consultant at hand. You will work with her; she, and finally I, will approve of anything you want to do regarding this, making sure neither I nor my business will be misrepresented, or you'll have to pay damages. You, not Ty, to make this clear."

For a full thirty seconds, the women only watched each other, eyes firing, bodies braced. Then Ty's agent leaned back in her chair slightly, folded her hands on the table. "You obviously know how to stand up for yourself. I'm sorry if we got off on the wrong foot. You're right, my priority is Tyler, which might have influenced my approach. I have a client here I care about. A man who first got a once-in-a-lifetime career chance, then has to deal with a personal tragedy. He manages, but then suddenly reschedules enough meetings and interviews to make my life — well my assistant's life mostly — a living nightmare. He suddenly flies off to California without an explanation and comes back engaged to a woman none of us have ever heard of before. To be frank, I was expecting some bimbo he got hooked on during a drunken night out."

Scarlette gave it a few seconds of thought, then nodded. "Acknowledged, accepted, and understood. Why don't we start over, then? Hello, I'm Scarlette Langella."

Ty's agent took the hand offered to her. "Hello. Viola Carlyle. Have a seat. Anything to drink for you?"

"A Coke would be nice."

"Diet?"

"No, regular is fine."

"Sure. Tyler?"

"The same, Vi. Thanks."

Judging the situation clear again, he came over as well. A moment later, he accepted the drinks from a woman in her twenties, who shyly carried them on a tray. He handed out the beverages and sat with Scarlette and Viola to discuss business and personal plans.

When they stepped into Tyler's apartment a couple of hours later, Scarlette turned on the spot and felt instantly at home.

He had kept most of the brick walls as they were, had hung up a few classical movie posters. A deep leather couch and a small office area made up most of the living area, the rest was covered in books and bookshelves, naturally. An open kitchen was separated by a counter, and there was a door leading into a bedroom. Outside on a small balcony, she saw a tiny table grouped with two iron chairs, and a few pots with blooming flowers strapped to the railing. "My upstairs-neighbor usually drops water down from above, when she knows I'm gone," Ty explained when he saw Scarlette peeking out the window at the plants. "It's not much, but sometimes a few bees come by."

"That is sweet. And I love this place."

"I do, too. It's small, but it's enough for me and my travel schedule."

"I love it. Maybe you could keep it. My place I can give up or over to Cora, but this is great. I love the loft flair. And if we need to spend a night in the city, together or alone, we wouldn't have to ask my parents for a place to stay. They would always let us, but this would be more private, we wouldn't have to plan around anybody else."

"You're right. Sure we can keep it. I bought it a few years ago, I'm glad if I don't have to put work into selling it."

"Great. Mind if I go through your stuff?"

"Feel free. I'll grab a few things, probably pack a suitcase or two."

"Okay."

. . .

On the way down to the garage and his car, Scarlette shifted one of the bags she had taken from him when he had finished packing, studied him critically.

"Yes, babe?" he asked.

"I don't know if I should be impressed or disturbed that I didn't find any porn or anything. Okay, I didn't really look, more at your books and music, but still."

"There's always the internet?"

"Mhm, true of course."

Interest and humor gleaming in his eyes, Tyler shot her a curious glance. "And what will I find at your place?"

She smirked. "Guess you'll have to find out."

At his car he let go of his suitcase and his duffel bag, took the bags from Scarlette and dropped them carelessly on the floor, boxed her in between his body and the car.

Her heart started to race, and she felt a hard tug of lust radiate from her lap all through her.

"You are dangerous to be around, you know that, Sparks?"

"And why would that be?"

His teeth nipped on her neck, and he felt a shiver run over her. "Because I'm very close to risking a citation for indecent behavior." His rough voice close to her ear was pure temptation. Holding on hard to control herself, she took a deep breath.

"Then we better get out of here, right?"

"Yes."

"I'll drive."

"Okay."

Ty fought the whole drive from his place to hers not to choke on a laugh, and when he finally opened the door and stepped out he nearly doubled over. "God, Scarlette, I don't think I have ever heard anybody curse that extensively, or inventively for that matter."

She was an excellent driver, he had learned. And about as patient as a recently caged wild tiger.

"Who thinks it's a good idea to hand any of those moronic, monkey-brained — no pea-brained, anything else is an insult to monkeys — fucks a driver's license!? I mean, did you see that anabolically pumped idiot at the last light? What was he doing, checking if any of his dick survived the steroids instead of punching it so normal people can still hit it when it's green?"

Still shaking with laughter, he took her shoulders and kissed her hard. "For you, I'd start writing novels just so I could pen down some of those insults. It's been an education."

She slowly calmed down and kissed him back with a chuckle. "Good to know I can still teach you something. Come on, let's get upstairs."

Her apartment reminded him of his own and had him grin. She had one brick wall left, too, and had highlighted it with some iron piping lamps. But most had been covered with drywall at some point. Framed and highlighted posters hung here as well, but hers mostly showed SciFi or horror movies, and when she gave her smart speaker a command and lights turned green and blue and a SciFi soundtrack started playing, he yanked her head back by the hair, plundered her mouth.

"Hell, I love you."

His hair curtained her face, and she fiercely gripped it, answered the kiss with equal intensity. "Same goes."

They stared into the other's eyes for a breathless moment, then dragged each other to the floor.

Hitching her jeans back over her hips, Scarlette grinned. "I guess that's one way to bid this place farewell."

"Are you sure you want to let it go?" Comfortably satisfied for now, Tyler ran his hand over her hair.

"Yeah. I don't have a problem with that. It's a decent place, it will be good for Cora. I had the platform above the living area put in and set up as my bedroom, and used the small room as an office. The living room was too small to combine it with my workspace. But if Cora and her friend put some curtains or something up there, it's private enough so both of them can have their own room and still share the living space. It worked well for me, but I won't especially miss it. I already emailed my landlord about it. He agreed. Plus, I have another home now, don't I?"

"You do. Want any help packing?"

"Sure."

She opened a closet in her small hallway and started to put clothes in her suitcase, but smiled over her shoulder at Ty. "You can go up to my bed; there's a nightstand with a box with drawers on it. We should take that. And the bottles and boxes on the shelf beneath."

Intrigued, Tyler climbed the stairs and found a much roomier level than he had expected. He found her nightstand and the box, opened it curiously. And almost choked.

Pressing her lips together to muffle her wild giggles when

she heard his reaction, Scarlette composed herself, called up to him very sweetly. "Ty, babe, is everything okay?"

"Woah... ah, yeah. That's an impressive collection." He stared at several plugs, dildos, vibrators, nipple clamps, and cock rings. Some sturdy-looking cuffs rounded the display, and the boxes on the shelf below she had mentioned held massage candles and lubes, some edible body paint, and toy cleaner.

She batted her eyes at him from below, all innocent and shy. "Well, you know, sometimes as a single girl, you get so lonely."

He had thought himself sated, but when she stood down there with that full mouth in a sexy pout, he felt himself go hard again.

"Come up here."

"Uh-uh. You know we have to get ready."

"Scarlette."

"Tyler. Come on, pack the box and the rest, we have all the time in the world to play with the toys at home."

"You are killing me, woman."

"I know, and for once I regret it. But if we don't get out of here within the next ten minutes, we'll hit rush hour."

He grumbled, mockingly kicked her bed. "Shit. Yeah, okay."

They hurried to get downstairs with their haul, and Scarlette made her way to the garage. "I can take my car and we drive home with both, then I have mine handy for..."

But when she saw the flat tire on her car, she cursed. "Damn it, what the hell?"

"It's okay. We don't have time to change it now, but I have another car at home, so you can take the pick-up next time you need to get into the city. We can take care of this sooner or later."

"I... yeah, damn, okay."

To distract her from the annoyance, Tyler let her drive and couldn't stop himself from going through the box again.

"What does this do?" He held up a sleek, black device with a few buttons and a somewhat funnel-shaped knob. Glancing over, she saw he had found her air pulse vibrator.

"I'll show you sometime. Probably a bit more fun for me, but you might like the view." She winked at him and focused back on the street.

Back at home, they carried their belongings upstairs, dropped the mail they had taken out of their mailboxes onto the desk in the office, then went further up.

In the bedroom, Scarlette frowned at her toy box. "Should we leave that out like this?"

"What? You think Lorraine and the housekeeper don't expect us to have sex?"

"It's one thing to expect people to have sex, another for me to move in here within a week of knowing you and put out my sex toy collection. I'm usually really comfortable with myself and my sexuality, but I don't have to rub it under people's noses."

"And you wouldn't. Scarlette, baby, I love how easy it is for you to talk about things like that, how happy you are in your own body. I have never met a woman who looks at herself in the mirror and thinks: 'Damn, I'm pretty hot.' Usually, it's self-doubt and nitpicking about some presumed flaws. I have the best sex of my life with you because you are who you are: a self-confident woman who isn't ashamed to say or show what she likes."

She cocked her head and considered his words for a second. "First, wow, thanks. It means a lot that you know and understand me so well. Then let me tell you, you are the only person I ever considered things like this for. Not even because of you directly, because with you I started out with all cards on the table, thinking it would be a fun night and that's all. It's a lot easier with a one-night stand. When things get serious, you start thinking about how the other person perceives you. In your case, I don't worry. I just worry about how your family will see me. And if their perception changes, whether that could change things between us. That's why."

Like her, he took a moment to think it over. "Yes, I see your point. Then let me tell you, it wouldn't change anything between us. But their perception won't change. Darling, your almost eighty-year-old grandmother sent us upstairs to have shower sex. Lorraine was the one putting her in the guest room on the far side of the house. She knows I'm far from innocent either. You think I didn't have a porn stash as a teenager before the internet made it easy? We're good."

Relief came out in a sigh. "You're pretty great. Okay, thanks."

When they had finished putting things away and Scarlette wanted to go back downstairs to check on Julia, Tyler took her hand.

"Wait, there's one thing I wanted to give you."
"Hm?"
He walked over to his own nightstand, opened a drawer, and came back to her with a velvet box. He showed her a

palladium ring with a dark red stone, embedded in the band to prevent it from catching on something.

"The jeweler needed a few days to change the stone. They called yesterday, and Lorraine was kind enough to pick it up for me today while we were in the city. July said the size should be right."

She stared at the ring and her throat closed. Taking a shaky breath, she lifted her eyes to him, and he saw tears shimmering in them.

"If you don't like it..."

"Oh, shut up. I love it. I'm close to crying because it's so perfect. Thank you, thank you so much, Tyler."

He laid his palm gently on her cheek, leaned in for a quiet kiss. "I'm happy you like it."

He took her hand, put it on her finger, and studied it. "It looks beautiful on you."

"Can I keep it?"

Tyler chuckled. "Well, that was the plan."

She snickered in response. "No, I meant as a wedding band. I never got the whole here's-this-gorgeous-engagement-ring-now-strip-it-off-for-the-wedding-band-tradition. Okay, I get it historically, but not today. This is perfect, thoughtful, and beautiful. Why would I want it replaced?"

"You know, you're pretty much the perfect woman. Yes, if you want to, of course, you can keep it. You'll only have to take it off before the wedding then, so I can put it back on during the ceremony. And I had something close to that in mind for me as well. All good."

"Okay. Thanks, seriously." She rose on her toes, gave him a deep kiss.

Downstairs, Scarlette found Julia going over a webpage and gave her friend a quick hug from behind. "Thanks for your help with Ty's agent today. Usually I don't like using our friendship like that, but your PR magic worked well in combination with Viola's ideas and I feel better about the results. And thank you for helping Ty with the ring size."

"Sure, no problem on both. Does the ring fit?"

"Yeah, perfectly."

"Show it, girl. He didn't let me see it, said that was for him and you first."

When Scarlette held out her hand, July went soft all over. "Wow, he did a terrific job. That's gorgeous."

"It is. And I convinced him to let me keep it as my wedding band. I love it."

They would have talked a moment longer, but Ty knocked on the doorframe.

"Josh just arrived."

Suddenly nervous, Scarlette shifted from one foot to the other. "Do you want to greet him alone first?"

"No, I really don't. Come." He held out his hand, and when she took it he lifted hers and kissed her knuckles. "It's gonna be fine."

As they reached the bottom of the stairs, they found Josh already being smothered in Lorraine's embrace. He managed to lift a hand about an inch to wave at them. "Hi."

Lorraine turned around a little, grinned. "Hey. Sorry, had to be the first. Here he is." She released the boy and, after ruffling his hair, left for the kitchen to keep working on dinner.

Tyler hugged his brother briefly. "Welcome back. How was the trip?"

"Okay."

"You should follow my lead and become a writer, you have such a gift with words."

"Ass."

"Missed you, too, jerk. Come, I want you to meet Scarlette."

She didn't know why, but it felt right, so she mimicked a gesture from a *Stargate* scene, added "*Comtraya*" with a grin and saw Josh's answering grin spread.

"You're cool. Hi." He held out his hand and she shook it. His grip was stronger than she would have expected from the slim, long frame, the gentle dark eyes he had also inherited from his father. *Eyes that showed too much sadness for a boy his age*, she thought. She couldn't change that. But she knew she'd help Tyler to resolve the whole blackmail situation soon to take at least that weight away from Josh.

"Where have you been? Tyler didn't say."

"Charlotte, and on the way back we stopped in Washington for a day, too."

"Cool. I hope it wasn't all boring."

"No, it was pretty interesting."

They spent dinner with stories from Josh's trip and updates on wedding plans, all of them carefully avoiding the darker topics.

And when the house became mostly quiet, Scarlette and Tyler detoured to the office to go over their mail before heading to the bedroom.

With the usual ads, Scarlette almost ignored one letter, but her fingers felt something hard in the envelope.

When she studied the handwriting she couldn't place it, and there was no return address.

"Weird."

"Be careful."

"What, you think it's a bomb now? It would defy the purpose to blow me up, wouldn't it?"

"Not if it's a small charge meant to scare you into paying."

She frowned at him. "That's really putting me at ease."

"I don't want you at ease, I want you careful."

"I am. But this feels like, I don't know, a key or something. And the handwriting isn't like the one on the note."

She very carefully opened the envelope, and inside she found a letter several pages long and an old key with some barely readable numbers on it.

She scanned the first page, then the last, swallowed hard. "Oh god, that's from my biological mother."

Chapter Fourteen

Dear Scarlette,

I'm so sorry if this letter turns your world upside down.

I'm sorry for a lot of things, but before I say anything about that, I want to say I have never been sorry that I had you.

I hope your family has been honest with you and you know you have been adopted.

I gave you up because I loved you so much, and I wanted to protect you. After I had given you away, I pushed a little to find out where and with whom you ended up, so I knew you have had a good life, and I'm so happy for you!

I suppose I should have known if I could track you, they could, too. And I'm not making any sense.

Let me start at the beginning.

Your biological family goes back to Eton and Abigail Barret. They were your great-great-grandparents. But before Abigail, Eton had been married to Cecille.

I looked them up. They were big names in the silent film era and were friends with another important couple. They shared a house outside of LA, where they threw huge parties. And at that house, articles say, Cecille killed herself. Eton talked to the press after, there was talk about depression or something because she couldn't have children.

Eton married again a few years later, and that's where our family comes from. With silent films dying, and the Great Depression, Eton never truly got back into the film industry, and he and Abigail lived a more normal life with their family.

I'm not sure what to believe of this or the rest.

When my father died, the letters started to arrive at my door. They wanted money, and they said your great-great-grandfather had killed his first wife, that all we had was built on a lie.

At first, I tried to ignore them, because, honestly, what could they do, what would it change, if they exposed any of it.

But then I got scared when they copied some law texts, showed me that the insurance company who paid Eton the money on Cecille's life insurance could come to me and force me to pay the money back, with interest, because I was a blood relative. Suddenly, the sum they asked from me didn't sound that huge anymore.

My mother didn't seem to know about anything. I think dad never told her about the letters to him before, because they wrote to me about that, too. That he had done it to protect my mother's vet clinic. They were threatening to publish things to hurt her business, and he couldn't let that happen.

So he had paid. And so have I. For years.

When mom died, I fell into this deep, dark pit. It wasn't right, but for a while, I let alcohol numb the pain. Then I found out I was carrying you, and I stopped at once. It's hard to tell you, I feel so ashamed, but I don't even know who your father is. When I needed comfort, I took it, but with the letters still coming, I never let anyone get close.

To know I had you growing inside me, it made me so happy. I loved you from the moment I knew you were there.

But somehow, so did they. They threatened me with the insurance again, and how I would be so poor Child Services would take you away, put you in a crowded foster home. How they would keep track of you and, once I was gone, how they would contact you.

And knowing what they had done for so long with the rest of the family, I made the hardest decision of my life.

I sold my parents' house so I could keep paying them — and I prayed hard they wouldn't ask for all of the money right away. I don't know why, but I got lucky and they didn't.

But I had to protect you from this. Who knew what they would do to you? So, even though it broke my heart and shattered my soul, I gave you away anonymously. As long as nobody knew where you came from, you should have been safe. I had a friend help me, she had contacts, and even though they weren't supposed to, I bullied them until they let me know the family they put you with, so I knew it was a good home.

I moved away, trying to draw the attention far away

from you. And I kept paying them. "Keep them happy, and when I'm gone, it's their bad luck," I thought.

For a long time they didn't even mention you with a single word, so I was sure you were safe.

Then I got sick. Ovarian cancer, fast-growing, and it had already spread. Like with my pregnancy, they seemed to know almost as soon as I did. They told me they knew where to find you, and how they would ruin you, your business, your adoptive family and their great work, so hopefully, you'd be a good girl and pay them, too.

Hon, please believe me, I loved you with all my heart, and I did everything to prevent you from getting involved in this.

I had this letter sent upon my death, routed through several friends I trusted, in hopes nobody would intercept it.

The key you find inside is the only thing I could find in my father's belongings going back to this. He had it in an envelope with my name, and a note saying "This has been in the family for some time, I don't know what it opens. But I hope they will leave you alone, then this can be forgotten. If not, you will know what I mean, and this might help you".

I could never find out to what the key belongs, but maybe you can. I hope it will somehow help you. I know all this will be a shock, but I hope the honesty will be more useful to you in the end than my dad's cryptic note to me, and I hope you can appreciate the warning, even if you can't forgive me or our previous generations for being involved in this situation. Hopefully, this letter reaches you before they get a hold of you.

I have loved you every day of my life!

Yours,
  Caroline

Scarlette had sat in one of the chairs in the office to read the letter, and Tyler had positioned himself so he could do the same.

When she lowered the pages, she let out a shuddering breath.

"Are you okay, baby?"

"I honestly don't know. With this arriving so late, it's hardly a surprise anymore. And I always knew about the adoption, and it was great for me. I never felt a real connection to my biological mother, even when you dug up some info before. I always figured she probably had a reason to give me away, but it never mattered to me, because I have the best family I could ever wish for. Now..."

"Now you realize she was a woman who loved and wanted you and did what she had to do because she loved you more and put your happiness and safety before her own?"

"Yeah. It won't change what I feel for my family. But, I don't know, it opened this other part in me, and even though I never met her, I think I grieve for her."

Tyler sat on the floor, held out his hands for her.

"Come here, let me hold you."

With tears in her eyes for a woman she had never known and from the gratitude to the only man she had ever loved, she got up from her chair and flowed into his lap, his open arms.

He pressed his lips to her hair, holding her tight in his embrace. He could feel the tremors from her sobs and gave her the time she needed. When she faced him again, the tears had stopped, but her cheeks were still wet. He ran his thumbs over them, gave her a heartbreakingly gentle kiss.

"I'm here for you."

"I know. Thank you, Ty. I didn't expect it to hit me like that."

"Grief doesn't follow a fixed recipe. What about this? When all this is over, we will work on finding out where she's buried and visit the grave to put some flowers there. It might not be much, but maybe it helps."

New tears flooded her eyes, and she pressed her lips to his. "Oh god, I love you. Marry me tomorrow. We can somehow manage that, can't we? Fuck those idiot blackmailers and their deadlines. Tomorrow will be for us. We already sent out license requests and all. We'll push, if we have to, but Ty, I really, really want to be your wife."

He cupped her face, returned the kiss, then smiled at her. "Then we'll manage tomorrow. Honeymoon might have to wait a little longer, though."

"That doesn't matter."

"Okay." He brushed some hair behind her ear, ran his fingers along her jawline. "Then we better get some things done tonight. We'll work on the key and all that after the wedding."

"Sounds good."

They woke up early the next morning to an impatient knock on the door. "Pull up the blanket or something."

Lorraine gave them about five seconds, then opened the door and strode in with a tray in front of her. "Today? Are you both crazy? How am I supposed to organize a wedding today? You opened that damn chat group after midnight. That's when normal people sleep."

Tyler rubbed his hands over tired eyes. "Yes, it is. But, apparently, we aren't normal. Which is why we were up until two working and preparing things, too, and which is why it's seriously inconvenient to be woken up at just past five."

"Oh, stop whining, here's coffee."

Scarlette tugged the sheets around her, held out her hands for the tray. "Thanks so much, Lorraine. You're a life-saver. Okay, Tyler and I went over most points. We don't need a special menu or anything." She was interrupted when her phone rang. "Looks like you're not the only early riser." Setting down the tray, she answered. "Hey, dad."

"Ciao, Bella. What's that I'm reading here? Today?"

"Wait." She adjusted the phone on a stand, patted the bed so Lorraine would sit beside her. "Yes, today – if Ty and I can push people into sending us the licenses and we find somebody who can do the ceremony."

Lorraine took Scarlette's hand, squeezed it. "If you really mean it, I can talk to Judge Walken. He plays poker with my husband every week. He can get the licenses, and do the ceremony."

"That would be amazing."

"Consider it done."

"Thank you. Okay, papa, about the rest. Would you be okay with closing the restaurant for today? And to help out with some food? We don't want fancy, and you have things prepared. Could you take some soup, and pizza things - you always have sauce and dough ready. Bring toppings along, too, and we'll make the pizzas here fresh. Lorraine and I will bake a cake. What else do we need?"

"Bella, of course, we will close today. But it's your wedding, and you want pizza?"

"Yeah, totally. I've grown up with it, it's one of my favorite foods in the world. Your wedding should be about what you love. I love you all, I love your food. So, soup and pizza."

Marco shook his head, then winked at Tyler. "I hope you know what you are getting yourself into."

That got a laugh from the groom and a narrow-eyed stare from the bride.

"Well, all right, we'll get the food. I suppose the wine will be no problem."

"None at all, Marco. If you let Lorraine know what exactly you'll be bringing along, she'll find the right bottles for it."

"*Perfetto.*"

Next to Marco, Cynthia's face appeared. "Girl, you'll give your poor mother a heart attack one of these days."

"Sorry, kinda."

"Uh-uh, I don't believe you one bit. I can bring along a bridesmaid dress for July. There's a shop that has something pretty in her size, I'll send you a picture. About your wedding dress..."

"Wait, that's grandma calling in. Hi, Granny."

"Ah, all of the mob's together, how fitting. Morning. What's the plan so far?"

They all quickly updated her, and the woman nodded. "All right. We'll manage. As to your dress, I will bring mine along, it should fit, and it will be very pretty on you. Up now, everybody, start working your butts off if we want this done today."

Lorraine grinned at the phone. "Bea, I like you. As to the rest, I'm looking forward to meeting you personally later."

It was a busy day, but with Tyler and Scarlette being the most relaxed – as long as they had the licenses and the judge to wed them, they wouldn't have cared if they had gotten married in jeans and t-shirt – it worked out well enough.

In the afternoon, the men came together in Tyler's old room to smoke a cigar, and share a drink. "By far not strictly legal, but here," Ty gave in and handed his brother a minute glass of whisky. They fell into a comfortable silence, before going over their suits and Ty over the tux Cynthia had handed him a few minutes earlier from the dressing room, as he had been banned from there.

The master suite had been declared the female realm for the occasion, and the women were using every inch. Shoes and stockings, jewelry and make-up, dresses, and a veil were scattered throughout the bedroom and the dressing room. Currently, Cynthia sat in one of the chairs by the terrace doors and dried happy tears from her cheeks. "My baby is getting married. I'm so happy for you. He is such a sweet man."

"Thank you, mom. Come, let's get your make-up done."

Scarlette faced her mother, fussed with some products, and when she was done she leaned over and kissed Cynthia's cheek. "You're beautiful. Dad will be tempted to renew his vows."

"Oh sweetheart, you are the most wonderful daughter anyone could wish for."

Grinning, Scarlette got up, then turned to her grandmother. "Okay, show me the dress, will you?"

"Of course."

It was gorgeous. Ivory silk was set in a wide, knee-length circle skirt, and the bodice was a slightly off-the-shoulder cut with a straight neckline in the front, a slight V in the back where a line of buttons ran down the middle. "The sixties brought on some timeless dresses. Here, get all this on, first," she told her granddaughter and pointed at a heap of lingerie and stockings. "Then here's the petticoat. The veil didn't survive, but Lorraine is a treasure, you can take hers, it will work with the dress. And like that you'll have something borrowed. The dress is something old. Won't protect a future *bebè* in your case, but let's transfer that to your young brother-in-law."

Scarlette couldn't find her speech at first, but then enfolded her grandmother in a fierce embrace. "Thank you, Granny. This means so much. And thank you, Lorraine."

The housekeeper smiled, ran her hand up Scarlette's arm. "You're welcome. Here is something else, then you have your blue."

She held out a braided white-gold necklace with a pendant of a heart-shaped blue sapphire.

"It belonged to Ty's mother, she would want you to have it."

"Oh god, Lorraine."

"No, no, don't you cry, or we'll have to fix your face, and it's so pretty right now."

Scarlette nodded, took a steadying breath, and huffed it out. "Okay. I'm okay."

Her mother came over, brushed her hair away. "And here is something new. I picked them up on the way when Ty told me what kind of ring you have," she said and held out a pair of ruby earrings.

July scanned her up and down, absorbing the happiness radiating from her friend. "You are stunning. Here, let's finish this off properly. You got super lucky, one of Ty's ancestors was a coin collector. I rummaged through the attic and found a real sixpence for your shoe."

It couldn't get any more perfect. Scarlette helped the others to get ready and allowed herself a glass of champagne before the ceremony. She felt a little uneasy about taking off her ring, but it was only for a short while, she told herself.

And in the early evening, with the sun providing a golden background that let her hair shine in its most fiery red, Scarlette walked outside to the flower garden behind the house.

Ty was speechless when he saw her, but when she put her hands into his, he smiled.

A rush went through them both, not unlike the first night in the bar. But now intertwined with the tingling and excitement there was the warmth and trust July had seen days before, the knowledge and comfort of a whole life together to come.

To please the judge, and themselves, they kept the ceremony short. And when Tyler put her ring back on her finger and drew Scarlette in for their first kiss as husband and wife, when her warm, sweet lips opened oh-so slightly for him, they forgot the world around them for a moment.

When he released her he leaned in, whispered to her. "You look beautiful, Mrs. O'Brien."

She managed a watery laugh, laid her hand on his cheek, and whispered back. "And you have no idea what's underneath the dress."

Laughing, he pulled back a little, dipped her deep down, and gave her another, playful kiss. "I'll find out later, believe me."

They used the back porch as a dance floor, and with lights strung up the adjoining outdoor kitchen and eating area was a perfect place for an intimate wedding party.

Scarlette had been right when it came to her parents. Marco was struck by his wife's beauty. And when he pulled her inside and upstairs, she cheerfully giggled and agreed to his proposal to renew their own vows on their 25th anniversary the following year.

Their daughter watched them, shook her head with a smile while swaying in Tyler's arms. Smile spread into grin when her brother-in-law let July go after a dance, then tapped Scarlette's shoulder. "Can I steal you from your husband for a dance?"

"Absolutely." Scarlette let go of Tyler and grinned when Josh smoothly led her into their dance. "You are a pretty good dancer, Josh," she concluded after a moment.

"Thanks. Mom made us take lessons and, well, the girls like it."

"I can confirm that. Are you okay with all this? It's been quite a rush."

"Yeah, it has, but a good one. We all needed something bright after everything that happened and what's still going on. You make Ty happy, so I'm okay with it."

"That means a lot, to him and to me."

For the day, they had put everything else aside, and when everybody was in their beds, Tyler made good on his threat to explore what his wife was wearing under her wedding dress.

Later, they both fell into an exhausted, endorphin-fueled sleep.

Chapter Fifteen

I n the morning, they both agreed that as newlyweds it was their right, that it was even expected of them, to stay in bed a bit longer and consume each other. And when they lay spent in the pillows after, Ty followed the lines of Scarlette's tattoo with his fingertip. "You haven't told me yet what this is about."

She let her eyes wander to her hip and the dragon nestled there. "Several things. First, dragons are awesome, obviously. Second, they're wise and powerful, and can have a dangerous temperament. I like that combination."

"And it doesn't remind you of yourself at all, I assume."

She snickered, kissed his cheek. "Never. Third, it's something that somehow connects almost every culture there is. A mythical being that never existed in reality, and still there are tales of them in one form or another all over the world. That's fascinating. And last but not least, I see it as a reminder to always have some room in my life for fantasy. Life is so serious, sometimes we need to have something epic to indulge in."

Tyler studied his wife for a long while, then gave her a deep kiss. "You're the most amazing person I know. You are the love of my life."

"And you're mine."

Since Scarlette's father and grandmother had mentioned their staff would take care of the early preparations at the restaurant, they all managed a family breakfast together.

At the table, Julia frowned at the happy couple. "I'm sorry to be the one to bring this topic back, but someone has to."

"No, you're right, July," Ty said, and topped off her coffee.

"Thanks. Okay. So, I thought about this, and well, actually, Lorraine gave me the idea, or more like seeing her here. With all this, I think we all agree this blackmail goes a long way back. I wouldn't be surprised if they got started with Eton and Charles. And who would be close enough to know so many things? They must have had staff at the house, right?"

After a moment of consideration, Julia got nods of agreement from everybody.

"I think I might be most useful, if I do a little research in that area. Try to figure out who was working for them back in the twenties, then find their offspring."

"That's a good idea. Scarlette and I have another line to follow, but you should do that. There's a trunk with old documents in the attic, I'll show it to you."

"That would be good."

After breakfast and her family leaving, Scarlette helped

Lorraine with some cleaning in the kitchen, while Tyler showed Julia the trunk upstairs.

When he came back downstairs, he saw his wife in running gear coming out of their bedroom. "Give me five minutes and I'll join you. That way I can show you around the property."

She learned aside from what she had already seen, there were a workshop and several sheds, and her favorite — an additional pool house with a hot tub and a gym — was marked as a big bonus.

On the last steps back, Ty took Scarlette's hand, drew her close. "Two of our winemakers will be at a convention in New York tomorrow. If you give me your car keys, I'll ask them to do us a favor and to change your tire, then bring your car here on the way back."

"Okay, sure. Thanks."

They went over the letter from Scarlette's mother again, but it didn't help. The key itself appeared to be quite old and the numbers on it were barely readable. Frustrated, Scarlette trudged up the stairway to the attic, had Julia hand her the trinket box.

Back in the office, she went through it but found no other key close to the one Caroline had sent her.

Twisting and turning it in her fingers, she paced the office and mumbled to herself. "There's something about it. I don't know, I can't place it. I think it's these numbers."

Tyler, about as frustrated as Scarlette, tossed his phone back on the desk. "Vi sends her congratulations to both of us.

She wants a wedding picture for publication, we'll have to go through the shots."

Scarlette froze for a second, turned on the spot and reaching over the desk smacked a loud kiss on her husband's lips. "You're a genius!"

He grinned, held her face to give her another kiss. "Thanks, babe, I like to tell myself the same. But why am I in this precise moment, again?"

"Picture! I knew I have seen those numbers. Get your laptop, I need to check on the photos you took of the mansion."

She ran downstairs to get more coffee for them, and found Tyler already staring at his screen when she came back.

"We need a coffee machine up here."

"That's *you* need a coffee machine up here, my addicted darling."

"So what? You don't want your coffee, I'm okay with two."

He held out his hand, curled his fingers. "Gimme."

Walking over, she got comfortable on his lap to search through the pictures. It took a while: Tyler had been thorough, but when they came to the shots he had taken of the dark passageway, Scarlette jiggled on his legs. "There! I told you!"

It wasn't easy to make out, but on one wall somebody had written the same numbers as on the key.

"There's something else, look." Zooming in and adjusting the brightness, they managed to make out three letters written below the numbers.

They ran a search and found out the key would most

likely belong to a bank box from an old San Diego bank. To their surprise, the building was still standing and in use.

"Holy shit, check this out. It's a hotel now, and they still have the vault there. Seems like it's used as a conference room now."

"Our luck is in, I'd say, and it sounds like we might take a short honeymoon after all."

"Kind of, even though I want a real honeymoon later. But with this thing taking up so much time, it will probably take a long time until I can take off from my own business again."

"I agree on all counts. We'll manage. Would you pack for us, while I make the reservations?"

"Sure."

Stepping out of the plane a few hours later, Scarlette put on her sunglasses. "I've rarely been on the West Coast, and I kind of know why. This whole state feels like a desert."

"I prefer the East Coast as well. Also, a lot fewer people running after you to try to get your signature for a movie based on your books. Back East, Vi doesn't even let them contact me, here I feel like they smell it."

"Babe, you're not exactly the typical shy, nerdy writer without any pictures online. Your family is loaded on top. People know you."

"You realize you're equally loaded now, too, right?"

"Don't talk about it, I don't want to think about it. Why did you tell your lawyers not to separate me from that?"

"Because I love you, because you are my wife, because I want to share all of my life with you. And I know you won't piss it down the drain," he explained easily.

"Okay, okay, fair enough."

They drove to the hotel, and Scarlette snarled when they entered the Gaslamp Quarter. "Look at this, how can they live like that? This whole city either portrays itself like some commercial for beachwear, or here like a cheesy amusement park. These are historic buildings, they could present all this in a respectful manner. Instead they're milking it. Why would you do that?"

Seeing exactly what she meant, Ty agreed with her. "I am constantly glad my family decided to live far away from here."

"Yeah. Just imagine us meeting had you lived here. Like we would have ever clicked, if you had been a West Coast beach boy."

"True. Yet another reason to prefer the East Coast."

The hotel welcomed them with open arms, and when they were shown to the honeymoon suite, Scarlette grinned despite their mutual cynical view of the West Coast.

"I couldn't refrain," Tyler told her and gave the concierge a generous tip, before closing the door himself. "I wish we had time to enjoy it."

"Me, too. But I want this over." She went through her bag and came up with the key. "Ready?"

"Yes."

Down at reception, the poor clerk went pale when Tyler asked for the manager. "Is there any problem? We will of course fix it for you. Can we do anything for you?"

God, he's close to hyperventilating, Scarlette thought with pity. She reached over the counter, and laid her hand on the young man's arm. "Everything is great. We merely have a personal question and will have to talk to the manager about it. But the room is fine, the hotel is great."

"Okay. Well, would you like to sit down for a minute? I will call our manager."

"Sure thing." Quietly chuckling, she walked to a small sitting area with Ty and thanked another clerk when two glasses of champagne were carried over. "Poor guy at reception. I think he'd rather jump from the roof than tell the manager the newest VIP guests want to speak with management."

"You're right. But at least we mean well. He'll have to learn to deal with others who don't."

"True."

"We could have a drink down here, later. From what's online, the bar sounds cozy, and I saw there's a pool table."

"Depending on what we find, we can do that, yeah."

When the manager approached them, they both got up and plastered on friendly smiles. After a minute of conversation, they found that they were talking to a woman highly interested in the history of the building.

"Well, this is extremely fascinating. We have kept that box untouched for nearly a hundred years. I cannot believe somebody is really asking for it. If you don't mind, I know it's an annoying thing, but is there any way you can show how your family goes back to this, Mrs. O'Brien?"

"Of course. We have recently been looking into this after my mother died. Here is the complete family tree."

She opened a file on a tablet she had brought along, told some details about her grandparents, then came to Eton and Cecille. "As you can see, while Cecille isn't a direct blood relative, the contract for this box was opened when they were married. With her death, Eton gained the right to open the box, even if it had been filed under her name." Not strictly correct after today's standards, Scarlette assumed, but back then it was a man's right to handle his wife's property.

"Yes, all right, I can follow that. And you have the key." The woman chewed on her cheek, tapped her fingers on the table, indecisiveness written all over her face. "I really should verify all this, but... damn... please excuse me. But I also really want to know what's in there."

Tyler shifted, gave her a friendly smile, his eyes beaming with benevolence. "Well, depending on how this goes, if I should ever decide to write about any of this, I would of course make sure to mention how very helpful you and your hotel have been to help uncover my wife's past." He finished it by taking Scarlette's hand and sweetly kissing her knuckles.

"Oh, well... uh, why don't we go down to the old vault and see whether the key fits at all. No reason to think about it all, as long as we don't know that, right?"

"Mrs. Delgado, you read my mind."

Leading the way, the manager elaborated on her own family, how her grandparents had come to the US from Puerto Rico, how they all had found a place to work in the same building over the years.

"You see, this building is as much personal history to me as this box is to you, Mrs. O'Brien."

"That's fascinating. Sometimes it's hard to believe how the world works, isn't it? Generations of your family have guarded my family's heritage." There wasn't the slightest trace of sarcasm or impatience in Scarlette's voice.

Beside her, Tyler smirked behind the manager's back. Oh

yes, she was good, no wonder Cynthia dragged her into the charity work now and then.

With a nervous laugh, Mrs. Delgado opened the vault door, led the couple inside. "Fascinating, yes. So, here it is. We replaced all boxes with empty ones over the years, when we managed to contact the owners or their heirs, or when somebody came in like you, who found an old key. Yours is the last."

Scarlette stepped over, carefully used the key she had brought along. An excited tremor ran through her, when she felt the lock give and turn, when the door swung open. Tyler merely glanced at the manager, who sucked in a quick breath.

"Oh, my. I think that's that. Oh, please, open it. Sometimes I forget we're not a bank anymore here. We take pride in our discretion and value our guests' privacy, but the boxes belonged to the bank, and from what I see, you're the closest relative to this in any case."

"Thank you, Mrs. Delgado. Would it be possible to take the box inside upstairs to our room?"

"Yes, yes, of course." The woman did her best to hide her disappointment.

"Once we know what's inside, we will tell you what we can about it."

"That's very kind. Thank you so much."

In their suite, Scarlette sat cross-legged on the bed, curled her finger at Ty. "Come here, I wanna see what's in here."

"Give me a minute to get us a glass of wine. This is a step forward."

"Okay."

With a toast, they finally opened the box and saw once again a pile of letters. "Deja-vú."

"Yes. Let's open them carefully."

The first one had Scarlette reach for another sip of wine. "They knew how to have fun, I'd say. Listen to this:

'Let them talk and complain about prohibition. When I took you to bed last night, when I tasted your skin, I knew I never needed a drop of alcohol again. Every time I am near you, you fill my senses, and I am drunk on you.

Your skin shines pure like a pearl and deep inside you taste like the ocean the pearl came from, and always I find you about as wet, only never cold.'"

"Sounds like they had some fun, yes. But where does that leave us? Cecille had an affair as well?"

"Yes, maybe. Do you think Cecille and Mary-Beth confessed to each other? You betray your husband for years, you'd need someone to talk to? Or not?"

"I don't know. But let me tell you, if you ever feel the need to try that, I'll probably end up killing you, too. Just a warning."

"Fair enough. Same goes, of course," Scarlette replied with a wink. "Okay, let's go through these, there isn't a signature here either, but maybe we will find something in the others."

They skimmed through several notes with the same explicit content, until Scarlette kept reading over one letter twice, lowered it, and gaped with huge eyes at Tyler.

"Oh my... I think you should read this."

She handed him the paper and reached for her wine.

Sweetest Cecille,

Neither do I know what happened. When we were alone and I watched you, a need I had never known came alive inside me. It felt like madness took over from me when you touched me. There is no rhyme or reason why I did not step back from your hands, from your lips. No excuse, as the meek amount of gin we had was nothing.

You touched me, and it felt so right, even if it was so wrong. Are we sick?

But how can something so wonderful be an ailment? You made me feel things I never felt before, and when you quivered under my seeking hands when my breasts brushed yours and you sighed, I knew it was the same for you.

I can privately write to you more freely, you are under less scrutiny than me, but whatever we make of this, for the public we need to remain friends for now.

There is a house outside of the city for sale. I will arrange a call with a realtor to visit and evaluate it. We can meet there and talk in private, once we tell him we need some time to go through the house again on our own.

For now, I can tell you, yes, things have changed for me as well.

Tyler gulped some wine. "I guess that means they did confess to each other."

"Uh-huh."

"They would probably make a cute couple today."

"Yes. But back in the 1920s... I can't even imagine."

"It would have caused a public outcry. An affair would have been a big enough scandal, but an affair with another woman — her best friend at that — from whatever side you look at it? It would have ruined everything for both couples."

"Yes. When did they buy the house again?"

"Ah, 1923, around Thanksgiving. But I don't know when they got started with the buying process or any early calls to check it out."

Scarlette ran her hand through her hair, drew a heavy breath. "What if their husbands found out that they were sleeping together? For years, probably every time there was a party and they drove up there a little earlier to "prepare the house." A house they had all bought together right after getting married? How would Eton and Charles react?"

"You think the blackmailers are right with their murder accusations?"

"I only think it's a possibility that cannot be ruled out at the moment. But it doesn't mean I'm ready to believe all this without questioning it. I still want them to show us proof, I still want you to write it as you see fit once we have every-thing, and I still want to hang the assholes for trying to get money from us."

"Then that's what we'll do."

They spent the evening with an update to Julia and were impressed when she showed them a whole case board including timelines and involved persons they knew about up to this point.

"You've been busy, sweetie."

"Yeah, well, meetings at the moment are tricky, and I had a few days off coming. I took them early and then could spend my whole day with this. I'll get into the details when you're back. But we have something to build on now."

"You're seriously awesome. We'll get back home tomorrow morning, then we'll discuss all this in detail."

"Okay. See you tomorrow."

When Julia had hung up, Tyler danced his fingers down Scarlette's spine. "She's a treasure."

"She really is. Okay, should we try to enjoy this trip even with all this mess?"

"Yes, I think we should. What did you have in mind?"

"Downstairs, having that drink and a round of pool, and the loser will have to screw the winner's brains out? Or the winner is allowed to screw the loser's brains out."

She saw it in his eyes, the amusement, the ego, and she squeaked when he pushed her down on the bed, scraped his teeth over her jaw.

"You will beg me tonight to take you, whether you win or lose."

Chapter Sixteen

It was good to be back at home, however much fun the night had been. But currently it didn't feel right to leave the East Coast for too long.

When Ty's phone rang while they were talking with Julia, he had a bad feeling seeing the number of one of his winemakers. After a short conversation, he hung up again with an order to let the cops know.

"Babe?"

"Your car tire didn't just go flat, it was slashed, and what we didn't see because we were on the other side of the car was that somebody let out his creativity and scratched "Bitch" into your door."

"Fuck. Damn it, I bet that was Patrick. He must have found out my new address."

"It wouldn't exactly surprise me. The cops will investigate, and I assume later today somebody will also come by."

She pinched the bridge of her nose with her fingers, squeezed her eyes shut for a moment.

"Shit, fuck, damn it! One thing to deal with is too easy or

what? Yeah, okay. But I swear to you, honeymoon will be a whole month of sun, sand, drinks with umbrellas, and banging each other into a coma."

"I can ignore it all and pack, we can leave in ten minutes."

She laughed, as he had hoped, then dropped her forehead on his shoulder. "Let's just figure all this out."

Julia was still reading over the letters and busy adding details to her timeline when Lorraine let them all know a detective of the NYPD was at the gate.

"That was fast."

"Mhm, yes."

When they walked downstairs and the door opened to a familiar face, Tyler shook his head. "I should have known. Bet you sped out here with your lights on just so you could punch it."

"'Course, what do you take me for?"

After a friendly one-armed hug, Tyler grinned at his wife. "Scarlette, this is Detective Luke Preston. We went to school together. Luke, my wife, Scarlette O'Brien, neé Langella."

Boyish charm lightened a face that told her he had seen more of his fair share of dark deeds done by humans. His dark hair fell a little over his ears, his brown eyes warmed when he shifted them to her, held out his hand. "Hello, Mrs. O'Brien. Nice to meet you. And apparently congratulations to the both of you."

"Scarlette, please. Hello, Detective. And thank you. I'm sorry you had to come all the way out here for this."

He easily shook his head. "Luke, then. No problem at all.

I'm always glad to get a chance to see Ty, and now I was curious, too, to meet you. How did you manage to tame that scoundrel?"

Her glance flicked to Tyler, and she grinned. "Mutual interests, I'd say. Do you two want to sit down and I'll get us coffee?"

"You only want more yourself, darling," Tyler teased.

"And if I do?" she asked innocently and quickly vanished towards the kitchen.

Luke peered after her and shook his head. "Still can't believe it. You of all people, married, and to a woman looking like a freaking princess."

When Tyler laughed loudly, Luke blinked. "What?"

"Nothing." He sometimes forgot that not everybody was as nerdy as he or Scarlette — and Luke's choice of words probably pure coincidence. "Come on, let's sit down."

He led his friend back towards the kitchen as well, and when Scarlette popped up in the doorway with a tray, he circled his finger. "Turn around."

"Why?"

"Because I like ogling your ass?"

"I get why, it's a great ass. Again, why? I've got everything."

"Yep, but the kitchen is more personal than the parlor. And we should find some leftover wedding cake here."

"Okay."

Lorraine left the kitchen discreetly after greeting Luke with a short wave of her hand, and the trio settled in the breakfast nook.

A few more minutes of small talk were followed by Luke frowning. "I hate to change the topic, but I have to. Let me say first, our lab has everything they need from your car. It can be brought back here, and the door can be repaired."

"Okay, that's good. Thanks."

"Sure. Now, when we checked the owner and your name and the RO against a Patrick Milton came up, we investigated in that direction right away but couldn't do more than talk to him briefly as of now. Unfortunately, we also have no exact time frame to work with. Could you help us out there?"

"Not since I left New York for a trip. Before that, everything was fine. That was about seven days ago. When Ty and I were there to pick some stuff up three days ago, we didn't see the scratches. We were in a hurry to get out of the city before the rush hour and only saw the other side of the car."

"Okay. That still helps. Have you had any contact with Mr. Milton since the RO was filed?"

"No. Shortly after, I moved to a new apartment, and I haven't heard from him or seen him since. Ah, my grandmother told me he showed up at the restaurant she and my father own together the day news of Ty's and my engagement came out."

As casual as he seemed at first glance, Luke took meticulous notes. "Do you know what happened?"

"No, sorry. Granny didn't go into detail, she only let us know he had been there, when she visited us later that day to make sure we'd be careful here."

"She's a smart woman, I'd say. I might need to talk to her and your father about this."

"Sure."

"Do you mind telling me what happened between you and Mr. Milton before things escalated to the night you called the cops?"

Scarlette leaned back with her coffee, more annoyed than upset.

"We had one date, and from my point, it didn't go well when he started planning our wedding after ten minutes, after fifteen he had basically named our three children. The fact that I don't want children, or that I wouldn't consider giving up my business or work in general to be his pretty little housewife, didn't concern him. I finished the date in the middle of our first course, stood up, paid for my part of the dinner, and left.

"After that, I got flowers, letters, emails to my company. He started to show up. My parents and I talked unofficially with a cop who told us that, unfortunately, until he did something to physically hurt me or broke any laws, they couldn't do very much. And he was careful to stay on the legal side of the line. He wasn't stupid, he was obsessed. I don't know what changed, but then he broke into my place. I assume you know the rest."

"Yes. Good job with the knife."

"Thanks. I almost had it framed."

Luke smirked. "I get what Ty sees in you. Okay. Thanks for the info. We'll check on Mr. Milton's whereabouts in detail again now that we have a rough timeframe. Is there anybody else who'd want to harm you?"

It brought on only a second of hesitation, but it was enough to have Luke's cop senses pick up on it. "I regularly help the authorities to get animals out of inadequate conditions. I suppose over the years several people have come to dislike me. But my private address isn't listed, you can't find it on my business page, and I'm not on social media. I don't say it's impossible, but it would take more than the usual quick online search, and I don't see any former clients going that far. In the five years I have had my business, I never had any problems after a case. At an apartment with the vets, sometimes the cops, sure, people get loud and angry, but after I'm usually out of it all."

Luke nodded for now and focused on Tyler. "What about you? Any jealous exes?"

"No. You know there was hardly ever anybody serious. Only Veronica, and that was years ago. By now she's married with a family if I remember correctly what my mom told me a long while ago."

Another nod. *Something here*, Luke thought, but couldn't pinpoint it yet.

He was about to dig a little deeper, when Lorraine came in again through the backdoor, her face hard, her eyes burning with rage. "Tyler, we have a problem."

"What is it?"

Instead of explaining, she opened a cupboard door, revealed the security monitor behind it, and zoomed in on an area close to the gate inside the compound.

Near the driveway, green grass was dyed deep red by blood. A lifeless bundle was lying there, intestines spilling out of its belly, the fur matted with filth. It took some imagination to make out that the poor gutted creature had once been a cat. Pinned to its head in some way was a note, and the camera zoom was enough to read it.

Curiosity killed the cat.
Stop digging up the past, just pay.

Scribbled under it was an email address and a payment service.

"No other people you two were saying?" Luke asked Scarlette and Tyler, who both looked up from the screen and at each other.

"Fuck."

"Those fucking assholes."

Ty ran a hand through his hair in his usual gesture of distress. "Goddamn it. I never thought they'd do anything like this. Luke, let's check on this, and then we should get upstairs. I'd say you got a second case dropped into your lap right there."

"Uh-huh, or one escalating one. I'll check it, you all stay inside. I will have your officers here come by, and they won't be thrilled to hand this to New York. Leave the pissing contest to me."

"Okay. We'll be on the second floor, my father's old office."

"I'll find you."

When Luke finally strode into the office almost an hour later, fury pumped off him and his eyes were fixed on his old friend as he ignored Scarlette and Julia.

"Tell me, now, all of it."

They did so together, and in the end, Luke pulled at his own hair so he wouldn't knock someone out.

"Damn it, Ty, have you all lost your mind? Why in the name of god wouldn't you go to the police with this?!"

Equally pissed, Ty shoved at a chair, had it rolling over the floor until it smashed into the wall. "Because I wanted to protect my family! Because for Scarlette, it meant nothing at first. And she figured, like I did, the worst they would do, would be to publish it. Would suck for my family, but we could spin it. And for Scarlette's family, it wouldn't matter at all."

"Ty is right. We never found any indication of violence, only vague threats toward reputation. I would probably have laughed about it, and it might even have benefited my business with clients signing up out of curiosity. Then I met Ty, and I wanted to help him, protect him, just as much as he wants to do the same for me. You know his family, and while I trust you, because Ty does, can you vouch for absolutely every cop there is that no one will leak the blackmail of the O'Brien family to the press?"

"Shit, yeah, I get your reasoning in a way. Still. You could have called *me*, Ty."

"With this, I would have, if you hadn't been here, believe me. Like I said, we never expected any violent outbursts. That's why we decided to check out the story, try to figure out what happened back in 1928 and how this started. We figured by the end of the deadline, they'd come to us with payment instructions, and would either give us more time when we asked for proof, or release what they had. When everything was over, one way or another, we would have handed it to the cops without paying."

Luke clenched his fists and opened his hands a few times to release the biggest chunk of tension, then nodded.

"Okay, here's how this will go from now. I'm on good terms with my boss Leroy, I'll manage him, tell him due to your recent marriage and most likely the outburst it provoked against you, Scarlette, that I'd prefer to stay here while investigating. I'll arrange for properly protected tech and start investigating on the down-low. This should prevent any leaks or curious eyes at the precinct.

"You guys will indeed ask for proof through the email address. It won't lead us directly to them, but it allows some form of a two-sided communication. We'll work on tracking the mail.

"I believe they'll give you more time, or some form of proof, because throwing a dead cat over your wall shows desperation: they need that money. They won't simply release information and lose their most valuable leverage.

"I will send a colleague to do the follow-up on Milton, it should be possible now. But while I can usually attest to the fucked-up mind of obsessed stalkers, when I talked to him, he sounded more like he thinks your wedding was merely a tragic mistake and you'd come back to him as soon as you see the error of your ways."

"And in all his grace, he would forgive me and take me back with open arms," Scarlette finished with sarcasm coloring every word.

"Yes. He sounds like a prince," Luke said to lighten the mood.

With a sigh, Scarlette sat down on the deep leather couch standing against one wall of the office. "Yeah. And all this had me rethink it. He would rather have either tried to lull me into a false sense of security or attacked Ty."

"That's how I see it. You two write that email, I assume they won't be surprised anymore to hear from you together. I will make some calls, then I'll go over that board with Ms. Stone again."

Julia looked over from where she had started to rearrange some notes.

"Make it Julia, or July. Sure, let me know when you are ready."

While Tyler moved with his laptop to Scarlette and composed the email with her, Luke took a seat at the desk and started making his calls. His eyes drifted constantly to the huge board Julia had set up, but if he was honest with himself, just as often as they scanned the notes, they also ended up on Julia, her wild curls, her back, her butt, and her legs. Man, the woman had gorgeous legs. Long, toned, nicely tanned, like the rest of her that he could see. She wore jeans shorts and a loose t-shirt. Nothing fancy, but it suited her.

Ty saw his friend's gaze wander, gently nudged Scarlette and barely lifted his chin to indicate it to her. She saw what he meant, shifted her eyes to him and lifted a brow with a grin nobody who didn't know her face inside and out would even see. For now, they both kept quietly working.

Lorraine interrupted their group session with dinner, and because he hoped to find out more about Julia, Luke steered conversation to more normal topics. With Josh having dinner at a friend's, he judged lighthearted ex-lovers stories safe enough.

"Ty, do you remember the brunette from New York with this huge eighties music collection on vinyl? You met her at some club, didn't you?"

"Ah, yeah... you mean Nancy, right? Nancy Gordon?"

Scarlette's eyes sharply came up from cutting her steak.

"Yeah, that's her. You think I can hit her up? I'm looking for an LP for my brother for his birthday."

"You might. For everything else, I think you missed your chance. I hear she's batting for the other team now and is happily married to Roselynn Jones."

"You're talking Nancy Gordon, the small-time Broadway actress," Scarlette interrupted.

"Yes. You know her, Sparks?"

"Uh-huh, you could say so. This is weird."

Ty cocked his head, lifted an eyebrow. "We haven't lived in completely different circles."

"No, but sharing my exes, well past one-nighters, with you is still weird."

He had taken a sip of iced tea, spewed it into Luke's face without a warning.

Luke accepted a napkin from Julia to swipe his face dry and awarded Ty with a perfect male interpretation of a resting-bitch-face. "Thanks, bro."

"Sorry. Let's get back to this. You slept with Nancy, too, Sparks?"

"Yeah, years ago. You gotta try to find out what you like, right? Was fun, but it wasn't really me, so you got lucky."

"I sure as hell did."

She punched his arm with a tease in her eyes. "Don't dare start imagining a threesome now. You're stuck with only me from now on. Your own fault, you started the marriage talks."

He gave her a smacking kiss, grinned at her. "And I couldn't be happier."

Taking it as a starting point, Luke peered amicably at Julia. "So, July, anybody we need to know about in your past as juicy as that?"

Grinning, she shook her head. "Nope, I'm tame. A few guys, but none of them really hit the right notes. And right now, it's complicated with me being in Australia for at least another month, more likely two months."

"Seriously? That's so cool. What are you doing there?"

"Helping my dad after an accident. My mom and he split up when I was young, but I have a close relationship with both. And when he needed someone around after his hip replacement, I managed to talk my boss into letting me work for the office there."

Luke focused his attention completely on her, and when he started asking her about life Down Under, Julia felt a strange pull, a warm flutter in her belly. No man before had shown that sincere interest. She knew she didn't look bad, and most of the time she even believed it, but that had usually turned out to be the problem. Guys were attracted to the tall blonde with the pretty tits. More than once she had found that any deeper conversation wasn't wanted by the guys or worth the time on her end.

"I always wanted to visit Australia. Maybe I should while you're still there; I'd have my own personal tour guide."

And when Luke freely talked about his family, about his problems with dating, or often the woman's problem with dating a cop, even about his family dog, she felt like she had known him for years.

Scarlette exchanged a knowing glance with Tyler, and smirked when she saw the same awareness in Lorraine's eyes.

When they hadn't heard back from the blackmailers after dinner, the group split up. Julia kept going through information on the former staff, and when Tyler told him he hadn't been able to pinpoint earlier payments in the bank statements, Luke decided to review the financials as well. Scarlette took the office that formerly had belonged to Ty's mother to talk to her own about the upcoming gala, and Tyler grabbed Josh, who had just come home, to go to the stables and check on the horses.

Tyler updated Josh on the way and felt yet another layer of innocence being stripped from his young brother when he told him about the cat. "Bastards. It's one thing to threaten us, or even to publish all they have, or say they have, but this? Hurting, killing a helpless cat, that's pathetic."

"It is. I'm sorry you have to go through all of this, but it would feel wrong to keep things from you."

Josh stopped, laid his hand on Tyler's arm until his brother turned to face him.

"It would be wrong. I know you want to shield me, and that's what a big brother should do. But Ty, this is bigger than some schoolyard bully. I need to know it all, it's a better weapon, a better protection. And I know how it hurt you when you got the first note, when you realized how our parents had been keeping things from us. It's made grieving so much harder on both of us."

A weight he hadn't even been aware of lifted from Tyler's chest, and he hugged his brother tightly.

"You are absolutely right, on all of it. You are pretty damn smart for your age."

"Thanks." When they let go of each other again, Josh shoulder-bumped his brother. "So, how is it to be married?"

A wicked smile spread on Tyler's face, and he hooked his thumbs in his front pockets. "Awesome, even with all the rest.

She is... I can't find enough words to describe her. She is what's been missing in my life until now. The day we met, something changed inside me, and after I had let her go in the middle of the night, there was nothing I could do to stop thinking about her. Not only her in bed with me, but how I wanted to get to know every corner of her mind."

"Yeah, she's cool."

"She is. And smart, ambitious, loyal. She has a huge heart, but she doesn't break easily. She can keep a distance, even when she is being friendly. The friendly is never fake, but she can separate herself from people. But when she lets you in, really in, I think there's nothing she wouldn't do for you."

Studying his brother's profile in the light of dusk, Josh grinned, and the beaming smile on his face still had something left of the seventeen-year-old he was supposed to be. "You are totally sunk."

"Yeah, but I'm good with that. Are you okay with her?"

"Sure. It's not like she's my stepmom or whatever, no problem there. As far as I've gotten to know her so far, I really like her. And her family is cool, too."

"They are. They never questioned her, or me for that matter. They simply accepted us. Scarlette and me, but also you and me."

"Yeah, they would."

At the stables, they went over the latest info sheets on each horse, inspected the schedules and checkboxes on each box, scratched necks and noses of happily neighing mares. However busy or screwed up life was, this was a good place, these were good animals. It put everything back into perspective, and both Tyler and Josh knew that whatever else work or school would bring, they would always come here and feel connected to this part of their family legacy.

More relaxed than they both had been in days, they made their way back to the house together.

"You wanna come to the charity gala with us? I'm pretty sure Cynthia would be thrilled, and possibly throw some ticket holder out to find a spot for you."

"Ah, actually, I've got a date that evening. It's only movies and a pizza, but..."

"Oh well, no problem. With whom?"

"Bonny Robins. I have History with her and we kind of got talking during the class trip."

"Anything happened, yet?"

Josh could feel the blush creep up his neck inch by inch. "Man..."

"Josh. No joking matter here. And nothing to be ashamed of. You're old enough to know if you're ready for it, and if you decide to have sex, I wanna know you're gonna be responsible about it. And I'm fairly sure you'd be a whole lot more embarrassed if Lorraine were giving you this speech, or making sure you'll have a box of condoms in your room within the next days."

"Yeah, probably. How did you know you were ready?"

"I didn't, really. Didn't think about it like that. I was horny, I shared a few beers I had stolen from dad with a girl, and we tumbled into the grass. It was okay for both of us. We kept seeing each other for a while, but I wasn't really in love with her or anything."

"You are so easy with it all. It never seemed a problem for you."

"What, to get a girl? No, I don't think that was a problem.

And I've always seen sex as a pleasurable way to spend time with a woman who wanted the same. But even with Veronica, there was something missing, although I didn't know it at the time. Then I ran into Scarlette, and with her it's something new for me, too. There's a connection now. It makes it brighter, it makes it more.

"I guess, what I'm trying to say is, don't pressure yourself. If you feel like it, and she does too, do it. If it doesn't rock your world at first, or with the next girl, don't think you're doing it wrong, or that it would be wrong to go on having fun. Someday it will really blow your mind, and then you'll know it's different with that woman."

"Okay."

They parted ways on the second-floor landing, with Josh going further up and Tyler swinging into the room where Scarlette was obviously discussing table arrangements with her mother. She had Cynthia on one screen, graphics of the ball room on another. "Why do I have to go over this? Isn't it enough I show up? Mom, I love your work, I'm proud of it, but I'm terrible at this."

"You're going over this with me because your spontaneous wedding had about twenty more bookings come in of people who desperately want to see you, talk to you. And with the man responsible for it behind you, and him giving a speech, we will find a way to adjust. Hi, Tyler."

"Hello, Cynthia." He ran his arms around Scarlette, rested his chin on her shoulder and studied the setup himself.

"You have a good setup there, though you might want to separate the Dicksons and the Hartfords. They recently had a... let's call it a 'disagreement', when the Hartfords' cat scratched and bit the Dicksons' son bloody upon being averse to be dragged along by its tail."

"Aren't you a fount of information? Thanks, Ty, I'll keep it in mind. Take notes, Scarlette, I'm pretty sure you'll be dragged into more charity work in the future."

"Only as much as she wants," Ty said and kissed his wife's cheek.

"You got damn lucky, girl. All right, I'll go over what we discussed, and we'll talk later. See you both," Cynthia ended the call with a smile.

Scarlette turned a little so she could face Tyler. "How are the horses?"

"Doing all right. When we have a little more time, I'll take you along and we'll go for a ride."

"Okay. It's been a while, but I would like that."

"Huh, and when has a city girl like you been out on horseback?"

"When I was out on field trips sometimes. More practical when there are no roads and the vegetation doesn't allow for off-road cars, but you still want to arrive before sunset."

"I think you and I should share campfire stories some time."

"Could be fun. How's Josh? You'd have been out with him to talk a little."

"You know me quite well already." His lips lovingly kissed her temple. "Yes, I wanted some time to talk with him. He's okay. Pissed about the cat, but thankful we don't exclude him but treat him like an adult on this. I'll give him a complete update tomorrow, I think. We talked about you a little, because I need to know he's okay with us. He is, he likes you a lot. I wanted to bring him along to the gala, but he told me he has a date. Which led to some semi-awkward sex talk."

"Semi-awkward for him or you?"

"Both. I think I just hid it better. It's not the topic itself, it's suddenly stepping in as the responsible adult on things like this. And let me say, thank god we both don't want kids. I couldn't do the whole deal with a kid of ours."

Scarlette chuckled, ran her fingers through his hair. "Oh, yeah, that would be weird. I'd probably dig out some nature documentary or something. Nope, we're good the way we are, just us."

"Mhm. We are." Her scent made him lose track of any rational thought, the quiet joy in her eyes made his heart leap in response.

"We are very good. I feel like I have hardly kissed you all day."

She hadn't realized it, but he had maneuvered her to the couch at the other end of the room, now gently pushed her down on it.

"Shame on you." She squeaked, when he rolled her under him.

"Let me make up for it."

His mouth found hers, and when hers answered, when she opened her lips with a quiet sigh, he tasted her. So sweet yet, her lips so soft.

With her lover's body on top of her, Scarlette sunk deeper into sensation, banded her arms around him. And innocence slowly slipped into demand. Exploring hands slid under clothes, and Ty could feel her taste become darker. His tongue played with hers, her teeth nipped with a teasing giggle.

Her fingers started on the buttons of his shirt; his hand slid into her pants.

And someone stopped in the doorway with a smothered chuckle. "Whoops, sorry guys."

Tyler managed a frustrated grunt, dropped his forehead against Scarlette's.

"Luke, what the hell?"

"His timing could've been worse." Resigned, Scarlette gave her husband a quick kiss, started to get her clothes in order.

"Mine was," July said from beside Luke with a grin, but didn't see the need to run out of the room this time.

Luke shot her a sideway glance. "Interesting, tell me later. Sorry again, but you got an email, supposedly with the proof you demanded."

Chapter Seventeen

It shouldn't be done, but nobody listened anymore. How had things gone so terribly wrong? How had they drifted from protecting their own family to pure greed?

Most of the older family had died or had left, safe in the knowledge they had never been involved deeply enough to be linked to anything.

Now there were two voices of reason left against a younger generation without restraint or focus. And a voice hadn't worked. It had started with the outrageously high demands. Never before had they asked for so much, or needed to ask for so much.

But even that could be overlooked, had they not brought violence to the table. First the car. And that had only come out during a casual chat.

Then the cat. They even bragged about it.

The blackmail was nothing to be proud of. It had always been a means to an end. And who could say if the house wouldn't have stayed in the hands of the O'Briens and

Barrets anyways, so they would have paid for it over the years themselves, too.

But now everything had become a twisted game. Admittedly, an anonymous payment service with an encrypted email address linked to it were easier to handle than the old-time drop-offs. But they had worked well.

Superior technical skills had worked so far, and had opened doors to jobs to stay close to the writer's family, had helped to have someone working in the same building as the woman. But they hadn't gotten close to the blonde friend, had they? But their arrogance prevented them from seeing the flaws. Arrogance was always dangerous. But watching them, it was clear they saw themselves as some kind of spies, some sort of evil geniuses. There was no reason penetrating the wall of their hubris.

Now they had decided to react to the email, to send over pictures, no matter what they had been told.

Well, they would have to find a way to deal with the consequences.

Chapter Eighteen

L uke allowed them to open the mail, but was adamant when it came to open the attached pictures.

"No, tomorrow, when I have my tech here. You never know what little extras they might have added. Hover over the preview, if you must."

"Yeah, yeah." Ty's mood wasn't the brightest, and when he read the taunting mail that came along with the pictures, it didn't get better.

It seems like congratulations are in order. What a pretty couple the two of you make, and to think we never even knew about you before. You have been very discreet.

Now, a wedding is such a happy event that we decided to give you an extended deadline. You have five more days to pay. That is, to pay our initial request plus another $100,000.

A little tit for tat you could say, and why should only the bride and groom get presents, right?

You know what they say: happiness doubles when it's shared.

So share your damn happiness and pay!

To show you our sincerity in these matters, we decided to grant your request for proof. We attached the pictures in our possession clearly documenting the hideous acts of the murderous men your families come from, along with the autopsy reports before palms were greased and facts were altered.

The small previews appeared to show ancient photos: in each one you could see a man and a very dead-looking woman. In one, dark splotches were covering the persons, the floor, and furniture around. But for any more details, the pictures were too small like this, and it was the same with the autopsy reports.

Scarlette stood behind Tyler, kneaded his shoulders. "Okay, I admit, right now this looks bad. But even if it was all true, who keeps this up for a century? There has to be more."

Luke had leaned over Tyler's shoulder, and was now scowling at Scarlette. "I've seen crazier things done for a lot less money. They're asking what of you now, 360K in total?"

"Yes. But here's the thing," Ty said and shifted so they could all face each other, "I told you I haven't found anything in our books indicating payments, but I focused on payments of this size. I'm no accountant, but I'm not bad with numbers. When I scanned the books, the biggest withdrawals I couldn't attribute to anything were always between ten thousand and twenty-five thousand max. Which would be the only reason I could think of, why my family never did anything other than pay." He shook his head in a disheartened gesture.

Luke nodded. "Yes, when I checked, I didn't see such a sum either and didn't go into more detail at the smaller sums, especially because there was no pattern. So."

"So. It seems paying the smaller amounts was easier, a lot quieter, and protected everything they had built. We have always been lucky. Even when Charles didn't move into the talkies as actor, or when he moved away with Elizabeth, he kept his fingers in the business, worked in the background as a producer for example. He kept quiet about his role in the charity work, but our family documents show it of course. And even when we really took on the horse breeding and wine business, the family still honored the charity work and kept it alive, began to talk more openly about the reason for it or, more, why we support that area. There have never been such big sums of money spent without a trace before."

Luke made notes, and Julia did the same on the board. "Taking a guess, I would say something has changed the status quo for them, has them demanding more than in the past. That's good," Luke stated.

"Because it makes them desperate, and desperate people tend to make mistakes," July concluded while still putting finishing touches on her notes.

Luke grinned in appreciation. "The woman is smart and thinks like a cop."

"Easy enough, my mom works for the FBI. I kind of grew up with stuff like this."

"And you become more fascinating every minute." The second he said it, he winced. "I didn't mean..."

Julia's lips quivered with the effort it took not to break

into a gleaming smile. After dinner, she had done her best to subtly check him out, had casually tried to stay close. And now the flutter she had felt earlier crept back. "I think you're the first guy fascinated by that."

"Then you know the wrong guys."

"Perhaps I do."

Luke had taken a few steps closer to Julia's board by now, and Scarlette was pretty sure she and Ty didn't exist in their reality anymore. She took her husband's hand, slipped quietly out of the room with him.

A few steps down the hall, she whispered to him. "We can't do anything anymore today anyway without properly looking at the pictures. And without knowing what exactly to search for, neither does it help us right now to know they have become desperate, or exceedingly greedy for that matter."

"Right. And you wanted to give Julia and Luke some time alone."

"Yes. The whole evening I had the need to pick them up like dolls and squish them together, chanting 'Now, kiss.' When he took the napkin from her and touched her finger, she jerked back so hard that I was afraid she'd fall out of her chair."

"You think they'll do it like we did and end up in bed tonight?"

"No, July isn't the type. But if they aren't both completely uptight, they could manage first base." She saw Tyler frown. "They are, aren't they? July... she can be open and outgoing, but only when she knows people, and not with a guy she's attracted to. She needs him to take a first step."

"Yeah, well, and Luke, he's a tech geek at heart. With you he's okay and can talk easily, because you're mine, meaning he's safe, nobody expects him to hit on you. But what he did most of the evening, stealing a glance, that's all he normally does for days. I'm actually surprised at how forward he has been already."

Scarlette could only roll her eyes. "You know what, they're grown-ups, they should be able to figure this out by themselves. I, for one, would love to take a late swim, but I didn't pack that part of my wardrobe yet, so I'll take a bath instead."

"Baby, you know one of the best things about having a private pool house?"

"What would that be?"

"You can always skinny-dip. We can lock the door, the windows are treated, nobody can see inside, you saw it yourself. Plus, I haven't shown you that, yet, but for cold winter days, or those days you wanna stroll over there in a robe or towel and nothing else, we had them built a tunnel connecting the basement and the pool house."

"You have a wise family. Since I don't know that route yet, I suppose you'll show it to me, huh?"

"Of course, darling."

"And since you can't be sure, yet, that I can really swim all that well, you wouldn't just let me alone, would you?"

They had given up on going upstairs first and were by now strolling through a short, well-lit tunnel after Tyler had guided Scarlette through a door in the kitchen leading further down and through the basement with its wine cellar on one side and additional food storage on the other.

"No. What kind of husband would I be if I didn't make

sure you're all right in the water? I think I should join you, for safety."

"I think that's a very good idea."

Meanwhile, Luke and July were flustered to find themselves alone in the office.

"When did they leave?"

"I have no idea."

"Well, why did they leave?" Julia, suddenly jittery, linked and unlinked her fingers, picked up a pen and put it back down.

Luke observed her, and his usual shyness evaporated. He grinned at her.

"On that I might have an idea."

"Which is?"

"Oh, I'd say they wanted to give us some time alone here, because I think it's been pretty obvious to them that I have wanted to kiss you almost since the minute I met you."

Her eyes rounded and she giggled nervously. Had she really just giggled? Damn it, what was wrong with her? "Oh, ah... I..." She huffed out a breath and only stared at Luke with those huge, gorgeous eyes.

He took another step closer to her, his eyes wandering down to her lips. He really wanted to kiss those lips.

"Are you okay with that, Julia?"

The air clogged in her lungs, and when she managed to release it, her breath came out with a shudder. "Huh?"

"Let's try this." At first, he only leaned forward, but his hands didn't touch her. Only his lips. They merely brushed hers, more a whisper than a kiss.

"Okay?"

She trembled; her heart thudded wildly. And she slowly nodded.

"More?"

Another nod.

His hands took hold of her hips now, slowly drew her against him, and when his lips came down on hers this time, he pressed them gently to her mouth.

He wasn't prepared for the heat pumping out from her, nor was she prepared to find her arms wrapped around him without her brain being able to intercept the move.

They clung to each other, her mouth opening for him, because, god, she wanted to taste more of him. Rich, dark, male; demanding, but not rough, and seriously skilled, she admitted.

They both panted when they finally let the other go.

"I usually don't do that just like that." She hated the need to say it but didn't want him to see her as yet another notch in his belt.

"Believe me, neither do I. What about this, why don't we go for a walk? Because I really want to kiss you again, but I also want to get to know you. And I figure we can't really do much more on the case tonight."

"Yes, sure, okay."

They went outside and strolled through the garden, followed a path along a group of trees, then veered from it towards the stables to peek inside. Talking all the time, Luke's hand at some point brushed against Julia's, and she took his without thinking about it.

They ambled back towards the main house when a cry from the pool house had Luke brace to run over. "No, wait"

Her grip tightened on his hand. "That's Scarlette, and I'd say that was likely for the same reason I was talking about earlier when I said my timing had been worse."

"Wha... Seriously?"

"Yeah. I stumbled in on them enjoying each other on a chair when I arrived from Australia and wanted to check on her in LA, well outside LA. Heard her scream and panicked, ran into the house. She didn't need help then, I doubt she needs any now."

And listening more carefully now, Luke shook his head. "No, I guess you're right, she sounds all right to me."

"Yeah, I'd say so." Julia suddenly realized her fingers were still tightly linked with Luke's and she made an attempt to pull her hand back, but he kept holding on.

"No, don't."

"Luke... Look, I live in Australia, and I'm not even sure for how long."

"So what? I have a lot of overtime, I'll come by next month. Until then, there's emails, texts, the good old phone, video. Julia, I meant what I said, I want to get to know you."

"You what? You'd come to Australia?"

"Yes, of course. If we find out that we might work together, and we both decide to give it a try, why not? I could get three weeks off, with some convincing I might be able to stretch it to a month. That would give us time after calls and chats to see how it goes in person. And at some point, you'll come back here, won't you?"

"Sure, yes. That's the plan."

"No problem from my side, then."

They were back in the foyer by now, and Luke snuck an

arm around her. "But maybe you need a reminder why I think this is a very good idea."

He tightened his grip on her, pulled her against him and had his mouth back on hers. She couldn't think, her body reacted in a heartbeat, giving her no time to think. Her lips opened, her tongue found his. Her hands dragged him closer, her fingers digging into the firm muscles of his back. Then she found herself with her back pressed against the wall and couldn't stop the moan.

His hands ran up and down her ribs, barely skimming the sides of her breasts, his lips traveled to her throat and his teeth playfully nipped at her neck and he heard her gasp.

He had to stop, he knew, or he would take her here and now at the bottom of the stairs of his friend's house. She did something to him that had him fighting for control in ways he never had to before. With great effort, he stepped back from her, heavily breathing.

She was shivering, her lips were swollen from their rough kiss. But she could see the change in his eyes, when he fought his composure back into place. "Don't you dare apologize, Luke."

He shut his mouth again, shot her a cocky smile. "Okay. Wanna do it again?"

She managed a laugh, while she still had one steadying hand against the wall. "Yes. But not now." She stopped him with a chuckle when he reached for her again. "Okay, I agree, very good idea. Let's see what we make of this. But I'm not Scarlette. She has a one-night stand and ends up married to the guy a week later. And I guarantee you, for them it will work out perfectly for the next five to six decades, I can see that with them. But that's not me, sorry."

"July, let me tell you the same you just said: don't you dare apologize. I don't want you to be like Scarlette. I'd be lying if I said I'm not excited about the idea of sleeping with you at some point, but I'm okay with taking it slow. I have never gone so far with a woman so quick, either. It takes me days or weeks to even ask someone for a date, and if I manage a friendly good-night kiss after that, I'm happy. Half the time I get lost in shop talk or tech talk, and the woman tunes out. You didn't, and I feel good around you, but I don't have to rush this to the bedroom."

"Okay. Then we probably should call this a night."

"All right."

They walked upstairs together, and on the second-floor landing, Julia stopped. "I'm here."

"Really?"

"Yes, I was working a bit on the side at first — okay, still am even though I'm on vacation now — so Lorraine gave me the suite with the guest office."

"Ah, that makes sense. Well, it wasn't planned that I'd stay here, guess I'll see what's ready upstairs."

"Okay."

"Ty and Scarlette have taken the master suite, I would assume?"

"Yeah. They decided to both move here. Keep his place in New York, but mainly live here for now."

"Okay. Goodnight, July."

She leaned in for a quieter kiss this time. "Goodnight, Luke."

They were sharing one more small kiss, when they heard a squeal and a deep answering laugh from downstairs, followed by quick running footsteps.

"Guess they finished their swim."

"Yep. See you tomorrow." Going with the impulse, Julia gave him another quick kiss, then hurried to her bedroom door.

Luke turned towards the stairs again and could barely stop in time, before Scarlette crashed into him on her wild sprint up the stairs. She was draped in a short robe, and he was pretty sure that was all she was currently wearing, her hair was still dripping wet, and she flung herself behind him with a loud laugh.

"Oh, good, Luke. Arrest him for me, will you?"

"On what grounds?" With Tyler coming up right behind Scarlette, Luke found himself caught between them, Ty trying to grab his wife, and Scarlette shimmying from side to side, using Luke as a shield to avoid it.

"Attempted murder-suicide? He nearly drowned us."

"Now, Sparks, didn't I tell you to hold on to the edge?" Ty commented in a sarcastic voice.

"You knew I couldn't. Don't tell me you didn't, Link."

"Mhm, perhaps. But it was still fun dragging you under with me. To..."

And now Luke held up his hands. "Nope, that's too much information. I'm sure when you talk about it like the adults you're supposed to be, you'll resolve the issue. I'm out of this."

He stepped aside, and Tyler grabbed Scarlette, picked her up, shut up her mocked protest with a kiss. "Okay, okay." She linked her hands behind Ty's neck, glanced at Luke. "Did you talk to Lorraine regarding a room?"

"No, I didn't. We were working, then July and I were taking a walk."

"Uh-huh, a 'walk,' that's what they call it now," Scarlette said to Ty, and poked her finger into Luke's arm, while the men were climbing to the next level and she let herself be carried.

"We were talking, and sure as hell didn't go for a swim like you two."

"You know I'll find out during girl talk."

"I'm sure you will, which means you don't need to hear it tonight from me," Luke told her with a teasing wink.

Scarlette narrowed her eyes. "And here I was, thinking I liked you."

"Oh, you do. I can tell you all kinds of stories about the guy you've married."

"Good point."

The guy she had married shook his head when they reached the next landing, shifted Scarlette a little to have a hand free to point at a door. "You can take my old room, that one is usually always ready."

"Cool, thanks. Night you two."

"Night."

"Night, Luke."

Chapter Nineteen

Julia opened the door of her room the next morning only to find Luke in front of her with his hand raised to knock.

"Well, that's timing." He kissed her sweetly, and she beamed a smile at him about as bright as the sun shining into the window behind her. "Good morning, July."

"Good morning, Luke."

Together they made their way into the kitchen, found the family already eating. Lorraine had made fresh croissants and Scarlette was discussing the recipe with her while Tyler was updating Josh on everything in detail.

"Morning, everybody."

Josh turned to the door, grinned. "Luke, hi!"

"Hey, Josh. Shouldn't you be at school?"

"Nope, class trip was scheduled to have us back right before break. We have to hand in tons of papers after, though."

"Guess that's still a good compromise."

"Guess so. Ty said you're gonna get some tech delivered today. Can I have a look?"

Luke shot Tyler a glance, and his friend shrugged. "We don't keep this from him. From my side it would be okay."

"Okay, then sure you can."

Scarlette probed Julia with curious eyes, but her friend shook her head until her curls covered her face. "Later."

"Definitely."

One of Luke's colleagues arrived with the tech delivery when they just had finished breakfast. Setting everything up took nearly an hour, but finally Luke decreed everything safe and ready to detect any underlying malware.

Tyler studied his brother. "No, I'm staying," Josh told him.

"Okay."

He opened the first photo, and they all were appalled by the gruesome scene.

His head was bent down so you couldn't see a face, but even without it, the man holding the bloody knife exuded pure rage, wild madness. What you could see of him, with the bed covering his lower body from this angle, was all covered with dark blood splatters. On the bed right before him lay the mangled body of a woman, blood covering her and the sheets, and even in the old photo you could still make out separate slashes and stab wounds all over her. Half her face was only a dark mass, the other half she had tried to protect with one arm, which now lay limp over it.

"Oh my god, that's horrible," July whispered.

Scarlette nodded. "Yes. He must have completely lost control after he had started on her."

Luke studied the black-and-white photo, shook his head.

It never got easier, whether you dealt with it live and in color or in an old picture. "I will have this analyzed, but since it's only a scan, the lab won't be able to tell me as much as I wish. Let's read the autopsy report. Who was this?"

"Judging by the bedroom, I think Mary-Beth," Ty said and opened the scan of the old report.

It was a cruel, written acknowledgment of the picture.

He began to read parts of it. "'Multiple stab wounds: face, neck, forearms, chest, abdomen. Deep lacerations, also on face, neck, forearms, outer thighs...'" Tyler had to take a breath before continuing. "'Inner thighs, outer and inner labia; internal cuts indicate penetration of vaginal canal with a blade, most likely perimortem. Cause of death with high probability: stab wound in the chest, penetrating left ventricle.' Good god. Please don't let this be true."

Scarlette could feel her husband shatter, could see her brother-in-law tremor with rage and despair.

"Come here, both of you."

She opened her arms, hugged Josh and brushed over his hair when his head fell on her shoulder. She did the same when Tyler, from his sitting position, had his arms around her waist and his head pressed against her ribs.

When they had recovered a little, Scarlette gave Josh a quick kiss on the cheek, then took Tyler's face in her hands, looked him straight in the eyes. "If there's anything, I mean *anything* to find in these that proves them to be faked, we will find it, I swear."

"Thank you, baby."

"Of course."

They moved on to the next picture and found a hardly less horrible scene. They couldn't see the face of this man either, but they could see his hands wrapped around the throat of a woman who might have tried to get around him to the exit after a severe beating. What was visible of her face was bruised and swollen, her bare arms showed more bruises. He pressed her against the bed frame, and it seemed like his hands and the bed were the only things keeping her standing upright. Her hands hung limply beside her body, her mouth gaped open from her last failed attempts to draw in even a tiny bit of air; her head would have fallen forward without the hands — bloody and bruised, too, from pounding on her first — still strangling her.

Scarlette shook her head, was glad for Tyler's hand reaching for hers, squeezing it, and running his thumb over the back of her hand. "I know I don't have a connection to my ancestors like you do, but I can't believe either Charles or Eton would have done this, however big a scandal they would have faced, however betrayed they would have felt. Open the other report, Ty."

"All right. 'Body shows signs of physical assault, blunt force trauma; injuries consistent with severe beating. Hematomas on arms with high probability stemming from fingers placed there. Further similar hematomas on inner thighs indicate legs were spread, vaginal injuries indicate forceful sexual intercourse.' Why don't they call it rape, as that's what it was, if this is true? 'Final cause of death most likely suffocation during manual strangulation.' Sorry, baby."

"No, not your fault. And I say again, I have a hard time taking this at face value."

"With all I know about them, so do I."

Luke scanned the faces in the office with him. Nobody was excited, but they were steady, and he knew he would have a hard time keeping them out of everything. But some part of this would have to be done by a cop to hold up as evidence later, even though he knew he was already walking on a tightrope by keeping things unofficial for now.

"Okay, I will start working on the sender, on anything I can find out on the tech side. I will have the photos and documents analyzed in as much detail as possible, without mentioning names. I have people owing me favors, they won't ask too many questions.

"You can keep following-up the history of the house, the staff. July, if you find anything I can use, or you run into a block while running names, let me know. The rest of you, you can try to unearth the original autopsy reports. Scarlette, I know that might be difficult on your end, but maybe something leaked back then, too, and ended up online today. Ty, your family will likely still have it somewhere in an old box."

"Most likely. Yes, we will check."

It took them most of the day, and more than once they took a break to escape the heat of the attic.

Scarlette and Tyler used the short interruptions to answer some calls still coming in to congratulate them on the wedding and discussed with Lorraine a Sunday brunch in a few weeks for neighbors who had sent over small gifts.

"Sure thing, we can do that. But you will still have a big party. Cynthia, Bea, and I are firm on that."

"We will, promise. With more planning, and after the summer heat."

"Fair enough. Now, here's your coffee, and up you go. Y'all find something useful to finish this."

"Yes, ma'am." Ty gave her a kiss on the cheek, walked back upstairs with Scarlette and a tray with fresh coffee and some chilled fruit salad.

In the middle of the afternoon, July jumped up from the old armchair she had claimed while working with the others up in the attic and danced in place. "Finally! Okay, so, I found the old housekeeper. They hired her when they bought the house, and she had already been working there for a long time before for the former owners."

"Okay, and you think she started this when the men killed their wives?" Scarlette asked.

"No. Here's where things get interesting. She died at the end of 1927, of pneumonia. They had to hire new staff, and they chose a family of four. It's a big house, they had huge parties. Apparently, it seemed like a good idea. With a family, they wouldn't need to find a working rhythm but could focus more on getting to know the house. That family was the O'Learys. They stayed on the payroll until Charles and Eton sold the house after their wives' deaths. After that, I can't find anything in here, because this is only the family documentation. Took forever to find the names and contracts, not just the expenses for the salaries in the household ledger. I've been at this for days."

"That's great work, July," Tyler said.

"I'll check what I can find online. I'll be downstairs."

Scarlette raised her eyebrows, smirked. "Uh-huh. And I'm sure research is the only reason you're leaving us alone up here."

"Shut up." July dashed out of the attic with a laugh after

jokingly punching her friend on the arm.

Scarlette and Tyler left Julia's piles of research on the housekeepers untouched and kept searching through old documents and pictures. Something constantly itched in the back of Scarlette's mind, but as hard as she tried, she couldn't put a finger on it. Something about one of the pictures of the murders, but what?

Frustrated, she gulped more coffee and was reaching for the next documents when an old picture attached to an insurance title from a joint policy shared by the O'Briens and Barrets for the whole house and interior fell down and landed directly beside Josh. When he looked at the picture — a snapshot of an old bed — he shot up.

"Shit, shit. I've got to... Wait, I know it's here somewhere, I used it for an art paper in school once."

"Josh?"

"Wait."

He frantically flicked through a box with old magazines next to them, finally pulled one out of the stash, thumbed quickly but carefully through it.

"I knew it!" With the magazine in hand, he ran downstairs.

"What's gotten into him?"

"No idea, but I want to know."

"Same."

When Josh stumbled into the office, he completely ignored Julia and Luke, who practically jumped apart as the boy had run in while they were caught up in a deep kiss.

He only spoke when he had found what he had been

searching for, then turned around the laptop since it wasn't synced to one of the wall screens and held up the magazine next to it.

Scarlette and Ty had followed Josh into the office by now, and they all saw the pictures of the same room side by side, with some small changes in the murder scene. Another carpet, other drapes, different sheets, but otherwise the identical.

"What do you see?"

"Eton's and Cecille's bedroom. So?"

"Look closer. Yes, there are changes, the magazine article is from 1926, they probably changed things all the time. But focus on the men in the photos."

The three adults stared hard at the pictures, tried to see what, for Josh, appeared to be clear as day.

"I don't get it, what do you mean? Yeah, in one picture you can't see a face, but everything else fits, same body type, same type of clothes."

"Right, Julia, but there is one very important difference. The article shows Eton giving a tour of the house, it was a piece they did together with the O'Briens, showing off the house after some redecorating. MTV weren't the first ones doing it. This was one of the rare occasions they allowed reporters on the grounds. And see, he's standing close to the bed, this pretty cool Art Deco bed with its high frame at the foot end.

"Now check the murder photo. He's equally close, roughly at the same spot, actually, and he seems a good bit taller."

"That might be because of the angle, the posture," his brother said.

"Angle will be easy to eliminate by some calculations. But not the posture, Ty. I would have accepted smaller, leaning a little down to strangle her. But taller? You think he suddenly started wearing lifts?"

"And over the years people became taller."

Josh pointed a finger at Luke. "You got it. I had a hard time believing we were the first ones asking for proof. What if we aren't? What if these pictures were taken decades ago, when it was a lot harder to check, to compare, to enter everything into a program and have exact numbers?"

Scarlette's eyes on Josh were full of pride. "I've said it to your brother before, I say it to you: you're a genius. And it made me realize what was nagging at me. Ty, the picture of Mary-Beth's alleged murder, it was taken in their bedroom, right?"

"Yes."

"Okay, but we don't seriously think he'd be okay with being photographed right after butchering his wife, so somebody would have needed to take the picture from one of the hidden passages. Look at this."

She brought the photo on screen again. "Ty, we were there. Behind that wall, there cannot be a secret passage, that's an outside wall, closer to the door was another window."

"Damn, yes, you're right!" He dragged her close for an enthusiastic kiss.

"Okay, cool. That's two for two not making sense. Let me see... Luke, do you have graphic software on here? I can measure some points, try to find out how much taller that guy in the photo actually is." Josh turned the laptop back to him, hunkered down with Luke over it.

And while they kept mumbling, Julia opened her tablet, checked on something.

"It says here the average male in 1920 was around 5'7". Now, what does your geek wizardry tell us about the strangler-guy?"

Luke fired a fierce grin at her. "Our boy-genius here just determined strangler-guy was a rough 5'10", which makes him significantly larger than Eton."

For a moment, relief washed over the whole group, but then Julia sobered. "Okay, great, so these are not pictures of your great-great-grandparents. Then who is this? And did they still kill somebody? You can't really make out faces, this could be anybody: killer and victim."

"You're right, July. And I will check on missing persons, once we can better define when these might have been taken. But I think, or more *hope*, these are only staged."

Scarlette checked the photo again and, cocking her head, tapped her finger against her cheek. "You could be right. Ty, call my grandma, please." She gestured to the screens hooked to the camera. "I think I have seen these curtains."

She took the laptop, adjusted the section visible on screen, then smiled at Beatrice when she answered the call. "Hi, Granny."

"Hello, Scarlette. Hello everybody, it seems."

"Kind of. I have a quick question. These curtains, you have them in your salon, right?"

"Yes. Kept them like a jewel. It was a special edition from the seventies, made up like old-time ones with some Art Deco chic thrown in. They work well in the old bar and seating area."

"They do. This is great, exactly what I needed to hear. Thanks!"

"Wait, girl. That's it?"

"For now, yeah."

"No explanation?"

"More details when we come to the city for the gala. For now, know you helped to strengthen our doubts about some supposed evidence."

"Good enough. I'll see you all soon."

When the call had ended, Josh quickly searched for something online, smirked – *so much like his brother. That boy will break more than one heart*, Scarlette thought.

"And the seventies put our strangler here at precisely the right average height."

"Perfect. In the seventies, nobody had lived in that house for almost half a decade. I'll bet you they cleaned up the rooms, staged them for these photos, because somebody from one or both of our families asked for proof at some point. Back then they didn't take enough care to set everything up with truly original props because you couldn't verify stuff like that so easily."

"Well, that sounds like a fine moment to break this up." Lorraine stood in the doorway, hands on her hips. "You've all done good work today. Come downstairs, I've put some meat on the grill."

With everybody feeling like they had made actual progress that day, they took their time with dinner, had some wine or beer, and Josh sneered at his brother.

"Wasn't it you who told me you stole beer from dad when you were a teenager?"

"And I didn't say it was right. You got a shot of whisky at the wedding, didn't you? And we have a cop with us at the table."

"As if Luke would arrest us."

"Be careful, Josh. Even if I'm impressed with your work today, that doesn't mean I'm deaf and blind. It's too long ago to throw him in jail, though, I'm afraid," Luke told the teenager with a shrug and pointed at Tyler.

"Figured. Okay, okay."

"What about you play taste tester instead? I got a text earlier to pick up the new bottle from the test distillery." Lorraine got it from the kitchen, filled a wine glass for Josh.

"It's the new alcohol-free version."

"Thanks, Lorraine."

"Sure. You're better than your brother here; you don't drink to get drunk like he did at your age."

"Thanks, Lorraine." And Ty's tone was very different from Josh's.

"Oh, shut up, boy. You had a wild phase. Your brother is very responsible. This way he can participate in that part of business, too."

"Yes, you're right."

Long days, a still-confused biorhythm, and constant excitement from being near Luke together with the regular wine made for a tipsy Julia at the end of the evening. So, while the others helped Lorraine to get things outside in order again, Luke offered to bring July upstairs.

"Make sure she remembers it in the morning, if you take advantage of her," Scarlette told him with a laugh.

"I won't, don't worry."

"Oh, I'm not worried."

When they were gone, Ty looked up from wiping the table. "You know she seemed more like she would take advantage of him."

"I know." Scarlette chuckled. "Let's see how strong his willpower is."

It was strong enough for Luke to carefully guide her to her bedroom, even answering the kiss when, giddily giggling, she pressed her lips to his, but then he stepped back.

"Goodnight, July."

"Don't you want to come in here with me?"

"Oh, very much, trust me. But not tonight, not when you're half-drunk and might regret it in the morning. Have a glass of water, get ready for bed, do your best to get some sleep."

"Oh, well, okay. Goodnight, then."

He kissed her forehead, then left her. God, he wanted her. But not if he wasn't a hundred percent sure she wanted the same. He had told her he didn't need to rush things, and he hoped he hadn't lied. But leaving her, not getting his hands on her, was damn hard — literally, he realized — and he hoped a cold shower would clear his mind.

Meanwhile, July managed the glass of water, brushed her teeth, and fell flat on her face on the bed.

. . .

Later that night, Scarlette slid down from Tyler, a smug smile in place when she saw she had given as well as she had taken from him. He drew her against him, kissed her lavishly when they both heard the stairs creak.

Ty whispered to his wife. "That's somebody coming upstairs."

"That's July coming upstairs."

"How do you know?"

"Hear that quiet tapping on the handrail? It's a little tick of hers."

"So Luke might get lucky after all."

"He might."

Julia had woken up a couple of hours after she had dropped into sleep, and most of the dizziness from the wine was gone. The constant inner restlessness wasn't. She deeply hoped she wasn't too audacious, that he wouldn't think less of her. But he had said he wanted her, hadn't he?

When she stood in front of the door of his room, she lifted her hand but then opened it without the knock and slipped inside. When she closed the door behind her and heard the latch snap into place, she was suddenly a little nauseous. What on earth was she doing here? How could she have thought it was a good idea to throw on her nightgown and sneak into the bedroom of a man she had known for two days?

She was about to turn when he sat up in bed, his hand reaching for his weapon by pure instinct.

When in the dim moonlight he saw the outlines of a

woman at the door, saw a mass of curls, and a long, lean body, he lowered his weapon. "July?"

She had expected the cop part, she could deal with that. What unnerved her was the low, charming drawl when he used her name, the hint of surprise in his voice.

"Yeah. Ah… god, I think I should go."

She didn't even get a chance to turn around completely, to reach for the doorknob, before he was out of bed and over at the door. His hands took her shoulders, very gently. Turned her to him again, very slowly. There was just enough light for her to see his eyes light up with delight, with desire.

"Why?"

She tried to find a reason, but only shuddered, when his fingertips danced up her shoulder, wandered along her throat. "I don't know."

"Good."

His mouth was warm, his hands careful when they roamed down her arms, up her sides. He was about to shift them away again, when hers took hold and placed his palms over her breasts. "Here, now," she whispered with a hoarse voice, then groaned when he easily picked her up. She would have been surprised by the casual strength with which he lifted her off her feet, but her brain had already given over control to her body. She wrapped her legs around him, barely realizing he was only wearing his boxers. Then she only moaned when he pushed her nightgown away, shifted his shorts, and was inside her.

He took her unhurriedly until she climaxed and dropped her head on his shoulder. Then he carried her to the bed and kept up the easy strokes. Kept them up until they were both sated and numb with pleasure.

Chapter Twenty

They had spent half the night enjoying each other and then had both slipped into an exhausted, relaxed sleep.

Now Luke woke up, the sun shining into the window, his legs caught between July's. Smiling, he played his fingers through her golden curls, thinking how pleasant it would be to wake her to make love again before getting out of bed. And he gasped.

The sharp noise, the sudden tightening of his body beside her, woke Julia with a jolt. "What? What is it? Is everything okay?"

"Huh? I... July, I'm sorry."

She immediately dragged the sheets around her, angry eyes blazing at him. "Fuck you, asshole."

Scurrying out of the bed, she wrapped the blanket tighter around her and wanted to get to the door.

"Wait! What the hell? I apologize and you cuss at me? What's gotten into you?"

"You really have to ask? All the stupid talk about how you

want to get to know me, how you don't want to rush things? Worked like a charm, A-plus for your acting skills. I tumble into bed with you, and now you try to make it sound nice and cozy and oh-so friendly that this was it? A polite apology, 'sorry,' but that's all? How could I be so stupid?"

Sudden, unexpected rage flooded through him. "Damn it, how dare you? How can you insult me, insult us, like that? How could you even think I would apologize for making love to you?"

"Oh, what then? Enlighten me."

"I was apologizing for the fact that the southern part of my anatomy took over and my brain didn't catch up, never made me get a condom."

They were both yelling, now stared at each other, breath heaving, and trying to process what the other had said.

It felt like a backhand slap in the face, and July's eyes filled with tears. "Oh god, sorry, Luke. I didn't mean..." Her lips quivered, and tears started falling.

"July, don't cry."

She sunk to the floor, burying her face in her hands. "Sorry. It's just... I came here because I wanted you, but once I was in here, I panicked. Then we made love, and it was good, so good. And I was afraid that this morning you came to your senses and thought I had been too forward, and that you thought I would sleep with everybody, or that you wanted out of this, period."

He knelt in front of her, cupped her wet face in his hands. "You have met quite the assholes before, haven't you?"

She sighed desperately. "Some, yes."

"July, I don't think less of you for coming here, and I know you don't sleep with everybody. I was more afraid that you would be scared when you remembered the same thing I did."

"Okay, yes, I see. Uh, I'm taking the pill, on that end we're safe."

"I think on the other end as well. It's been some time for me."

"For me, too."

"New try then?"

"What do you mean?"

He kissed tears from her cheeks. "July, last night was wonderful. I'm sorry I wasn't as responsible as I should have been."

She huffed out a relieved breath, managed to smile at him. "Luke, last night was great. I think we're good, but maybe we both try to be a bit more responsible from now on until we're sure where this is going."

"Deal."

They were late for breakfast but didn't care, and when Scarlette kept her friend in the kitchen and sent the men upstairs, July didn't mind and updated the women on what had happened.

"I'd say enjoy yourself, honey," Lorraine told July with an arm around her shoulder. "Take the good things, see if you both can make them better together. And if it doesn't work, you at least had some fun. I get the feeling you were used too often. He won't do that with you, trust me. I've known him a long time."

"Thank you, Lorraine."

When they rejoined the guys, they found Josh reading a report on the laptop while Luke was on his phone. Tyler was nowhere to be seen, and Scarlette's inquiring look was met by Josh gesturing in the direction of the other office.

While July stayed with the others, Scarlette took a step back out and made her way down the hall. She waited in the doorway, but Tyler smiled at her, held out his hand for her.

He was on the phone and had a file on his own laptop open, but still pulled her down into his lap.

"Yes, Vi, I'll still hit that deadline, don't worry."

Scarlette saw several dates on screen, all with corresponding notes regarding steps for his current book.

"No, it's all coming along, I managed a few quick questions over the phone with him this morning, I can finish that chapter in no time."

The voice over the phone became a little quieter. Before, Scarlette hadn't been able to make out words, but she had clearly heard the agitation.

"Have you spoken to Cynthia?" Tyler asked. "She told me she'd find a spot for you at the gala."

The distraction worked, and Ty's agent answered in a friendlier voice now.

"Good, great, we're looking forward to seeing you there. Yes, she came in a moment ago and I have her sitting on my lap now," Ty elaborated and let his fingers glide under his wife's shirt to feel the skin of her belly under his hand.

The embarrassed sigh was clear enough.

"You asked. Vi, let's talk about that at the gala or after, that'll be easier. Bye." He hung up, with one hand saving the document, the other now playing with Scarlette's hair. "Hello from Vi. She was a little concerned about the book not moving forward. And she still wants us to talk to one of her other authors who is currently suffering from writer's block, and she thinks our energy and telling him how we met, might help him."

"Do we get a counseling fee or something?"

"Ah, a businesswoman at heart, I like that."

"Always. You've been busy already. I'll have to make some calls to my staff, too. But nobody has called me yet to tell me there's an emergency, which makes me hope everything's okay. But we need to stop this soon, I have to get back behind the wheel."

"Very much agreed. Although it's pretty awesome to have an excuse to spend so much time with you at the moment."

"Fair point."

She shifted to straddle him, dragged them both into a deep kiss.

"It's pretty awesome to do this, too."

Her hips rocked a little, his hands ran down to cup her butt. Their next kiss was interrupted by Luke calling for them.

Silently cursing, Scarlette got up, took Ty's hand on the way out.

"We've got more info." Luke was in cop mode it seemed, and it fit him like a glove.

"Scarlette, let's talk first about Patrick."

"Okay."

"I got in contact with your family, and they said when he came to the restaurant he was sad, but rather calm. He asked them to tell you that when you understood that you had made a mistake, he'd be waiting for you. He knew everybody was entitled to mistakes and it took time to be sure where you belonged."

"I don't know where he gets that from, I swear. That's totally crazy."

"No argument there. I had my colleagues do follow-ups, and we know now your car was intact until after he showed up at the restaurant. A neighbor who hadn't been at home the first time could confirm that on a second round of interviews.

"And we know that, after his brave display, Patrick went to his therapist, and had a breakdown that had him in the hospital until yesterday, which is why we couldn't extensively interview him before."

"Right, you said earlier you could talk to him only briefly at first," Tyler recalled and felt resentment for the lack of information rise inside him.

Luke must have seen it on his friend's face because he answered with a heavy sigh. "Yes, I stopped at the hospital before coming here. But his doctor wouldn't give me more than a few minutes with him. Look, man, I'm sorry, but I have to do my job. I couldn't just give you information on where to find a suspect, so I didn't mention the hospital earlier. I know neither you nor Scarlette or her family would hurt him, but still."

Feeling her husband seething beside her, Scarlette tried to defuse the situation. "Ty, Luke is right. I have worked with enough authorities to know their rules and protocols suck sometimes, but he has to follow them."

Ty still scowled but nodded. "Yeah, yeah, I get it. We're okay."

Scarlette gave his hand a quick squeeze, then focused her

attention back on Luke. "Okay, so the car wasn't Patrick. Well, we figured, right? But it's good to know."

"You're right. Now, while I was talking to my colleagues, Josh, you checked on the first feedback on the autopsy reports, right?"

"Yes, I did. It's hard to say from a scan, and they of course can't analyze the ink, the paper, all that. But a first examination points to the reports being falsified. Whoever created them did work with the originals at some point or had a template, the lab assumes, because the layout appears to be authentic. But from the scan, it appears like some ballpoint pen was used, and those, while in existence for some forty years by 1928, weren't great for writing with yet, meaning not many people used them. Meaning, while not impossible, it's unlikely they would have written the original autopsy report with one.

"Also, the handwriting wasn't precisely what the lab had expected. They'd need an expert there, focusing on how writing has changed over time, but they had the impression it was more likely written by somebody trying to mimic an older style."

Luke nodded in approval. "You're really good at this."

"Thanks."

"And this is good news for us, I'd say. I'll keep working on the email; they aren't stupid when it comes to tech, but I'll see where I end up. July, anything on the housekeepers?"

"No, they vanished after '28, at least from the documents I can find online. I would probably have to try my luck in some old physical archive."

"Maybe let's not go there, yet."

"Didn't plan to, but I'll keep it as an option in the back of my mind. I thought I'd follow yet another line, though. The house has been kept the way it's been for decades, right? But somebody had access to it for the photos. Could be they're tangled in there, and that's another way to find them."

"That's good. I never dug deep there," Tyler commented. "but I can get you some starting points."

"Perfect."

The group separated, and seeing everything in capable hands, Scarlette followed her plan to check on her own business. Meanwhile, Tyler shot the info regarding the house to July and took some time to prepare his speech for the gala the following day. He still wasn't sure how he had been talked into that.

July worked through several years of ownership changes, additions, amendments. In the end she had several companies and some old studios she needed to check out in more detail. But once she got started, she quickly ran into the first roadblocks and would need a more official background to get further details. Well, her official background was downstairs and had told her to let him know when she needed his badge, hadn't he?

She wasn't entirely sure how wise it was to set up in the office space she had been given in the guest suite, but Scarlette was working in one office, and Josh and Luke in the other. Tyler was nowhere to be seen, but as she had heard he wanted to write, she assumed he had found himself a quiet space for that.

Crossing the offices, she curled her finger at Luke to follow her. It shouldn't have surprised her that she was caught in an embrace and her lips were entrapped by Luke's when he stepped into her office with her.

"Mhm, I wish that was why I called you here."

"It can be." He nuzzled her neck, brought her closer against him.

Chuckling, she linked her hands behind his neck. "No surprise there. But I need the cop right at this moment."

"Okay. What can he do for you?"

She explained her findings to him, and once they began, they both got lost in the work.

Hours had gone by when Scarlette brought them back to the here and now. "I'm getting a vat of fresh coffee up, you two want some?"

"Ah, yeah. But we'll come over to you all; I think we're okay to update you on this. I'll just get some papers from upstairs," July said.

"Okay."

Luke carried over some of the things they had been working on to the main office of this investigation, and checked on some things he had decided were legally okay for Josh to pursue and could still hold up in court.

Scarlette had come in with the coffee a moment earlier, and Tyler almost bumped into Julia in the doorway.

"Sorry, didn't see you," she said and adjusted the papers she was carrying.

"No wonder. I'm more surprised you didn't break your neck coming down the stairs."

The pile of documents she was balancing towered higher than her face.

"No, it worked, but I want these, or parts of them, on the board. It will help us all keep track."

She and Luke began to present their findings with more enthusiasm than anybody had expected.

"Okay, we'll go into more detail in a minute, but let's say all this," she waved her hand over the documents, "began with the strangely unknown old film studio 'Studio Royale.'"

"Which coincidentally is an anagram for O'Leary," said Tyler.

"Ten points for our writer here. Yes, it is. To link this one hundred percent to the O'Learys will take the aforementioned personal search in some archives, though, because what we can find is vague and even back then things were covered under several layers. No owner or anything was directly mentioned by name. Which is just super suspicious."

"Very much so," Luke took over "July and I kept going forward in time, and the pattern for that holds. With every decade, there were more companies, other studios, more layers. But what they all had in common is that they all appear to be about as fake as any of the evidence they have sent you.

"I would love to say that now that we know this, we can quickly find them. Unfortunately, they weren't stupid, and to uncover some of it we will have to follow this up with financial investigations, and for those I will need a warrant. We've come pretty far, and that's great, because I will need this to substantiate the need for said warrant. But to keep going deeper, Scarlette, Ty, I will need to take this to my superior at some point soon."

Tyler nodded. "Okay. Once we have everything we can

get under the radar, we'll talk how to approach the next steps."

"All right. July, would you pin everything to the board while I explain the details we found? Your system there is solid, I don't wanna mess it up."

"Sure."

It took nearly an hour. A hundred years of lies and secrets, red herrings set up for curious eyes, and technically more elaborate mazes over time needed a lot of illustration. The board and the papers helped indeed, and July had just picked up the last with some relief that they finally had a reasonably complete picture when from the back of the paper a note fell to the floor.

"Oh. I guess I picked that up accidentally. It's not part of this."

Chapter Twenty-One

Tyler reached for the note, then realized he had seen it before.

"That's the one from inside Eton's suit. I put it on a table, then it probably got buried under everything else before I remembered to check it. Okay, let's see..."

October 13th, 1928

My dear Eton,

Death means freedom.

I wished bedding down where I have experienced love and happiness for so long would feel right.

But it was stolen from us.

You have always understood me, you have always been by my side. For that I will treasure you for all eternity.

I regret your sorrow, but life has become unbearable, and I must follow my heart.

Fear not, you will be happy again. That I know in my soul.

You are a good man, you will find love, you will have what I could never give you.

Yours truly,
  Cecille

"That sounds very much like a suicide note to me."

"It does. And it's dated the day after Mary-Beth's death. I bet she meant her when she wrote that she must follow her heart."

July came back to the group after pinning the last sheet of paper, then scanned the note again.

"I think you're right, Scarlette. But what do you make of that last part? Do you think she really was infertile, that she still slept with Eton, and she couldn't give him a child? Or what? Did she sleep with him and had found a way to secretly use some form of contraception?"

"Did they have something like that back then? I mean, I know condoms have been around for some time, but something secret for women to use?" Luke eyed the two female members of the group with raised brows, some doubt and some curiosity in his eyes.

The women shrugged in a baffled gesture that asked how they should know that. Since Josh was still sitting in front of the laptop, he ran a quick search.

"Hm, it says here there were some diaphragms around at that time, if you could find a way to get them. Not sure how secret that would be."

"Well, that depends on the guy, I'd say," Scarlette

smirked. "No, joke aside. It's hard to say from this letter what the state of their marriage was, whether Eton even knew about her and Mary-Beth. For us, it makes sense to assume what she means, but for him, I couldn't say."

"No, that's true. But it sounds a lot like the suicide claims from back then were true for Cecille and, maybe I'm a little naïve here, or too optimistic, but I hope that means the same for Mary-Beth. It's pathetic, but it would help me to know our family's history wasn't based on lies."

"Josh, honey, that's not pathetic, it's natural. And I feel the same, for your part of the family, and for mine. And as much as it hurt them back then, I still hope it was suicide because anything else would hurt you and Ty, and I don't want that."

Scarlette enfolded her brother-in-law in a warm hug, kissed his hair. He was good at compartmentalizing, she realized. While working he could focus on the task at hand, but after, he was a gentle young man who had already dealt with more than he should have, and he needed people to lean on.

Josh took the comfort gratefully, ran his arms around her. He had told Ty she wasn't his stepmother, and he was glad about it. She felt like a sister to him, like he had known her for years. It was soothing to have her here, to know she'd stay. "Thanks."

"Of course."

And she realized this needed to be finished very soon. Not only for business, not only because of the escalating violence, but because of the hurt it had already caused and would go on causing the people she loved.

"Tyler, can we talk for a moment? Privately."

"Yes, of course."

In the office that had unofficially become hers now, she sat on the edge of the desk, waited until Tyler had closed the door and came over to face her.

"What is it, Sparks?"

"I know we want to dig, and would be happy to do it all by ourselves, but Link, this needs to stop. Josh hurts, you hurt."

"And you don't?"

"I do. Mostly for you both, but some for my biological mother, for the generations before her. This is a constant rollercoaster, we're all torn between hope and despair. How much do you trust Vi? You haven't told her about this."

"No, I haven't. Because when it started, I thought I could shut it down quickly; find some neat and tidy clue to say 'fuck you, whatever you publish,' or, even better, to prove them a fraud and hand them together with the proof to the cops. But to come back to your question, Vi I trust a great deal. But I wouldn't talk about this in her office; you never know who hears what. Remember our engagement."

"Yes, I know what you mean. Do you know Luke's boss?"

"Hm? Ah, a little. He seems competent, and during the short acquaintance we've had, trustworthy. I know Luke thinks highly of him and he's usually a good judge of character."

"Okay. What about the following plan? Tomorrow we invite Vi to your place or my parents' home before the gala. We explain everything to her, only her, prepare a first statement in case anything leaks to the press. We also explain to her the wonderful next book you can write about all this, family biography, autobiography when it comes to today, to you and me. It has it all, doesn't it? Love, death, crime and, hopefully, punishment. And that from her favorite writer, whose name alone already guarantees success.

"Today we talk to Luke, tell him we need this handled officially now, and ask him to talk to his boss tomorrow. We all drive into the city early enough, July can visit her mom, Luke starts the official investigation, we involve Vi. We all eat together at our restaurant, or Granny will kill us. Then we all get ready for the gala. And I, to be honest here with you, will feel a lot better to have Luke there, too, because I'm scared they might try something that evening, even if we still have time according to their deadline."

He saw the façade she had put up in front of the others crumble and could've slapped himself for not taking time earlier to console her.

She had hidden it well from the others, but he had seen the stress, the raw nerves under the surface. She was so damn strong, had offered a shoulder to him, to Josh, had kept the mood light for Julia so as not to burden a friend already worried about her father, had relaxed her when she was nervous about a guy.

He had already made up his mind to kidnap her early to take a bath with her, perhaps give her a massage. Now he saw that first she needed a shoulder, too.

"Baby, come here." Wrapping his arms around her, his hand tenderly stroked her hair, his lips pressed to her temple.

"I think you are right. This needs to come to an end. You have a good plan, let's follow through with it. It's close to dinner time, so we talk to Luke, we eat, and after, because we all need it, we'll watch a movie or play a game."

"Yes, okay." She burrowed deeper into the embrace, sighed deeply. "Thanks, I needed this."

Luke was pleased to learn they would take off some of the shackles the secrecy had put on him.

"I'll talk with Leroy outside of the precinct, far away from any ears. He knows whom he can trust, we'll handle it discreetly."

"Thanks, Luke."

And when Lorraine called them to dinner soon after, Tyler quickly shot a short text to Vi letting her know they needed to talk to her privately before the gala and to keep it to herself, and that he'd tell her where to meet.

"She'll think we broke up, came to our senses, and realized what a crazy idea our wedding has been."

"She'll be disappointed, then. I think it was the best idea we both ever had."

"So do I." And knowing that was true, Scarlette reminded herself to add something to the bag she had to pack later.

A movie night, in theory, sounded like fun to Josh, but he also knew he'd be sitting there with two new couples, no matter their age. He'd seen each couple through the day, sharing quick kisses, or undressing the object of their desire in their minds. He knew he'd be sitting there between them, trying to watch a movie while they were necking beside him. That was too close to nights with friends, and now he'd have people around him considerably older. Not cool.

Scarlette saw the doubt in his mind when she carried popcorn and soft drinks, candy, and nachos upstairs to the family room. She put herself into his spot, then had an idea.

"Josh, would you help me push some of this furniture around?"

"Huh?"

"I haven't had a girl movie night with July in ages, so we'll have two camps. You guys get the corner over there, you can get the extra hot nachos, too. July and I will sit over there, get a blanket, have our girls' night."

"Okay, yeah, sure."

The other three had been debating what movie to watch, and were a little put off when they saw what was going on, but caught on quickly and helped get everything into place.

Once the setup was complete, Tyler got out his phone for a quick check, then glanced at his wife.

"Sparks, one last thing, you got a minute?"

"Sure. Guys, get things up and running."

They walked over to one of the offices, and Scarlette glanced at Ty. "Everything okay? Did Vi text back?"

Ty made a noncommittal sound, closed the door when they were both inside.

And had Scarlette with her back against it. His mouth greedily devoured hers, and his hands filled with her full breasts. Her hips pumped instinctively against his and they both groaned. Lust burned painfully through them, and Scarlette aggressively dragged him closer.

With the fire still raging inside him, Tyler took a deliberate step away from his wife, had to shake his head to get back to reality.

"Okay, better, I had to get that out of the system when I can't get my hands on you during the movie. But I appreciate what you're doing for Josh there."

"Huh?" She was still panting, finally managed to draw a

full breath, clearing her mind a little with it. "Of course. I don't want him to feel like the fifth wheel."

"Thank you. My watch tells me the movie will end late, probably after midnight, but I'm sure we'll still find time and energy to pick up where we just left off."

"Yeah, uh-huh, sounds great."

"Perfect. Guess we should get back."

In the living room, they got the expected comments from friends and family. "We had to adjust some more plans for tomorrow." *And it wasn't even a lie he had told*, Scarlette thought and fought hard not to let the giggle rising in her throat bubble out.

And after midnight they all cleaned up together, put back the furniture, before finally saying goodnight.

In their bedroom, Ty did pick up pretty much exactly where he had left off and had Scarlette weak and mindless again within seconds.

Later, it took considerable effort and concentration to finish packing her things but she somehow managed it right before her husband grabbed her and dragged her back into bed.

Chapter Twenty-Two

Ty wasn't entirely comfortable leaving Josh alone, but the boy almost physically shoved his brother out the door in the morning. "Just go. I'll be out of the house half the evening myself, and after that Lorraine said I could sleep in their guest room. The situation sucks, but we can't stop living our lives."

"Okay, okay. Remember what we talked about. Did you find everything?"

"I will, I did. Thanks."

"Good. Have fun tonight."

"You guys, too."

They dropped July off at her mother's first, and Luke got a little nervous. "Don't worry, it's not meet-the-parents-day. Not with all this going on. I don't want to explain to my mom why I'm seeing a cop I met when I stayed at Ty and Scarlette's. She doesn't even know why I came over from

Australia. I told her it was because of the two of them, which isn't really lying, but not the specifics."

"Okay. It's not that I don't want to meet her, it's the current situation."

"I know, and once that's resolved, trust me, I will totally have you meet her, leave you to her mercy." With a wink and a kiss, Julia jumped out of the car. She'd come to Scarlette's parents' house later as well, to get dressed there for the gala.

That had become the meeting place for the day, and after letting Luke out at his stop, too, they made their way to the Langella home.

Since they still had time left before Vi would come by, they helped Cynthia with some last-minute preparations, solved the usual emergencies. Scarlette shook her head when she was on a video call with one of the decorators.

"What's your problem here, Sue?"

"There's a cracked tile right next to the entrance!"

"So what?"

"So what? It ruins the impeccable look of the whole room when people see a crack first thing when they enter."

"Woman, I can see the flowers on pedestals behind you. Next to the damn crack. Move them a foot closer to the door on each side, cover the crack. It's not our room, not ours to fix. Use some damn make-up to make it pretty for the night."

Silence dragged on, while the woman considered the advice. "Yes, I guess we could do that."

"Good."

Scarlette hung up, glared at Tyler who chuckled silently. "Oh, you take the next call for that. It's the third time that incompetent bimbo called. Mom, where the hell did you find her?"

Cynthia glared up from her laptop, understanding her daughter's frustration. "Didn't. Her mother is the actual event manager, but she had a biking accident last weekend and now has two broken legs. Her daughter was the only one who could fill in on such short notice because the co-owner of the company went into labor day before yesterday and is now at home with a little baby girl."

"Wonderful."

Luckily for everybody, Scarlette was spared from any more calls when Viola rang the doorbell.

The trio settled into the living room and, with a coffee for everybody, they went over everything after Vi had been sworn to secrecy.

When Scarlette and Tyler had finished, the agent stared at them, huffed out a heavy breath. "Well, that's a fucked up situation."

Scarlette laughed. "I like you a lot better like that. Yes, it's fucked up, you're right."

"It's good that you have the cops in on it now, too. We can use that for the statement "full cooperation with authorities" and such. Scarlette, can I trust I will work with Ms. Stone on this as well?"

"Yes."

"Wonderful. She's sensible, easy to work with. All right, let's get down to this."

They drafted, redrafted, texted, and spoke with July while she was in a cab from her mom's place to the house.

It took longer than Scarlette had expected, but Viola and July were both perfectionists and aimed for something that would be thorough yet superficial enough not to interfere with a possible investigation – here July's background with her mother turned out to be highly useful on all accounts.

Finally pleased, Vi left to drive back home and get ready for the evening entertainment.

And, checking the time, Scarlette hauled the rest of the house to the restaurant, so they'd all get some real food to hold them over through an evening of canapés and delicate finger food. She knew the drill well enough to foresee neither her mother nor Ty and herself getting a chance to have a bite of the actual dinner later. Hosts, co-hosts, and apparently for this one, showpieces, always drew the short straw.

Beatrice had set a big table for them and, knowing her family and friends, she had already prepared most things they'd need and was now getting everything in the oven or into a pot.

They had all entered through the side entrance, and Scarlette got a glance at a couple leaving the restaurant.

"Huh, that looks a little like Vi's assistant."

The group followed her gaze, and Ty agreed. "It does. I think I remember Vi told me she has some family somewhere around here."

"Small world."

"Yes."

Now July got a glance at the man accompanying the young woman. "Mhm, strange."

"What?"

"That guy with her? He almost looks like law firm guy."

"Wait, what?"

"I said almost. I really didn't get a good look. It could be a coincidence."

"Or not. Come."

Scarlette hurried her friend through the restaurant and onto the sidewalk, but all they saw was the back of the man climbing into a cab beside the woman, and the car driving off before they could do anything.

Tyler flew out onto the sidewalk right behind them.

"Shit!" Scarlette cursed.

"Yes. Don't do that again, just take off like that."

"What?"

He took hold of her arms, turned her to face him. "You can't take off like that with things the way they are. What if something had happened to you?"

"Ty, babe, broad daylight, open street. I wouldn't have jumped in a car with them, and they didn't seem like they were carrying a concealed weapon. I told you I can watch out for myself."

She saw fury rise into his eyes, felt it with his fingers digging deeper into her arm. Understanding him, she tried to ease it. "But I appreciate you coming after me, seriously. It's good to know you're looking out for me now, too. Give me some more time to get used to having someone doing that. Sorry, if I scared you."

Ty rested his forehead against hers, sighed. "It's okay."

Luke ran into them when he got out of his car. "Guys, I thought we would meet inside."

"Yeah. But we thought we saw somebody."

"Who? What?"

"Nothing happened, we're okay. But I thought I had seen the assistant of Ty's agent leaving the restaurant, and July wasn't sure if the guy the woman was with might have been law firm guy who hit on her in Australia."

Julia shifted a little, ran a hand through her hair. "I'm really not sure. I got a glimpse, maybe half a second. It might have been somebody who looked similar and my brain projecting."

"Or it might have been the same guy and he tried to hit on you to get some info on me. They know me, they will know you're my best friend."

It sunk in, and July shuddered. "Oh god. You're right. That's so fucking creepy."

Luke draped an arm around her shoulder, squeezed. "It is, but it's also a good lead. Did you get the cab number?"

"No, sorry. There were several cars in our line of sight."

"It's okay. I'll note the time, the address, it will take a lot of work to find that cab, but it's not completely impossible. Also, July, I need to know all about that law firm guy, and why I haven't heard of him before." Luke said and leaned in, tauntingly biting her lower lip.

"Because nothing happened? But yes, I'll tell you. It's something to follow up on."

"Exactly. Let's go in, I'm starving, and I want to try that allegedly awesome pizza I was lured in with."

"Come in, then." Scarlette held the door open for them, found her family all anxiously waiting. "All good. Sit down, everybody," she told them

Now that he wasn't running after his wife, Tyler took a moment to focus his attention on the restaurant.

It was a homey place with about twenty tables and a small bar area close to the entrance. Nobody had tried to enforce a too modern or too fancy style here; instead there were cozy chairs or booths with comfortable benches, plain but clean, good-quality tablecloths, wine bottles with candles in them on the tables, and pictures of Italian scenery on the walls. He knew he would always love coming by here once life had become more routine again.

But today, they talked and updated each other in low voices. Luke told them his boss would start working on the case today but would need to put things together in a manner that would get the right judge to sign off on the warrant. It would take a day or two longer, but with the possible connection between Vi's assistant and law firm guy, Luke could start with a superficial run on them or, in law firm guy's case, try to find out who he was to begin with. July could provide the law firm he had usually walked into, and that his first name was Jake, but that was all for now.

"Well, I have started off with less in some cases. I'll see where it gets me. But now, Mrs. Langella, I have to thank you, your granddaughter didn't oversell. This pizza is amazing."

"Thank you. And please make it Beatrice, I have the feeling we will see you here more often in the future."

"I sure hope so."

Scarlette was happy to hear one of her aunts would cover for her dad for the rest of the day so he could leave the restaurant with the rest of the group and attend the gala with them.

And when she saw her mother after getting ready at her parents' house — Cynthia looking gorgeous in a long and straight red dress and wearing a bright smile — Scarlette could understand the sparkle in her father's eyes as the women all went downstairs to where the guys were waiting for them. Tyler, on the other hand, decided Luke was just as lucky as Marco when Julia walked down beside Scarlette in a green one-shoulder-style dress, her mass of hair partially tamed with a clip, and her face pleasantly highlighted.

But studying his wife, he was sure had won the jackpot. She wore a long, dark-blue dress with carefully draped wider straps off her shoulders. It clung to her body, showing off her sumptuous figure, and with every step she took it softly shimmered, reminding him of a deep ocean slowly moving. She had curled her hair, too, and some strands she had left out deliberately, but for the most part, she had put it up and had pinned a shining comb in there that went with the earrings and the bracelet she wore.

She was always beautiful, but this image of her took his breath as effectively as her walking down the garden path in a wedding dress.

"So, would you guys take us along like this?" July asked playfully.

Luke held out his hand for July's and kissed it. "Of course, you all look wonderful."

When Ty stayed quiet, Scarlette cocked her head. "What about you, Mr. Man of the Evening? Are we presentable?"

It took him another five seconds to find his speech. "I think it's been a very smart idea to get dressed here. We would never have left our place. You are stunningly beautiful, darling. Cynthia, July, you both look fantastic as well, of course."

Ty's phone vibrated with a text and he smiled after checking it. "I hope you all don't mind that I took care of our transportation for the evening. It just arrived."

They would have been stupid to complain about the elegant black limo waiting at the curb.

Later that evening, Scarlette counted it a success when she managed to eat one small plate of appetizers without being interrupted.

Ty's speech had been well-received, and he was currently being dragged along by Vi. His own fault, Scarlette figured, and was about to reach for her food when a hand stole the last piece from her plate. Marco practically inhaled it, beamed at his daughter. "Thank you, Bella."

She frowned at him, gave him a mock punch. "You're lucky I like you."

"Ah, a father's dream to hear those words. How are you, my sweetheart?"

"Seeing as we had pizza before this, luckily not too hungry or I would be starving by now. This is more to buffer the champagne people keep constantly putting in my hand."

"I know exactly what you are talking about. And how are you and your husband? We have hardly had time to talk."

"I know, papa. We will take the time once we finish all the unpleasant things going on. But I'm incredibly happy with him. Within all the chaos, he keeps me steady. When I read the letter from my biological mother, it shook me because I learned she only gave me away to protect me. I love you and mama so much, and I never thought I needed to know the why, but when I did, it made my heart a little bigger to fit her in there, too. And when I cried for her, Ty held me, suggested we find out where she's buried and to bring her flowers."

Marco gazed at his son-in-law. "He has a very good soul. I am terribly glad you found each other." Then a boyish smirk appeared. "And I'm glad for you and me because I hope we can now push him to these events together with your mother."

Laughing, Scarlette hugged her father. "Oh, that would be perfect."

Cynthia came over to them, stole her daughter. "I have a few more people you need to talk to."

"The quiet couldn't last forever. Yes, of course, mom."

She survived, and when Ty finally came back to her, they managed to escape the constant small talk by sauntering to the dance floor.

His eyes had followed her whenever he had gotten the chance, and holding her in his arms now, swaying with her, her soft curves leaning against him, Ty had very clear pictures in his mind for their personal after-party. "Let's get everybody home later, then grab the bags from the car and have the limo drive us to our apartment."

"Any reason we shouldn't sleep at my parents'?" Her cheek was lying on his chest and he couldn't see the smug grin on her face.

"Multiple, I hope."

"Okay. Yeah, we can do that, sounds good to me."

"Perfect."

Considering their surroundings, they finished their dance with a modest kiss. Scarlette had hardly gotten off the dance floor when her personal nemesis of the evening, the event manager's daughter, stepped in her way.

"Mrs. Lange... Mrs. O'Brien, there's somebody who wants to speak to you outside, just say hello really."

"Who?"

"He didn't say, only that he was an old friend. I think he works here maybe. He wears a service uniform with some lightning bolts on it, some cables hanging out of his pocket."

Running it quickly through her head, Scarlette came up with a couple of electricians — no surprise Barbie here wouldn't know the job title — from when she had updated her office, who sometimes took jobs for hotels.

"Okay, thank you. Where?"

"Outside the ballroom, there is a small corner next to the cloakroom. If you'll excuse me, I have some things to check on." With fear exuding from every pore, the woman fled.

Ty played his fingers down Scarlette's arm. "Want me to come?"

"Ah, no, seems like mom and Vi want you. I know a few people who could fit, I'll check. Probably only a quick 'hello and let's get together sometime again' situation when they heard I'd be here."

"Be careful."

"I will be." Strolling out, she saw the man in the corner. He had his body turned a little and she couldn't make out his face until she'd get a bit closer.

"Hi. You wanted to see me?"

When he turned, she knew the face immediately. "Fuck this. I'm leaving; you better do the same."

"No, no, Scarlette, my little butterfly, wait."

"I'm not your damn butterfly, get that through your head."

"You are confused. I understand. It's this strange uniform, isn't it? But you see, I had to get into this area, and with your event, they don't let anybody in here without an invitation."

"You didn't get one, get a hint."

"Well, I'm sure it got lost in the mail. You know how terrible the postal system has become. But look, it's me, honey bunny."

He took a step closer to her, and she automatically took one back.

"Fuck it, Patrick, I know it's you, I'm not confused. How stupid do you think I am that a stolen uniform would confuse me? I have tried this the nice way and told you we don't fit. You didn't get that. I filed a restraining order against you. What else do you need to understand I am not yours, have never been yours, will never be yours. I don't love you, and I never will. Move on."

"Oh Scarlette, my beautiful flower, you don't know what you are saying."

She stopped herself from dragging her hands through her hair. She had to get back to the party after all.

"Patrick, I know exactly what I am saying. I love Tyler, I am married to him."

"He is hurting you, isn't he? Makes you say those things you don't mean. He forced you to marry him. I know it. You can tell me. I will help you. There are lawyers to help you annul the marriage, it will be like you were never married, not like a divorce. We can start clean and pure with our wedding."

Take a deep breath, you don't want to cause a scene, girl, Scarlette told herself.

Inside the ballroom, Tyler listened to the same praises and congratulations he had heard half the evening and replied in the same friendly manner. But inside he felt uneasy. Something was wrong, even though he couldn't pinpoint what exactly.

Then he heard scraps of conversation. Electrician, dangerous job... Scar... Hand...

He didn't bother to excuse himself, just turned on his heels and strode to the exit to get to his wife.

She did her best not to yell at Patrick. There were people coming and going every other minute, it wouldn't be appropriate for her to lose her temper with some poor maintenance worker, as that was what people would see. "Again, there will be no wedding between us. Ever. I am not your damn soulmate, pretty little wife, birth machine or whatever."

"Oh, that is all right, we can adopt if we should find out you cannot conceive. It would be sad, but we could love them like they were ours, I'm sure."

"None of this is getting into your head, is it? I do not want you. I do not want children, not even one child. I especially do not want *your* child. I don't know what else to tell you. Go away for heaven's sake."

She was on the verge of turning, when his hand reached out for her arm, grabbed her wrist.

"Sugarplum, what's wrong with you? Are you having your time of the month? I know women can be a bit senseless during those days."

"Shit, did you really just blame my period for your fucked up brain? You are even crazier than I thought."

She tugged to get her hand back, but his grip tightened.

"We will talk about this at home."

"No, we will not. Let go of my wrist, Patrick. Now."

"Now, Scarlette, I am sorry, but I must put my foot down on this. Come along now, precious."

She blinked at him, tilted her head. "Funny, I was thinking about putting my foot down, too."

She did, with full force and her spiked heel crushing into the thin top of the shoe he hadn't bothered to change to a sturdier one going with the uniform.

He would have screamed, had he gotten the chance, but at the same moment that her heel hit his foot a fist punched him straight in the face.

"Let the fuck go of my wife!"

Crumbling and curling into a ball on the floor, Patrick wailed bitter tears.

"Fuck, help me get him away from here."

"He can wait. Are you okay?"

"Yes, I am. That's why you will help me now to get him into that office over there."

She had already begun dragging Patrick up and across the hallway to a door, so Tyler went along. But once they had him in the room, had the door closed behind them, he let the weeping man fall to the floor, turned Scarlette around. Keeping his hands on her arms, his eyes ran her up and down, examining her for any marks of violence.

"Are you really okay?"

"Yes, I promise. He had only just reached out for me, he didn't touch me before. Thanks for the assistance, though."

"Anytime, Sparks. Looks like you left him with another hole in his body," Tyler concluded when he saw a pool of blood spread on the floor around Patrick's foot.

"And probably a broken bone, it crunched under my foot." She checked her shoe. "Let me see... yeah, okay." She reached for some tissue on the table, cleaned her heel without mercy for the whimpering mass on the floor. "Can hardly go in there smearing blood over the floor. And I assume you won't leave me alone with him and get Luke."

"Not a chance in hell."

"Okay, then I'll be right back with him."

When the office door opened and Cynthia, Vi, and Luke stared at the scene, Scarlette shrugged. "Or this works. Luke, the bundle on the floor is Patrick Milton."

She quickly and precisely relayed what had happened, and Luke huffed. "Guess the fun part of the evening is over for me. Scarlette, I'll need to get your statement again officially, but we can do that tomorrow. For now, I'll get him out of here, have him examined by the doctors. I'm sorry I can't tell you anything else, but I think he'll end up in a psych ward."

"Better than nothing. Thanks, Luke."

"How did you all know to come?"

Cynthia frowned at her son-in-law. "Ty, do you think we're brainless? You tell us Scarlette is out here talking to somebody alone, and all of a sudden you run off in the middle of a conversation? Easy enough to put two and two together, to know something was off. And you can hear the crying in here from the hallway."

"Fair."

"And how did you know to come, Link?"

"People saw you speaking to a guy with a scar on his hand, I caught part of their conversation. And also being good at math, I figured chances would be good I finally could meet our friend Patrick."

"Yeah. Okay, uh, Luke, can we help you with anything?"

"No, I already called in a uniform to assist me with him. Would you let July know I'll contact her when we're done with booking? I'll see if I catch her here or what we'll do."

"Yes, sure."

After getting back to the ballroom, neither Cynthia nor Viola complained when Tyler hardly took a step away from his wife for the rest of the evening.

They had to stay several hours longer, but after he had seen Scarlette being absolutely capable of looking out for herself, Tyler slowly let go of the tension the interruption had caused.

And when she was dancing with him again, felt him relax, Scarlette brought her mouth close to his ear. "The plan for later still stands, right? I think you need to explain those reasons you mentioned in detail."

His fingers tightened on her back, and using the slow dance as an excuse Scarlette rubbed against him, felt his pulse spike when her lips pressed to his throat. Who knew torture could be so sweet?

He swallowed hard, forced his hands to stay where they were and not start roaming over her exquisite body.

"Oh yes, the plan still stands."

"Terrific."

It was almost sunrise when they finally stepped into their apartment after dropping everybody at their homes.

Tyler helped Scarlette quickly with the bags, then left her to lock the door properly.

He didn't care how long the evening had been. Half the

night his mind had played with ideas on how to get his wife out of that dress, it was time to turn those ideas into reality.

God, she was gorgeous, and she was his. Sometimes that still gave him a jolt. However perfectly things had fallen into place with them, he knew she was the greatest gift he had ever been given. Her love, and her willingness to merge their lives, to be there for each other no matter what. Even that could make his head spin, and then he looked at her and saw how freaking beautiful she was on top of it.

Now he followed her to the bedroom again, saw her standing in front of the mirror. He stopped her hand when she reached back for the zipper of her dress.

"No, let me."

Scarlette inclined her head to give his lips easier access to her neck, when he stepped behind her and bowed down a little, his hands carefully unzipping the dress. His warm breath on her skin had the first tendrils of desire creep over her body, his lips wandering to her ear, his teeth delicately nipping at her earlobe had lust bloom deep inside her.

She leaned into him, into the solid body she had come to love as much as the man it belonged to.

Drawing away the dress from her body he revealed the thin layers of lace covering her beneath it.

His eyes feasted upon her in the mirror, light skin against midnight-blue lace, emerald eyes going dark.

She had put on pasties as an addition because lace and dress had been so very thin. Now he reached inside her bra, peeled them off. But when she wanted to turn around, he held her in place.

"No, I want to see you like this, I want you to see yourself."

His thumbs began to circle over nipples that were peaking under lace now, his mouth caressed her shoulder, and when he trailed a hand down her belly, his other lightly covered her throat, his fingers holding her chin.

"I want you to see how you look when I make you come."

The man was incredible, knew exactly what would make her long for everything that he could give her. Her pulse pounded hard in her lap, she could feel how wet she was already.

And when his fingers crawled under her panties, slid inside her, her eyes fluttered closed, her head wanted to fall back. His hand held it level.

"Open your eyes."

She did, and saw herself rock against his hand, saw her eyes light up and at the same moment go blind when he teased her to a slow, deep orgasm that crept through her whole body. Her moan made him drag her closer, and his teeth sank into her flesh. "I want you. I will want you for the rest of my life."

Now she turned and shoved him playfully towards the bed.

"I want you, too. Get out of that damn tux. I've got to get something."

She left him speechless when she strode off into the bathroom to go through her toiletry bag.

When she came back with the vibrator he had asked her about a few days earlier, she cocked her head.

"You aren't naked. Well, it's more for you to watch, anyway, but now you'll somehow have to manage to get your clothes off, while I get started on my own and distract you."

She one-handedly opened her bra and let it fall on the way to the bed, then wiggled out of her panties.

Climbing onto the bed, she turned around to face him, knelt in the middle of the sheets.

One hand she let run over her breast, the other switched on the toy, brought it between her legs.

Her husband was better, sure, but the air pulses playing around her clitoris still had her panting quickly, her hips moving against her hand. And knowing Ty observed her brought a new thrill to it, filled her with excited pleasure.

He stood there, watched her lose control, watched her hand race down and her fingers slip inside her. She was dripping wet, and completely lost in her own passion. He was near to exploding. His mouth had gone dry at first, now with her guttural groan, saliva began to pool. His hands, he had to make his hands move to undress so he could have her.

Somehow he managed to lose the tux and find his way onto the bed with her.

He dipped his head to suck on her breast, his hands running to her butt. She was wild, her voice rough, when she focused on him, demanded from him. "Touch me, touch yourself."

She slid her own fingers out of her, guided his inside, then took his other hand and closed it with hers around him, began to stroke.

"Good god, Scarlette!"

He was so hard, so ready for her, she could feel his hot blood throb under their joined hands. And when she came again, he overbalanced her, simply threw the toy away, and plunged deep inside her. She screamed, and another climax topped the last one. With the frantic burst, she left bloody streaks on his back with her nails.

"More, take me!"

The pure heat off her burned away any civilized boundaries he had so far always held on to.

With all reason abandoned, he forgot about gentleness, about control, about holding himself back. His hands groped, bruising her skin, his teeth left marks over half her body, but she didn't care, only urged him on, meeting each of his thrusts with the same mad energy.

And when she shattered yet again, her whole body forming a tight arch under him, her muscles fisting around him, he broke with her and spilled himself inside her.

"Are we dead? I feel like we might have killed each other with that one," Scarlette managed after a long period of gathering her melted brain.

"I don't know. Don't care either. That sure as hell was one for the books."

She giggled. "Oh, it was, but don't you dare go into that much detail in the biography."

"Okay. You never stop to amaze me, Sparks."

"Same goes for you. I was pretty sure you'd like it, but not a hundred percent. Some guys get touchy when it comes to toys or female masturbation, like they're afraid they aren't enough."

"Then they're idiots. I have never seen anything as hot as you kneeling there and pleasuring yourself, to know you were so acutely aware of me watching you."

The memory alone stirred a wanting he had been sure would need at least a full night's recovery.

"To watch you like that, to know you trust me enough to let yourself go like that in front of me is something special. And watching, I could focus on everything about you, your face, your voice, your body. I love your body, give it to me." He rolled back on top of her, slipped inside her again. She gasped, then started to move with him once more.

Chapter Twenty-Three

While the rest of the family enjoyed the gala, or he assumed they did, Josh was nervously waiting for Bonny. He knew he was a little early, but at home he had gone crazy. She had told him they'd meet at the theater, so he wouldn't have to deal with her parents right away when he picked her up.

Should he have brought her flowers? Would she expect that because she knew he wasn't the usual broke teenager? But she had also been the one talking movies and pizza, nothing fancy, even though she probably knew he could get a table somewhere.

He saw a street cart with flowers and made up his mind to try for something in the middle. He felt foolish to buy only a single flower, but it kind of felt right.

When he turned around, he nearly bumped into his principal Ms. Adams. The woman had to be ancient, but she had always been kind and had offered an open and understanding ear when Josh and Tyler had talked to her after their parents' accident about having Josh first exempted for a short time, then assigning him remote sessions so he could stay in New York while Tyler had been organizing things.

"Josh, good evening."

"Ms. Adams, good evening. How are you?"

"I'm well, thank you. Oh, have you bought this one for a girl?"

"Ah, yes."

"That's very sweet of you. Who is she?"

"Bonny Robins, ma'am."

"Well, she will certainly appreciate this. Are you two going to the movies?"

"Yes, ma'am."

"You have fun then. I will see you in school after the break."

"Thank you, Ms. Adams. Yes, we will surely see each other then. Have a nice evening."

"You, too, Josh."

As if his nerves hadn't been raw enough. Running into the headmaster when you were on break should be forbidden by law, no matter how friendly the person was. It just made you itchy.

But any thoughts about school vanished when he saw Bonny coming around the corner.

She wore a bright yellow summer dress with short-capped sleeves and a slightly flaring skirt in contrast to her soft, dark skin. Her hair was held back with a clip on each side, but she had left her curls untreated. He smiled at her, shyly waved.

"Hi, Josh."

"Hi, Bonny. Ah, this is for you." He handed her the single daisy he'd bought, and she cooed over it.

"Oh, that's so sweet, thank you!"

When the teenagers had chosen a film and were sitting in an otherwise empty row, Josh felt a new nervous rush roll through him. Would she expect him to take her hand, to kiss her?

Sure, they had talked a lot on the class trip, had gotten along well. She was easier to be around than other girls because with her he could talk movies — actual, substantial movies, not girly rom-coms. She was intelligent and she didn't try to hide it like some other girls still did. He didn't understand that.

So they had talked, and somehow they had agreed to this date, and yes, she had given him a few kisses during the trip, and the last one had definitely been more than a friendly peck on the lips and had him dreaming very explicit dreams that night.

But this was a date; there were rules for things like that, weren't there? He probably should have tried to squeeze more info out of his brother instead of trying to stuff the topic back in its box.

Bonny apparently had thought about all this before, because during the last few ads she leaned over, gave him a soft, lingering kiss. "Sorry, I'd say we can neck during the film, but I really wanna see this one. So necking is off the table except if the film sucks. But after, we should grab the pizza as a takeout and find a comfy place to eat it. Okay?"

"Yes, very okay."

"Cool." With another quick kiss, she turned in her seat again to watch the opening sequence.

After the movie — that hadn't sucked — they were eagerly discussing it while waiting for their food.

With the pizzas on her lap, Bonny let him drive, guided him to a small forest. "This is part of some of my dad's farmland, there's a little pond and, since I begged forever as a child, now there's also a pretty cool treehouse. Come, we can eat up there."

Had she planned this? Had she done this before? She seemed so sure about everything. It was a comfort to him, but it also made him queasy. What if he did something stupid? What if...

"Josh, relax. I can see you overthinking this. We have had a great time together up to now, I feel good around you. If you feel the same, I'd really like you to be my first. If this is too fast or too forward or too much pressure for you, I understand that, too."

And watching her — her smile spreading, her dark eyes gleaming at him — he took her hand, kissed her palm.

"Oh, my..."

"I really want you to be my first, too, Bonny."

She huffed out a small, relieved breath. "Good. Ah, did you bring something along for protection? I have some, too, but I figured you guys might know better what you want or need."

"I had the reduced version of the talk with my brother a few days ago, he gave me a box of condoms."

"Cool. First pizza?"

"Sure."

They stayed in the forest until close to midnight, made love several times.

"I wish we could stay here, and to be honest with you, my family knows I went out with you and where we would go, if things went well. But we have some guests coming tomorrow and I have to help my mom get the house ready, so I have to get up early."

"Okay, I understand that. But please tell me I can see you again. Not only for more of this, even though it's really nice. But I also feel good around you, and I would like to go out with you, spend time with you."

"That's really good because I want the same. You wanna come to dinner the day after tomorrow?"

"Umm, yeah, okay."

"My family is pretty cool. You'll be okay, just be yourself."

They had climbed down, were facing each other beside the car and holding hands.

"I think I can do that."

"Cool."

"Come, I'll drive you home."

"Thanks."

And when Josh quietly slipped inside Lorraine's house, she heard him and sent his brother a short text that the boy was home, safe and sound.

Chapter Twenty-Four

Scarlette woke up and felt utterly, gloriously used. Sore muscles and bruises sang and pinched, and she grunted contentedly. She was about to roll over to steal herself a morning kiss, when the doorbell rang.

"Damn. I'll go."

"Thanks. Wait, this first." Tyler drew her mouth to his, then let her get out of bed.

She hadn't brought a robe along, and instead wrapped the sheet around her. She checked the security monitor, and saw July and Luke. After letting them into the elevator, she opened the apartment door a moment later.

July saw bruises bloom on her friend's skin, hissed. "Oh shit. Scarlette, what the hell, Luke told me Patrick had hardly touched you. And I didn't see any bruises come out the rest of the evening, either."

"What? No, he didn't, and there weren't any bruises."

"Then why the hell do you look like this today?"

"Hm?" Scarlette peered down at her shoulders, her arms.

"Oh, that was Ty. We got a little carried away after the party."

"Holy shit."

Luke pinched the bridge of his nose, squeezed his eyes shut. "And again I say, that's too much information."

"Come on, I didn't go into detail."

"Oh, but you will, girl, when we get this good drunk going," July declared.

"Sure."

"You girls do that, I'll drag off your husband to a ball game then or something."

"Whatever works for your male bonding rituals. Make yourselves at home. Ty and I will get ready."

Half an hour later, all four of them were on the way out of the city, after Luke had let them know he would keep working from Scarlette's and Ty's home. "Leroy agrees with me on this, we don't know what they're gonna do next, so somebody should be close by. And having a cop right there might help keep things low-key, too, should anything happen. I can handle it without dragging in the locals right away. Leroy is working on those warrants, we will carefully choose whom to involve and how to set it up."

"Okay. What about Patrick? You said you needed an official statement."

"Yes. But we can do that at your place, too. He has two broken bones in his foot and a broken nose, by the way. His lawyer made some noise about bringing up charges of physical assault. He became very quiet when I told him why the RO had been issued in the past. But, unsurprisingly, they'll go for diminished capacity. And frankly, in his case, I understand why."

"Yeah. And if he had stayed away, I'd probably even feel bad for him, but not like this. Maybe he'll get the help he needs now, who knows."

Back at the family estate, Ty briefly checked with the distillery and the stables and swore to himself to pay more attention there once things had calmed down. For now, he was relieved his parents had always taken care to hire some of the best people in their fields and to treat and pay them well to have their loyalty.

Inside, July and Luke had retreated to the office and were working on compiling and filing more info on the companies and studios owning the mansion in California. Having the details in order would make it easier to systematically work through everything once Luke finally had his warrant.

Scarlette was talking to Lorraine in the kitchen, had a pile of mail in her hands, when Ty joined them.

"Hello, Lorraine."

"Hello, Tyler. Your brother is fine, he's off with friends. He came home when I texted you, and going by the grin on his face this morning, I'd say he got lucky yesterday. I hope you talked to him first."

"Yes, I did, gave him condoms and all."

"That's all right, then. Catch up with him when he gets back."

"I will. Thank you for looking out for him."

"'Course. Scarlette, sweetie, you want more coffee?"

"Always. If I hadn't fallen for Ty, I'd take my chances

with you, Lorraine. Thank you." She made the cook laugh and gratefully held out her mug to her, then turned to her husband and showed him the mail. "You are popular, babe. These all came in yesterday."

"Hm, it's that time of the year. I bet half of those are invitations to Thanksgiving events or winter balls already, asking for a kind donation along with it of course. They start earlier every year. I've helped my mother go through these for years by now. Mostly deciding who needed a written thanks, but no thanks.'"

"Seems like it, yeah. We get some, too, but nowhere close to that many. But these here," she held up some other letters, "should be some of the notes we couldn't read that you sent off for restoration."

"See, much more interesting. Let's take those upstairs."
"Okay."
When Scarlette slid down from the high chair at the kitchen island, Lorraine scowled at Tyler. "And draw your wife a bath later or have her soak in the hot tub for making her look like that, bruised all over."

He threw up his hands in exasperation. He had already heard accusations from July on the drive home. "Does anybody care how I look? It's not like she was any more careful or restrained, just saying."

"It's true." Scarlette shrugged with a clearly faked innocent smile. "We'll take a bath together or something. But thanks for your concerns."

She quickly rounded the island, pecked a kiss on Lorraine's cheek. "Sure. But to make this clear, I will not be cleaning up after your dead bodies or have the housekeeper do it when you drown in the tub."

"We'll be sure to kill ourselves very decently and far away from your realm, so you don't have any extra work."

"Better. Now, up you go, see what those notes are about."

Outside the kitchen, Tyler became silent and studied Scarlette mournfully. "Ty, what's wrong? I'm sorry if the talk upset you."

"No, it's not that. I just realized how perfect you are for this family – and how much my parents would have loved you. I'm not totally sure, but I think my mom even mentioned you once. You said you met her for about a minute at some function or other, and I think you impressed her. When we were talking on the phone one day, she was telling me about an event and this smart, gorgeous redhead full of life and ambition I had to meet one of these days.

"I only put it together now, because I watched you yesterday at the gala, and I saw how easily you can show all your sophistication and decorum. But that energy, and everything else you are, is always there, right under the surface.

"And when I see you with Lorraine, joking in the kitchen like you've lived here forever, like you've always belonged to the family, I merely wish my parents would have met you like this, too, as the woman I love, the woman I made part of this family."

For a long moment, she was speechless and felt tears burning behind her eyes. Then she laid her hand on his heart.

"I wish I could have met them like that, too. But I feel like I meet part of them every day I spend with you because they'll always be in here." She tapped his chest with her fingers. "They will always be in this home, so I will know them from that, too. And to know your mom likely told you about me, wanted us to meet, Ty, that means the world."

Overwhelmed, he banded his arms around her, buried his face in her hair. He breathed her in, reveled in the texture of her. "You undo me, you know that? I will have to insist on that whole month of honeymoon."

She only nodded, and wished she had both hands free to hold him. But since she was carrying the mail, she instead made do with pressing her lips to his throat.

"A month sounds great. I love you, Tyler."

"I love you, too, Scarlette."

Very gently they let go of each other and made their way upstairs with their fingers firmly linked.

They found Luke on the phone with his boss, and July apparently picking up on some work and engaged in a conference call in her guest office.

"Guess it's only us then."

"Yeah, let's take my offi...." Scarlette cut herself off. "Sorry."

"For what? For accepting and finding your place here? Make this house yours, too? Baby, my mom would have loved to see you working there. It's your office, not just unofficially, you should know that by now."

"Okay. Thank you."

"Of course."

Settling in at the desk, Tyler opened the first envelope and carefully took out the notes. Along with the smell of aged paper, reminding them both of old libraries, there was an underlying chemical scent. They both saw more now than they did the first time, some words were rather clear. But it was still hard to make out complete sentences.

"These are the treated originals. They told me they'd send them back, but we would have an easier time reading the reproductions. With the process they used, these require some specific light sources to better read them."

"On to the second envelope, then?"

"I'd say so. Let's put these back." He fiddled a little to protect the old paper, then reached for the other envelope.

Inside were pictures of the notes, freshly treated and apparently scanned or photographed with the correct lights set up. They had enlarged the notes in the pictures, and it still took some concentration to make out some parts. But there was enough to make sense when you knew what had been going on.

You looked so very involved, I did not want to interrupt.
But I took this photograph, it shows you so clearly enjoying
yourselves.
I presume you will want me to keep this a secret.
Leave a case of the gin you secretly brew for your parties out
by the pear tree tonight,
Or this filthy picture will find its way to a newspaper.
For the gin alone I could hand you to the coppers,
But what good would it do, knowing the Chief of Police
attends your little parties?

"Oh god, that must be one of the blackmail notes. They kept them?"

"Maybe they were trying to find a way to stop them, much like we are. It's a threat all right, but it doesn't ask for too much. With prohibition looming over the country, there were all kinds of home distilleries to brew bathtub gin or homemade wines for personal use. It wasn't strictly legal, but it wasn't followed up on as much as on people selling alcohol. Especially not if the Chief of Police could get his share, I'd think."

"True. I guess they destroyed the picture."

"I would have. And probably hoped that only the one existed."

"Yes. Here, this is a different handwriting." Scarlette picked up another note, read it together with Tyler.

1923

Dear Charles,

Thank you for your letter.

I agree with you, it is a precarious situation, but what can I say? I grew up with Cecille next door for so long, she is family to me. I see her as a surrogate sister.

When she confided in me, and it cost her dearly, she was bitterly afraid and unspeakably ashamed. I could do nothing but open my heart for her. Is it an illness? I cannot say anything about that, I can only say I have never seen her truly happy before. Now, no matter the burden, she finds those moments of glee, and isn't that what we all strive for?

She came to me, to ask me for this marriage to provide her a cloak of security, and I find myself not being able to deny it to her, because she deserves love.

Do I expect you to do the same for Mary-Beth? No, I don't expect it, but I hope in your heart you cherish the friendship you have shared for so long enough to wish her the bliss she seems to have found.

I cannot tell you what to do, or how to decide, I can only tell you I can't see harm in making a friend happy.

Details can always be explored, and should one of us find a woman to fall in love with, to consider a family, there would be ways. For me, it is easy at this point in my life. I need to focus on my career for now, I could not start a family.

I understand all your doubts and concerns, Charles, and I shall not tell you what you have to decide on your own, I can only tell you my decision and my reasons.

Your friend,
Eton

"Holy shit! They knew! They went into these marriages as a cover for their friends. That's incredibly sweet."

"It reads like it, and yes, it is. I would say this also completely crushes the murder theory, by the way."

"Well, you could always argue they changed their minds,

but I find that highly doubtful after five years. Okay, let's keep reading."

The following notes gave them a testament of the strong friendship between the men over the years, even though they had only Eton's written side to go on. Career advice, recaps of some premiere, much the same complaints about some boss or other you might hear today, some sports chat, discussions on prohibition.

"This is awesome, it shows they were people, same as you and me. I think that's something we always forget when we study history, when we study what survived through the ages. Those were people too, with the challenges of their time for sure, but they had their everyday lives, their friendly chatter, too," Scarlette said.

"Yes, you are right. It's absolutely charming."

Tapping one of the notes against her palm, Scarlette looked Ty in the eyes. "You know, I think we should see if we could get that house up and running again and turn it into a museum. Kind of honoring them, and banishing the years of neglect by the O'Learys and their descendants."

"I like that idea. We'll check it out."

"Okay."

They found another note, and their mood sobered again quickly.

1928

Dear Charles,

Cecille told me about a note Mary-Beth got the other night.

I advised her to destroy or at the very least lock every-thing she might have kept of her correspondence in a bank box, at the most leave only a hidden clue somewhere should she be afraid to forget the numbers.

I would advise you or Mary-Beth to hide or destroy everything that could incriminate us all as well. I know you keep these letters in the safe, but we cannot be sure they don't have access to it.

Just think about it, who would have been able to take the photograph Cecille mentioned? Nothing like this ever happened before, and now with this new family as housekeepers, they know the villa inside and out, like we do.

This sounded like a small request, but I am not sure it will stay that way.

Your friend,

Eton

"This must have been after the first note."

"Yes, and Mary-Beth had apparently hidden everything under the gazebo after that. I think Eton was right, I severely doubt they stopped after that. She hid the box when? Summer?"

"Yeah, there were roses in bloom. My mom gardens a little," Scarlette explained when she saw the question in Tyler's eyes.

"The new housekeepers had been on for a few months by

then, maybe Mary-Beth and Cecille got a little careless, and the first note came in," she speculated.

"And it goes on and on until Mary-Beth can't take it anymore, kills herself."

"And Cecille follows her a day later."

Tyler nodded. "Yes. No wonder the O'Learys did everything to keep the house. They couldn't know whether the O'Briens or Barrets knew for certain it was them, but they would probably have felt the distrust and paranoia rising."

"And didn't know if there might still be a small hiding place they weren't aware of, hadn't found, where some form of proof of their blackmail scheme was kept, a scheme ultimately sending two women to their deaths."

"Exactly."

"You'll have some family past to write about, Link."

"Yes. But currently I'm more concerned with the present. The second deadline ends tomorrow."

"And so far, we have an old family name, layers and layers of false owners, maybe a vague suspicion of your agent's assistant, and some guy hitting on July."

Luke stepped in, humming a happy tune. Work had obviously been successful for him.

"Ah, sounds like we're all on the same page again. I'm interested in your work there, but I can tell you when it comes to mine, the vague suspicion has gotten a lot more definite for the two you just mentioned there."

"Has it? We're all ears."

"Let's take this back to the main office for this and wait for July. She is downstairs getting fresh coffee for everybody."

"Awesome."

As it was more urgent at the moment, Luke began with his update.

"So, Ty, good news, your agent appears to be clean. And don't even pretend to be pissed that I ran her, too. Likes to drive fast, that's about it. But her doe-eyed, unassuming assistant, going by the company photos and your input, seems far from clean, once you dig a little deeper. Everything an employer might check holds: address, bank account, social security number, even a very tame social media profile. But when you start cross-referencing those, try to follow them further back, there's either no data to find or so much that it's impossible to sort through." Luke opened another file, smirked at Julia. "As for your boyfriend Jake here..."

"Huh, I thought the boyfriend was you. Oh well, that's okay, I'm sure Jake and I will enjoy the stay at the Tantra retreat I booked for next month very much."

"Well played, and I will be heavily disappointed if there isn't a Tantra retreat scheduled when I come to Australia. In any case, the same goes for Jake. With a description and the name of the law firm, I could find him. He hasn't been there long. And running him, I got the same superficially correct data, but then it gets wild for him, too.

"I talked to my boss about this already, we're getting several warrants. I need to check on travel for Jake, need access to financial information on both, get into their social media accounts, and so on. The warrants will need a little time, but at this point, we're fairly sure to get them. I know it doesn't sound like much as of now, but it's a good thing to start with."

"No, Luke, it's great. This is a lot more than we had before. We have figured out most of the past, I think. But as

Ty said to me earlier, the present is more concerning right now. This is a good point to start, and with some luck, they don't know we know about them, yet," Scarlette told him.

"Agreed. I'll keep you all updated on this. Now, what did you two find out?"

They explained everything to Luke and July, and all four studied the board with the latest information pinned to it after.

"Okay, that wraps up what happened between 1923 and 1928. But how did we get from 'We'll expose your ancestors' wives' lesbian affair' to 'Your ancestors freaking killed their wives?'"

"Good question, July, and we have no idea. It must have happened sometime in the seventies, but why, no clue. I feel like, on our side of the game, every generation constantly destroyed everything or almost everything, and hoped things would stop with their death at some point."

Ty ran his hands absently up and down Scarlette's arms. "Maybe the other side has kept some records. We'll see. For now, we have to wait until you get these warrants, right, Luke?"

"Yes, pretty much."

"Okay. Then let's get the living room ready for an after-dinner battle. I have to prove my wife wrong and defeat her in *Mario Kart*."

"Ha, you wish. I'll kick your ass!"

While they were busy arranging the living room, Josh came home. Ty managed to talk to him before dinner and counted it a success when they both didn't die of embarrassment.

"Oh, tell Bonny she's always welcome here, too."

"I will. But I want things finished and kind of back to normal here before I invite her over."

"Might be better, yes. Okay, dinner, and then we'll see who'll be the champion in this house."

Ty grumbled, but had to agree when later Josh crowned Scarlette said champion.

"How? Seriously, you could probably drive the damn *Rainbow Road* blindfolded."

"Can, did. There are audio clues."

"That's just bragging at this point."

"Link, I warned you. But I'm proud of you, you didn't cry, you only threatened to divorce me twice, and only once to kill me. I had expected worse."

The daggers shooting from his eyes clearly said *I'll show you worse later* and had her laugh wildly.

And her phone pinged.

Chapter Twenty-Five

S he checked the screen and jumped up from the couch.

"Oh, shit! That's an alarm from my security system. Luke, send someone to my office. There's a break-in." She rattled off the address and was already running out of the room.

Luke called it in right away, followed Scarlette and Ty, who had been out of the room as fast as his wife.

"Wait, both of you. What are you planning to do? I have cops on the way, they'll be there within minutes. Even punching it, it would take too long to do something useful. Scarlette, show me your phone. Is there camera footage?"

She was angrily pacing, impatient to get into a car, but handed her phone over.

"Yeah. I had a system installed when I started to work with the authorities. Like I said, I never really had problems, but you still get hollow threats from time to time. And depending on the case, some files might become relevant in court hearings, so I protect everything."

"That's good. Okay, we got a video feed of the guy, but he is wearing a mask. Anything familiar about him?"

She leaned closer, checked the screen herself. "No, it could be anybody. Sorry."

"No need. What is he doing there?"

Tyler leaned in from the other side, studied the video. "I think he's carving something into the desk. And apparently, that's too much work," Ty concluded when the perpetrator grabbed a piece of paper, scribbled something on it, and pinned it to the desk with the knife he had used for the carving. Then he cocked his head as if listening for something and fled the office.

"That will be my colleagues interrupting him."

But when Luke got a call a short time later, he exploded.

"What do you mean you couldn't find him?! He must have run into your damn arms! No, I don't want to hear you're sorry, I want you to find him, damn it."

A moment of listening didn't help to calm him down. "No, you do not see the point, apparently. And you don't have to understand why this is important. Do your goddamn job and find the man." Another pause. "Do I have to tell you how to do that, now? Get the freaking super, get the landlord, find out the security system for the building, check the damn cameras. If he didn't run into you, he's probably still somewhere in the building! How long have you been a cop? Five years?! That's... oh, really? Stellar records? Not after this, believe me. Do the job, then call me back!" Luke dragged a hand through his hair. "Damn idiot. Scarlette, we'll get this figured out, believe me. And this moron won't be able to rest his lazy ass on his performance reviews anymore."

Luke's furious outburst had surprisingly done a lot to

calm her down, and she laid a hand on his arm. "I believe you. And even if they don't find him, it's another lead to work with. If it's connected, which, okay, I think we're all sure of."

"You're right. But, as annoyed as I am, I meant it. Help me start working on this from here. Even if you were there, you couldn't do anything. We'll have a Crime Scene team go over it, get everything to the lab. Would be best if you kept the place closed tomorrow, though."

"Ah, yeah, I can arrange for that. Should I be there for anything?"

"No, you don't have to. It's enough to let your people know there was a minor incident, you need to keep the office shut down for a day. Getting in and out isn't a problem. Can you tell me anything about the building's security?"

"Some. Usually, the alarm system is switched on at seven in the evening. That's when every office should be closed and empty. We and some other offices offer Saturday hours and instead close Sundays and Mondays. Easier for people with regular weekday jobs to come see us, then.

"Also on Saturdays, one of our vets offers a medical consultation as a group info night – that's prepping future owners on what's important, like vaccines and stuff, or what breeds need special attention, but no actual exams or anything. That runs from seven to eight. But you'd only know that if you make an appointment, or maybe if you work in the building and have seen people come in. So on Saturday, the alarm is switched on shortly after eight."

"Okay, that's helpful. Anything else?"

"Ah, you will trigger an alarm when you go in after these hours, but as tenants, we have a key code to prevent that. And if you find yourself inside the building after hours, there's also a key to get out without triggering the alarm, but you'd need to be on the inside for that and only the tenants know it."

"Even better. Can you tell me about the companies there besides you?"

Scarlette huffed out a breath. "Not really. There's a nutritionist, and some interior decorator, I think. But honestly, we're on the second floor, below us is the super's office, a small coffee shop with another entrance. I don't really pay attention to the other offices, because I never had problems with them."

"Completely understandable. I'll look them up."

Ty felt terribly useless and paced next to them, until Scarlette took his hand and stopped him. "Babe, I wanna do something, too, but Luke is right. Go tell July and Josh things are okay, there are cops at the scene already."

"Yes, all right."

Her gaze followed him, and she dug her nails into her palms. Someone would pay for screwing with them like this. She turned back to Luke when his phone rang again.

His eye roll and the growl in his throat told her how close he was to crawling through the phone to strangle the caller. "Yes, send them over. I will have someone come by and take over from you."

He hung up with a barely contained curse. "They'll send me pictures from the scene, I'll get Leroy on the line, send him over."

"Okay."

Scarlette got back to the others, pushed them to clean up to keep everybody busy.

When Luke called them to the office, Scarlette saw he

had hijacked one of the wall screens, had put up the picture of her desk.

Carved into it were the words *"PAY BITCH"* and on the paper, the intruder had scribbled *"You both have until 8 pm tomorrow."*

"No new instructions, that's good, right Luke? They have kept the payment account online, then. They might not know how long we've been working on this with a cop on board. Even after today, they'd think it would take longer to get where we are."

"Yes, you're right, July. And I will have to keep working on this."

"I can help you. You know I can," Josh said when Luke wanted to wave it away.

"Yeah, you probably could. The rest of you..." Luke sighed. "I honestly don't know what you could do at the moment."

"Hm, okay, what about this?" said Scarlette. "Ty, you're behind on your schedule, right? Why don't you see if you can focus some of that anger on work instead? Luke, if there needs to be someone at my office after all, let me know. My mom or dad could get there. I will have to make a few calls myself, and after that, July and I will be in the gym. We haven't trained together in forever. With all the crap going on, it might be a good idea to wake up the muscle memory."

"Oh, I'm all for that. Plus, great way to relieve some of the anger."

"Yep, my thoughts exactly."

A very edgy group split up for the evening, hoping to be productive in one way or the other.

Chapter Twenty-Six

They had given the O'Briens a deadline, now it was time for a family meeting of their own to talk about what to do, how to make things public should there be no payment. For now, everything was secured in the apartment, though. If they truly needed to publish anything, they could still get it, but so far everybody had crumbled under the pressure in the end.

After picking up the second sensible family member, they discussed the right approach on the way.

But at the meeting, any "right" way seemed to vanish. The cat. The car. Those had been bad enough. But they had hardly entered when they heard a gloating voice talking about a break-in, about leaving a message. About how close it had been with the cops, and the only chance to flee had been to hide in a huge transport box smelling like cat and piss until the cops had left the office to talk to the super, making it possible to sneak out.

No, this wouldn't do anymore. They had to be stopped.

"What do you think you were doing? We have a plan, we

will follow that plan."

"About that. We figured the old plan sucks. They have a deadline. They pay. If they don't, we will start hurting them. Beginning with the whiny little brother. Once we publish, there won't be any leverage left. This way they will pay to keep their bastard families safe in a much more real sense."

"Oh, oh no. You cannot do that. We have never hurt anybody in all those years. It isn't right."

That got a derisive sneer. "And look where we are. Creeping around some small apartments because we constantly need to pay for that stupid pile of junk in California. Needing to work, to keep up a charade. We could be swimming in money! If any of our previous generations — that includes you two by the way — had had any vision, we wouldn't have to be so fucking aggressive. We softened, they hardened, how is that right? Their families messed up with the women screwing each other. We were protecting them! We were fair enough not to make it public back then, others would have. We gave them a choice."

"It was never right what our family did back then, you cannot believe that. We keep doing this because we now need to protect our family. There might still be proof, and if it comes out, can you even imagine the damages we would have to pay?"

"Ah, but it will never come out. We are cleverer than all of you ever were, and we will start to really live. And we're sick and tired of your cautiousness, of you constantly trying to hold us back. That ends now."

The gun pointed at them so quickly, the bullets hit their targets fast as lightning.

Reason was gone completely.

Chapter Twenty-Seven

Scarlette and July were about to finish their extended one-on-one training after a warm-up on the machines, when Tyler appeared in the doorway. He saw his wife executing a well-aimed kick that sent Julia skidding back on the mat. The women bowed to each other, and Ty inclined his head.

"I didn't know you'd be doing a karate session."

"I said we wanted to get back some moves."

"Yeah, but I wasn't aware you do martial arts, both of you. Very impressive."

"I always did some, beefed it up when Patrick got started with the stalking. And July, you know her mom is FBI."

"Yes, and it reminds me you were right when you first said she could get them to open a file on me."

July grinned. "Totally could. I'd say I don't need to anymore. But it is like it is, and my mom taught me self-defense from early on. What we do is mostly karate, but also other things thrown in. In the end, what style or method you use doesn't matter as much as getting out of a dangerous situation."

"And what you can use might depend on your surroundings, too. Like with Patrick. Sure, I could have used different moves, also some with little movement and more making use of angles and levers. But given the dress, the heels, it was easy and efficient. July gets that, that's why we work out together. It's always surprising, keeps you on your toes when you don't know what technique will be applied next. And it keeps you aware that the outside world doesn't always come with people attacking you exactly like you learned it in the dojo."

"I have a damn smart wife."

"You do. What brings you here? I thought you were working."

"Was. Then your mom called. She had some news and texted you to call her. When you didn't read the message, she got concerned, and called me."

"I must have missed the notification. Thanks, I'll call her back."

Scarlette put the phone up to have a camera and connected it for the call to the screen on the wall for a bigger picture. Grabbing a towel and water, she cleaned up a little, then Cynthia answered.

"Mom, hey. Sorry, July and I were training. What's wrong?"

"Baby, I'm glad you're okay. It's... I just heard they found Dr. Branson dead in his apartment."

"What? How? Did he have a heart attack or something?"

"No. It seems like there was a break-in, and he was killed while trying to stop it."

"Oh my god."

Tyler saw Cynthia battling composure into place over the shock of losing a colleague, and Julia and Scarlette gripping hands, paling a little. But for him, something began to hum in his mind.

"Wait, is that the same Dr. Branson you told Scarlette you had seen in LA a few days ago, July?"

"It must be. Our old pediatrician, right Cynthia?"

"Yes. LA? What do you mean?"

"Ah, when I came over from Australia, I bumped into him at the airport by coincidence."

"Mom, was there any major conference or something?" Scarlette had picked up on Ty's suspicion already.

"No, not before later this year. But why would he..."

Scarlette held up a hand to silence her mother, and turned to her husband.

"Your agent's assistant, probably somebody in my office building – I have seen the wheels in Luke's head turning. Generations of blackmail. Wanna bet fifty he was in on this?" Turning back, she faced her mother on the screen again. "Mom, did you by chance talk to him before or after I flew out to California?"

"Ah, yes, we bumped into each other at one of the hospitals we both volunteer for. He asked how you were doing, how your business was going. Normal questions, small talk really. I only mentioned you were taking a little deserved time off, were taking a trip West. Baby, I'm sorry if..."

"No mom, no. It's all good. Trust me, if he was really part of all this, he would have found out any other way."

"Okay. Oh god. I brought you there as a child. I..."

"Mom, there is absolutely no way you could have known. He knew I was adopted, right? But at that time my biological mother was still alive, was the one being pressured for money. Right now, we don't even know if it's true. It might all be a freak coincidence."

"But you don't believe that. Is Luke still there?"

"Yes. And we should talk to him."

"Then do so."

"Okay. Mom, be careful, all of you. This gets crazier every day."

"We will be."

Scarlette stomped angrily over to the main house. "Fucking assholes. This will eat at her, she'll blame herself for giving them a close line to me."

"Yes, and we will make them pay, baby, I promise."

"Thanks. Is Luke upstairs?"

"I heard him mumbling to himself when I walked down, yes."

"Okay. Where were you working?"

"Our bedroom. I only needed my laptop. Can't call the UK at this hour, so I refined some paragraphs, went over the notes I got back."

"If you need more room while your office is blocked, let me know. I'll shuffle over and you can use my desk, too."

"Thanks, Sparks."

They took the last steps, heard Luke speaking with his boss. "Yes, Leroy, I know a murder is more important, and you'll get more pressure from above when it's a prominent guy like the doctor. But I would appreciate it, if you could make sure you route the findings of the break-in at Scarlette's place to your and my desk only."

In a strangely simultaneous gesture, Scarlette, Ty, and

July all cocked their heads, and Luke frowned at them. Tyler picked up a pen and a piece of paper.

Leroy – Branson case?

He got a nod from the detective, so he scribbled something else.

We think it's connected to all this.

Luke suddenly stopped talking to Leroy, looked from one to the other, and only huffed out. "Shit."

Focusing back on his call again, he interrupted his boss. "Leroy, wait. The others just got in and told me the murder might be connected. I'll put you on speaker, and they can explain everything to both of us directly."

There was a long moment of silence when they had finished. "Damn." It was all Leroy said at first, then they heard a few steps. "Okay, I needed some privacy. Luke, usually I'd say get your ass here, but depending on if and how extensively they are watching you all, that could give them the idea we know more than they expected. For now, you have a few days off, visiting a friend after his wedding. Congrats, by the way. Shitty way to celebrate, though."

Scarlette bubbled out a sarcastic laugh. "Yeah, you could say that. But thanks."

They couldn't talk long with Leroy needing to work the crime scene, but arranged for a call in the morning by which time Leroy hopefully would have more to work with.

After hanging up, Ty watched his friend with pity in his eyes. "Sorry, man. Seems like your evening just became a whole lot busier."

"Hardly your fault."

"Still. I don't assume we can do a lot to help you with anything?"

"No, not really."

"Okay. We'll leave you to it, then. I think Josh will stay here with you. And the rest of us have some work to catch up on."

Scarlette and Julia both nodded in agreement and left the room together with Tyler so the geeks could keep digging without interruptions.

Chapter Twenty-Eight

The morning began — much to Scarlette's delight — with a flood of coffee. Lorraine had also prepared a breakfast buffet to feed half of a third-world country, and Ty stared at the display she had set up in the office.

"Now, don't be so skeptical. You all have a lot of thinking to do, that takes as much energy as other things. You need to eat to stay sharp so this can all finally be shut down. And maybe I feel a little useless otherwise at the moment."

"Lorraine, you are not, you know that."

"Knowing and feeling are different things. Let me do this, I'm good at this."

"You are seriously amazing at this," Scarlette corrected, and shoveled some bacon and eggs in her mouth.

"Girl, where do you put all that food?"

"Awesome metabolism, high-energy personality, lots of sex."

"You're a lucky one. Well, I can't complain either, I know. If you need anything else today, tell me."

"We will. Thanks, this is much appreciated."

They were still fueling up when Leroy called in. He sounded equally pissed and pumped. "Morning everybody. As I know Luke will update you anyway, let's get the most important things out.

"Branson wasn't shot in his home. Nobody heard any shots, but they clearly heard the noise when the place was tossed. And there's nowhere near enough blood for him to have bled out here. The ME is examining the body now and will get back to us. We did find traces of cocaine. Any chance you would know if Branson was using, Mrs. O'Brien, Ms. Stone?"

"No. I don't know, but I wouldn't think so. But I also wouldn't have thought he might be involved in a blackmail scheme." Scarlette turned a little toward Julia, and her friend nodded.

"Yes, same from my end."

"Okay. Coming to that involvement. Witnesses called the police when they heard the loud clatter and saw light beams moving in the house. They didn't see anybody flee but thought they had seen at least two light sources. Seems they left before they found what they were searching for. There are enough valuables here, easy to carry ones, that were left behind. An open safe is empty, possibly some money is missing, but that appears to be it. From what it looks like, they took advantage when they found it while hunting for something else.

"Going over the scene with the idea this could be connected to your case, I also searched for some less obvious places to stash potentially incriminating things. I found a switch opening a hidden compartment behind a wall socket. It contained a box with an old ledger, some notes. I had a quick glance, sounds like it would be helpful to have you read them over. I'll be on my way to you soon."

"Okay."

They used the time until Leroy arrived to get some work of their own done, with Scarlette filling out some discount forms for those having to reschedule appointments planned for that day. Beside her, Tyler shot a text to Vi, urging her to be careful.

Scarlette tapped her fingers on the desk in an annoyed rhythm. "Remind me to sue them for damages when the cops bag them. This day alone costs me a couple hundred dollars, and I will have to replace my desk or have it repaired, the locks checked, and possibly replaced."

"They won't have a cent left. Our lawyers will make sure of that."

"It's small of me, but that's a bright spot."

When Leroy arrived, the women learned he was about five years older than they were, sported a scarred black leather jacket with jeans and t-shirt, and his short hair burned an even brighter red than Scarlette's. They were all on a first-name basis before they even reached the office.

When he stepped in, he whistled. "Impressive work, I have to say. This will help us to tie this all up with a pretty bow for the DA. Let's see what you make of this."

He set the box on the table, and when Scarlette checked with him, he nodded. "Go on, we examined everything already, took prints where we could."

"Okay."

She reached for the ledger first, scanned a page, then the

next. "These are notes on what they demanded from them. They were damn meticulous. Listen to this:

- June - 1 crate of gin (6 bottles), delivered on time
- June - 1 bottle of perfume, delivered a day late (C. arrived 1 day late at house; compensation demanded)
- June - Compensation (red lipstick) left in dressing room after departure
- July - New dress for cousin Lucille's wedding, delivered on time

This goes on and on. Middle of August they ask for money for the first time, and the sums they demand keep growing every time. This would be a fortune today."

Tyler shook his head. "Four and a half months before they couldn't take it anymore."

"Yes. Four and a half months until they knew this would never stop."

"And it hasn't for almost a century. It will now."

Leroy took back the ledger, nodded. "It will. But where does the alleged murder come from?" He held up an old photo of two women in bed, caught in a passionate kiss. "How did we get from abusing something nice and actually pretty hot to the kill shot photos on your wall?"

Luke surfaced from a note he had been reading. "I think I might have something on that. This is dated 1964."

No evidence found in mansion, yet. Family discussed new strategy and extending the requests to next generation. Payments have arrived later with every request. Possibly due to progression of Eton's and Charles' mental decay after both their experiences in the war.

Other reason discussed: state of society. Focus too much on the war. Publicly revealing women's affair might not be a sufficient lever in the future.

Possible to stage murder by husbands? Careful planning and infiltration needed to evaluate how many family secrets have been shared.

"That's just sick."

"So when the lesbian affair wasn't enough of a scandal anymore they decided, 'screw it, we have already fucked with them for forty years, let's see how we can make it even worse in the future?'" July was outraged on behalf of her friends and threw her arms in the air. "That's more than sick."

"Yes. And then you do some math and realize they still had years to squeeze money out of Charles and Eton: they died around the same time. And also years to set up the plans for their little murder shooting," Scarlette added.

"And now they have gone even further and killed a man for real – one of their own family," Tyler finished grimly.

"Yes. We will find them, believe me. They will be brought to justice. Julia?"

"Yes, Leroy?"

"I looked you up, I saw your mother is FBI. The feds will want to be in on this, seeing as this reaches over state lines and over decades. Do you think she'd work with me on this once we have them and wrap this up, so we can be sure justice and Scarlette's and Ty's families will be paramount and not the tug-of-war between cops and feds?"

"Yeah, I think so. She's still on medical leave after a knee operation, but she's supposed to be back on duty next week or the week after. Desk duty at first, which wrapping up will probably mean mostly. I guess it should work."

"Great. We'll talk in detail later. For now, I gotta get back to the city. You try to have a more or less normal day here, if they have eyes on you, we want them to think you have no idea about anything."

"Yes, all right."

Chapter Twenty-Nine

"If they don't pay this evening, we will need to make a bigger impression. So far they think we might hurt a little kitty, that's not exactly scary."

"Like I said, he has this little brother. What do you think he would do to protect him? Losing mommy and daddy was already so hard, wasn't it? Can't lose the little bro."

"And what do you have in mind?"

"I picked up some things along the way. A little firework should be very convincing. I persuaded the old hag to put a tracker onto the boy's car, I'll get to it and fiddle a little. We text the brother from a burner phone, let him know something will happen to the boy at 8:01 pm, if they don't pay. Send it right before 8 pm, I bet they will pay to protect the brat. I need that money."

"So do I, so stop whining. Yes, we can do that."

Should it be so easy? The threats, the blood on their hands? A human life suddenly was nothing anymore, because they needed money. Self-preservation and greed, they could distort a person until you couldn't recognize them anymore. A long tradition, based on right or wrong didn't matter right now, discarded and overtaken by something much darker.

This was calculated madness.

Chapter Thirty

Josh was thankful to Leroy. The comment about a normal day had made it a lot easier for him to convince his brother to let him accept Bonny's invitation to dinner. Tyler had at first become more reluctant to let his younger brother go, with the murder now more than likely being connected to all the rest.

But even with all the ongoing threats — maybe especially with them — normal had sounded just like what Josh needed. And his day had only gotten better when Bonny had texted him to come by a little earlier, then had dragged him out into the heat of the late afternoon for a walk. They had done their best to ignore the knowing glances from Bonny's parents, but as soon as they had reached the little summer house at the other end of the yard, they forgot about anything else other than getting their hands on the other.

Nervousness overshadowed by the rush of falling in love for the first time and still tasting Bonny on his lips, Josh enjoyed dinner with her family. Her parents were kind but didn't treat him like a cracked egg that needed to be handled with the utmost care, her brother liked comics, too, and her sister got starry-eyed when he told her that sure, she could come by one day to see the horses.

It was a nice evening. With everything currently going on at home, it was a great evening, if he was honest. He loved home, and he was happy for Ty and Scarlette, but it was crazy at the moment. This evening gave him the chance to relax a little, be the teenager that he was.

After dinner, he smiled at Bonny's parents. "Mrs. Robins, Mr. Robins, thank you again for the invitation. My brother, his wife, and I would be happy to have you and the rest of your family over to dinner or a barbecue soon, too." Okay, technically Ty had invited Bonny, but Josh knew it wouldn't be a problem to have her whole family over.

And he was sure it was going to be more fun than the neighborhood brunch they more or less had to give soon. That was okay, too, but with Bonny's family, he really got along.

"Josh, that's really sweet. We'll be sure to schedule that in."

Bonny grinned, took Josh's hand under the table. "Perfect, mom. So, can I stay over at Josh's?"

"Not tonight, sorry. Every other time, though. Your dad and I talked and we don't have a problem with it, as long as it's okay for Josh's family, too."

"Ah, yes, it is, my brother already told me it would be."

"Good. We all know you're responsible, and we trust you to keep being responsible. That's why, in general, yes, you can, but not tonight. I need you early tomorrow to help me prepare for the market day."

Bonny scowled a little but nodded. "Yes, okay."

"Thank you, sweetie. Why don't you two enjoy a little more time outside, while your siblings and your dad help me clear the table?"

Since this didn't get any complaint, groan, or even a hidden eye-roll, Josh was pretty sure Mrs. Robins was leading the household with an iron, but fair hand.

And being on the receiving end of the fair hand that night, Bonny thanked her mom with a kiss on the cheek, let Josh say goodbye, and led him to the front porch.

Chapter Thirty-One

Scarlette and Tyler came to the house after checking on the horses together, and she was relieved she could still find a reason to laugh. "'Course you'd name her Epona, why am I not surprised?"

"Like you would have given her any other name."

"True."

"She liked you, that's good. We'll have to find one for you, too. I want to go on that ride with you."

"Okay."

They found Lorraine in the kitchen, anxiously folding and refolding a dishtowel.

"Lorraine, what's up?"

"Ah, I just hung up on a call with a friend because we wanted to plan a shopping trip. She told me Ms. Adams didn't show up on a staff meeting call today. Usually, they don't have calls now, but there's an extra program during the break this year. Anyway, she was the one who had organized the call, and you know she always attends meetings, Tyler."

"Yes."

"Who is she?"

"The principal of my former school, still Josh's principal." And a damning suspicion crept up his spine. "Josh told me he ran into her while waiting for Bonny on their date night."

Lorraine shook her head in disbelief. "You can't think she'd be part of this."

"I bet Scarlette and her family didn't expect a doctor with supposedly high moral ethics to be part of it, either."

They couldn't argue any longer, because Luke and Julia came into the kitchen.

"Ah, good. I need coffee. But now I can update you. We got the first warrants for some of the tech side. The email address brought me back to Josh's school when it was used to create the payment service account. Now, I'm not saying Josh..."

"No, and you don't have to. His principal, Ms. Adams, coincidentally missed a staff call today."

"Really now?"

"Yes."

Tyler's phone pinged and he was about to ignore it, but something told him to check.

"Fuck! I need to call Josh!"

He was already getting started when Scarlette handed him her phone. "Use mine, Luke and I need to see this."

She stared at the screen with Luke, felt the same icy panic run through her that Ty was battling down while calling his brother.

Tick-tock, it's 7:59, you better pay right now, or there'll be some pretty fireworks at 8:01.
Your brother and little Ronny are just saying goodbye, what timing.
Ah, young love. What do you think she'd say to see him blown to pieces right in their driveway?

"Josh, get away from your car!" Ty yelled it into the phone, already running to the front door, grabbing his keys.

He could hear the explosion loud and clear through the phone, and so could the others. Scarlette yelled to July while following Ty. "Take care of Lorraine, we'll call you and let you know!"

The cook had gone white as a sheet. July levered her to the floor, watched after her friends, and prayed Josh was okay.

Chapter Thirty-Two

The explosion was amazing. So much force with so little effort. It might have gone off "accidentally" even if they had paid. But this was better, now they had to take the blame for it. They could have stopped it with only a few clicks, a little money being transferred. And really, what did it hurt them? They swam in it.

Too bad the boy's phone had rung just before he had been in the car. But it had looked like he had still been hit hard. Was it bad to hope it had been hard enough to kill him? No. His brother needed to learn his place. It was a shame there was no time to watch him fall apart. But the cops would soon be here.

And killing turned out to be so... thrilling. Such a rush. To have the power to decide about life and death. Was there anything more important?

Chapter Thirty-Three

L uke got into his own car, Scarlette jumped into the car with Ty. "You drive, I don't know where we're going. Give me the phone."

She listened for anything and could hear muffled yells. Bonny calling for Josh. She heard a deeper moan, hoped fervently it came from her brother-in-law.

Tyler flew down the drive, Luke followed. Before he could ask, Scarlette updated him.

"I can hear a girl, and there's groaning and hissing. Okay, there's Josh's voice. He seems clear enough from what I hear. It's muffled, but he's talking. Probably in shock, but coherent. There are other voices. Bonny's parents, I guess."

She switched to speaker now that she was somewhat assured of Josh's state, and they both heard some scratching, then the voices became more distant.

"I think they're bringing him inside. The phone must be lying on the floor or something. How much further?"

"Nearly there, they live close."

It only took a minute or two longer, but time was flowing

by like thick syrup. They were racing down the main road, skidding around curves, but it felt like a crawl.

Finally, they could see the destruction in front of a house, and Ty braked with screeching tires. They were both out of the car almost before it came to a complete stop, and Luke followed them with his own phone on his ear calling for the locals and the fire department.

Ty hardly stopped at the front door, ran straight in.

He jerked back and threw up his hands when he had a shotgun pointed at him. "Woah, okay. That's my brother over there. I'm Tyler O'Brien."

From the living room came a hoarse mumble. "Yeah, that's Ty."

Bonny's dad let them through, and Tyler sank to his knees beside the couch, ran his hands over the boy.

"Oh god, Josh. Are you okay? Have you called an ambulance?" he asked Bonny's mother.

"Yes, I have. They'll be here any minute. I'm a trained nurse, I checked him out. He's in shock, has some scrapes and bruises, probably a light concussion from hitting the pavement, but from what I can see here without more diagnostics, that's it."

"Thank you, thank you so much."

Ty and Bonny both focused on Josh. Scarlette ran a hand over the boy's hair, kissed his forehead, before turning to Bonny's father.

"Mr. Robins, thank you for taking care of Josh, for bringing him in here and trying to protect him from whoever did this."

"Of course. We have no idea what happened. He and Bonny were outside, saying goodbye, and suddenly there was this explosion. Do you have an idea? How did you know to come?"

"We actually do. And we're sorry you got involved in this."

"What do you mean? This isn't some sick racist attack by some of your rich neighbors or family, is it?"

"No, that's not it. But..." She glimpsed over at Ty, saw him and Bonny both holding Josh's hands, and made the decision to trust a strong family foundation. "... this is sensitive, but somebody is trying to blackmail Ty and me. This was their latest incentive to make us pay. Without their taunting message, we couldn't have warned Josh. It could have ended way worse. We never figured on anything like this, and with the police investigating, we were supposed to let it seem like a normal day."

"Then you don't have anything to be sorry about. This is sick, and don't get me wrong, I'm worried for my girl, so until this is finished, she won't be visiting you. But you are much more the victims here than we are as I see it. And don't worry, it won't leave this house. From what I see over there, the kids have something sweet going on, I wouldn't want to ruin it with bad blood between us."

"Again, thank you. Sorry, I hope it's okay, but I have to." Eternally grateful, she leaned over and gave Bonny's father a light kiss on the cheek that made him smile.

"That's all right."

Late in the evening, after Josh had been cleared by the doctors, he had nagged and begged long enough for Tyler and Scarlette to agree to take him home.

Lorraine ran out of the house as soon as Tyler's car was slowing down and had her arms around Josh before he could even get out.

"I'm okay. Scarlette and Ty called you and told you. Some scratches, a sprained wrist, that's it."

"Oh, stop acting brave, stop bullshitting me. You must have been awfully scared, honey."

He knew it was useless to argue, so he gave in and took the comfort her embrace offered.

"Yeah, I was. I just want this over."

"It will be." Luke came out of the house, checked the boy out again. He had already talked to Josh and to Bonny and her family, had left the rest of the scene to the locals and the explosives expert they had called in. Sometimes you needed to play along to get forward.

"Leroy let me know we got more warrants coming through; we'll track them, we'll take them down."

He had a hard time controlling his rage when he saw the wounds all over Josh's face, arms, and legs. He had always liked the boy, they had worked closely together the last few days. He felt like he had let down a partner. "Josh, I'm sorry. I thought it was a good idea to let you go out. I underestimated them."

"Luke, we all did. Or we all didn't figure they'd go down this road. Even when we assume they killed one of their own with the doc, all they ever threatened us with was exposure. We couldn't know they'd do this. It's stupid. With Branson, they had to hope it would be seen as a burglary gone wrong. How or why would we connect him to this? But now, after a violent attack on one of us, and someone in Scarlette's closer environment being killed, somebody in ours gone missing —

Ty told me about Ms. Adams on the way back — they have to know we'd connect the dots sooner or later."

"You are right."

Inside, the group, including Lorraine this time, had just gotten back into the office, when Luke's phone rang. He paced up and down while he listened, acknowledged something with a somber nod. "All right, thank you."

Turning to the others, he ran his fingers through his hair. "That was the County Sheriff. His cops were checking the woods for somebody hiding there after the explosion. They found the body of Marigold Adams, gunshot to the heart. The coroner will examine her. They found her car trashed, it appears like it came off the road a few miles down towards New York on a poorly visible stretch. They assume a carjacking: she was killed, the assailant crashed and fled. I will keep an eye on that, convince them to work with our ME. Maybe we'll find that bullets from the same gun killed her and Branson."

"Good god." Lorraine ran a hand to her throat, and Josh laid an arm around her shoulders. Tyler got her a whisky. "Here, have a drink, Lorraine."

"Thanks, boys. Your mother did a lot right with you."

"So did you. You should..."

"Don't say go home."

"I wasn't. I was going to say you should call your husband, stay in one of the rooms upstairs. With Luke bunking with July by now, you have free choice."

"Thanks, Tyler. I will."

For about an hour they kept busy. Tyler and Scarlette switched from watching Josh to helping Lorraine and her husband get things over for the night from their place. July updated her board with news coming in to Luke – traces of cocaine found in the principal's crashed car, parts of the car bomb discovered, bullets recovered from Adams' body. Luke attached some notes himself to highlight where he would need to convince the locals to work with the city. Josh was annoyed to be under constant watch but figured it was easier to swallow it than put up a fight. At least he could text with Bonny.

Exhaustion had taken its toll and Lorraine's husband had carted her into bed with pity in his desperate eyes. Josh, after a consultation from Ty with the physician who had treated his brother, had crawled into bed, and July was lying curled up on the sofa in the office.

The night was getting heavier every minute until Luke suddenly jumped up. "Fuck, yes!"

"What?" Scarlette and Ty turned around as one from the pot of coffee they had been plundering. On the couch, Julia stirred herself awake, rubbed her tired eyes. "Hm?"

"I managed to get down to the first birth certificate for them. Jake and Tracy, as they go by currently, were born as Todd and Summer Branson. Family business there, I'd say. I have to dig deep on Branson when I have time. I don't know how far back those fake identities go. Their parents apparently live in Alaska, if any of this is correct. And... damn, it says here they were born as triplets. There's another brother. Reed Branson. I don't know by which name he goes by now, but I'm still working on the electronic traces."

"But this is good, really good, already."

"It's progress."

It took almost another hour, but finally, the tracing paid off. "Gotcha! Okay, number three now has a PI office under the name Corey Jacobs in your office building, Scarlette. Easy for him to get information on bombs, to get a license for a gun, if you say you need it for a case and your protection. Do you know him, Scarlette?"

She rounded the desk, studied the picture Luke had opened.

"Shit, yes. Well, not know, but yeah, I have seen him in the building from time to time. PI, right. We never wondered when he carried weird equipment looking like he was preparing to go on a photo safari or equipment to follow a tracker. Damn it."

"You couldn't have known."

"No, and in my head, I know that. But."

"I understand. I will send cops to his official apartment, but it will most likely be empty. I'll keep following this. At some point, it will give me a location from which they have most often worked with it."

"Okay."

Luke was right, he got feedback shortly after that the apartment was as empty as the others had been. But when Scarlette glanced at him, he didn't give off an air of resignation, not even disappointment. "I think he has something," she whispered to Ty.

He watched his friend hack onto the keys, grumble, and give the desk a kick every other minute. "You think?"

"Oh yes, he's getting more and more agitated."

Luke suddenly whipped up his head, shot a fierce glance right at them. "Got the bastards. There's an old warehouse. I already shot Leroy the info. He wants me to come in for the takedown. If I leave now, we can hit them when they're most likely asleep."

"Then you better go."

"On my way."

July got up from the couch, watched Luke gather his keys, his wallet, his gun. How many times had she seen her mom doing the same? Odd, she had always thought she wouldn't fall for the hero type leaving the house in the middle of the night to save the world. It was honorable, but also pretty damn inconvenient for the person staying back at home. But seeing him light up with fresh vigor in anticipation of closing the case, of getting justice for his friends and even for two criminals whose murder was still plain wrong, only opened her heart further for him. She rushed down the stairs with him, dragged him in for one short, intense kiss. "Be careful, I want you to get back to me."

A seriously smug smile spread on his face. "I'll get back to you, baby, don't worry."

Chapter Thirty-Four

L uke had been gone for an hour, and with the knowledge that an update would take at least another two hours of waiting — with the rest of the drive and then the actual action ahead of him — Scarlette ushered July out of the office.

"Sweetie, we have updated the board, we have cleaned up the mugs and all, we need some rest. Go take a shower, lie down for a little while. We'll do the same."

"Okay, okay. I know you're right."

July had hardly taken a step to her room when Ty's phone pinged. She pouted a little, thinking Luke was contacting him rather than her, but then she saw Ty's face.

Chapter Thirty-Five

"You did what?"

"Sis, chill, it's just a text. Untraceable, like the other. They can't make it here in time on the road, you know that. They deserve to pay, and knowing they can't stop this will make them pay so much more. Leaving us hanging dry instead of giving us the money. They need to know everything happening is their own fault."

"You are right about that part, but you're still a moron. Give me that."

A gun exchanged hands, bottles clinked in a bag.

Chapter Thirty-Six

"Oh no." July read the same message as her friends, felt her stomach sink.

Really, you should have just paid.
You decided not to give us the money, so you shouldn't have
any, either.
Let's see what you think about losing your money machines.
It's really nice out here. How about a late barbecue?
You won't make it here in time, and neither will the cops, all
still scattered in the woods.

"The stables, the breeding stables," Ty said.

Scarlette gasped. "We have to get there."

"They are right, from here by car it takes at least twenty minutes because there are no back roads, only fields and small woods."

"Is there any other way?"

"No... wait. Stables, yes. We can take the horses from our retirement stables here to get there."

"Then we will. July, call the cops and the firefighters, stay here and make sure the others are okay."

"Fuck. Yes, all right."

Scarlette and Tyler ran out of the house like the wind, both reached the stables of the compound at the same time.

"You take Epona, she knows you now, she'll listen to you."

"Okay."

Ty was running to the tack room but stopped himself when he saw Scarlette simply opening the box and leading the horse outside and away from the estate, jumping onto the mare's back without a saddle.

"Move, Link!"

She was impatiently waiting for him, and as soon as he had a horse under him as well, she had Epona flying over the grass like a mad thing. Ty and his horse caught up and she let him take the lead, as he had to guide the way.

Over his shoulder, he yelled at her. "Holy shit, Sparks, when you said you could ride, I didn't expect you meant like that!"

"Where's the fun in doing anything half-heartedly? Let's hurry."

"Yes."

The horses felt their riders' urgency and eagerly ate up the ground. It was deep in the night, but the full moon hanging low provided them with enough light to navigate through the backcountry. The ground was mostly flat from there to the breeding facility, but there were small creeks and little groves to pass and Scarlette was glad Tyler knew the terrain.

Thighs pressed into hot flanks, heavy breath came out in huffs and puffs from animals and humans, but they kept moving like shadows in the night, like arrows aiming for their target.

And with Ty knowing every inch of the stable grounds, he was aware there was a small stretch of fence they could get over without stopping.

"We'll have to make one jump. You up for that?"

"'Course."

It felt like only a few seconds later when she saw Tyler and his horse take a leap in front of her, and she fleetingly thought it was good he knew her well enough to be sure she was okay with this because she had no idea how she could have done anything else than jump anyway, considering their speed and direction. Hoofs hit the ground, and they still kept racing, racing toward the beam of a flashlight.

Right in front of the stable doors they stopped, opened the doors further, and saw two men and a woman, all with their hands closed around bottles with rags hanging out of them.

Neither Tyler nor Scarlette wasted any breath with words. They directly ran to the men, who were standing a little closer. But when Ty saw the woman reach behind her back, draw a gun, he changed his target.

For a breathless second, he was sure he heard the shot when he saw her finger closing over the trigger. In his mind, he could already see the bullet flying in Scarlette's direction.

But then his brain realized there was only an empty click, and he heard the woman screech out a frustrated scream. "You idiot! You've been high for days, you haven't reloaded it!"

While Ty reached for her wrist and wrestled the empty gun from her, throwing it over into a heap of straw, Scarlette, on the other hand, was starting to enjoy herself.

Both men tried to grab her, but neither got a proper hold. Instead, Scarlette managed to turn into one of them, rammed her elbow under his jaw, and heard the satisfying sound of teeth crushing hard against teeth.

The other man felt her other elbow jam into his stomach and folded over with a groan.

She felt a hand grip her hair, but before the guy could yank her down, she lifted her foot, kicked hard against the inside of his knee. The lateral displacement had him stagger and release her hair to find his balance and reach out for a hold.

Energy, pure adrenaline, was pumping through her whole body, and when the second guy was coming on to her again, she grinned fiercely. "Try it."

Meanwhile, the woman had managed to get out of Tyler's grip by slipping out of her jacket and was drawing a knife, rambling on. "I have to do everything by myself, like killing his fucking parents and her damn mother. You idiots. Get her!" Running over she was aiming to plunge the knife into Scarlette's back. Ty sprinted after her, tackled her to the ground, and without a moment's regret planted his fist into her face. When she still moaned, he hit her again, then a third time after her previous words processed in his brain.

Scarlette registered the moves, called out to him, and

with that brought him back to her situation before the red haze of rage spreading through him could take control over all his actions. "Thanks, Link! Now, back to you." She adjusted her stance, facing one of the brothers, and Ty wasn't really sure he should intervene.

"Want any help?"

"Nope." She gleefully brought her hand up when the guy came at her, crushed the ball of her hand from beneath into his nose, pushing cartilage against bone. Blood spouted like a fountain. Her hand came down in a fist, punched him hard in the stomach again. It would have been enough to have him retching on the floor, but the final knee to his balls disabled him completely.

She would have joyfully taken on the other man again, but he had sunken to the floor, held his already swollen knee, and was rocking back and forth. "She killed your parents. We didn't know. Oh god, what have we become? I'm sorry, I'm so sorry."

When he actually started to cry, Scarlette drew up her eyebrows, goggled at her husband. "What the hell is this?"

Ty just grinned at her. "You're fucking amazing. I hear cars coming."

Cops and firefighters came running in, and Ty left the unconscious or babbling siblings to the police to take them away, managed to find all potential Molotov cocktails with the firefighters, and checked for any other surprises.

Scarlette gave a first quick statement to one cop while she was getting the horses, who had trotted a few steps away with the commotion, to lead them inside to water them after the race.

"Yes, you both will get an extra treat once you're back at home." One sentence and she had made friends for life with both horses, had both their heads rubbing and playfully nudging against her.

Epilogue

The next morning, Scarlette and Tyler were sitting around the dining table with all the rest of the family and friends. They had said they'd come to New York, but nobody had listened to them.

Too revved to sleep, they had been up the rest of the night, getting the horses back home, answering questions from the police, letting the family know they were okay — which had ended with everybody deciding to come by.

Lorraine had joined Scarlette in the kitchen in the early morning hours, and together they had cooked up the feast for breakfast that every person around the table was now feeding on while they listened to Luke's summary of the preliminary interviews.

"From what we know so far, and what I can share with you, the woman, Summer, owes a huge gambling debt, and her brother Reed has a drug problem and owes money to the wrong people. Their brother Todd was dragged into it, pressured with their own family history into working to get information. He claims neither he nor the rest of their family knew about his sister killing both of your parents. The triplets' parents supposedly never had their fingers in the blackmail business, that's why they moved so far away."

"So, for all before them, it was trying to protect the family name after things had gotten started, much like everybody in our families tried to by paying," Tyler concluded.

"Yes, that's what it sounds like so far. Then the huge debts for two of the triplets came in, and they wanted to up the game. Branson held firm against it, and because it took too long in their eyes to get to the next generation — you — to try for a larger sum, Summer finally struck out on her own. She visited your biological mother in the hospital where she was treated for her cancer, and because treatment was expensive, the payments had slowed significantly. She gave her a morphine overdose. I'm sorry, Scarlette."

"Not your fault, Luke."

"Still. But I'm glad you had switched on your phone's recorder when you were getting to the stables, it helped to get the confession from them that quickly.

"Ty, with your parents, she loosened the lug nuts on two tires. It was a rainy night, and with the unstable tires, they lost control. From what I heard, I personally think she was close enough behind, probably to finish what she started if she had to, but they both died on impact. I am terribly sorry. They will pay for everything, but she will pay for this especially."

"Thank you, Luke."

They talked about a few more details like the blood they found in the warehouse — still to be determined, but likely

Adams' and Branson's — and the cat's blood they had found on the knife from Scarlette's desk, and bullets being matched to the gun from the stable. But around noon Scarlette's family and Viola made their way back, and Josh said he would be off to explain things to Bonny.

Deciding to give Luke and July some time alone, Ty took Scarlette's hand for a walk. He stole a bottle of wine from the parlor, took two glasses and, grabbing a blanket from the stables, he sat down with her next to the meadow where Epona and the mare he had ridden the night before were playing around.

"I don't care what time it is, we deserve this," he said and handed her a glass.

"Me neither, because you're right. This is nice."

"It is. Vi gave me a first draft of the contract for my next book, the one about all this."

"Fun. But it's good that it will come from you."

"Yes, it is. Now, about our honeymoon..."

"Let's talk about that in a month, when we have found more of a routine than the last two weeks. Right now, I just want to enjoy being your wife in our normal day-to-day life."

"Deal." In agreement, they clinked their glasses.

Ty played his fingers through Scarlette's hair.

"I looked into buying the villa..." they both said at the same time.

Laughing, Scarlette crawled onto his lap, wine in her hand, horses grazing behind them.

"You know, we really are perfect for each other. So, for all the times you're off traveling..." She set down her glass, framed his face with her hands, studied his eyes. "It's dangerous to go alone! Take this." And gave him a sweet kiss that ended in a warm laugh when he rolled her over and himself on top of her.

Acknowledgments

Thanks to my amazing husband Chris for believing in this book, believing in me, being proud of me. Thank you for all the coffee you always bring me and the amazing food you make to keep me going and, most importantly, for loving me.

Thanks to my awesome friends supporting me, reading the early work and sharing their opinions with me.

Thanks also to my wonderful editor and publisher, Jessica A. Scott, from Tuxtails Publishing. Without your input and support, this book wouldn't be what it is today.

About the Author

Lyv Lamere grew up in Germany and still lives there with her husband, their two cats, and her snake, even though they plan to relocate in the future.

Lyv successfully studied veterinary medicine and worked at a laboratory before following her other interest, which has her currently working as a contractor in the tech industry.

One day she found she had developed yet another passion – writing – and her first novel was completed sooner than expected.

Today she's still working at her "day job," but continues writing and hopes to bring a smile to people's faces with her stories.

To learn more about Lyv, visit
www.lyvlamere.com.

instagram.com/lyvlamere

www.ingramcontent.com/pod-product-compliance
Lightning Source LLC
Chambersburg PA
CBHW051246210726
48287CB00002B/364